Extreme Consequences

Imogene's Past Lives

Christine Sherborne

Extreme Consequences

Imogene's Past Lives

Christine Sherborne

Copyright 2014 by Christine Sherborne
Published by Colourstory Pty Ltd
Edited by Don McNair
Cover Image by Hugh Sherborne

ISBN 978-1-921501-24-1

Print Edition
All Rights Reserved

TABLE OF CONTENTS

CHAPTER ONE

"Doctor Schneider, please stop. I don't want to do it." Imogene watched as he held up the syringe and squirted the liquid. Cold drops fell on her bare arm as she tried to push him away, but he grabbed her, stuck in the needle and pressed the plunger. She clutched the edge of the white leather couch.

"Hush, child. You'll be fine, close your eyes. You are safe here, remember it's just a dream."

Her head swam, and she felt slightly sick. She fought back the waves of darkness, but it was no use. Her fingers relaxed, and she let go.

Kukulcon came for her.

With her arms bound, the young woman stumbled toward the bottomless limestone sinkhole and stared into the pit's black depths as the Shaman pushed her closer. She fought against him, how could this be happening?

The drummers' bright feather headdresses nodded and chanted as they beat the taut leather, and sweat gleamed on their backs in the firelight as they swayed in unison. The girl's heart raced as she struggled. She didn't want to die.

The Shaman gripped her harder and bowed low before the new king. He lifted his spear. "Yum Kaax, God of the Harvest, we offer you this sacrifice. Bless our crops and our people."

1

He bowed again and dragged her to the edge of the sinkhole. The girl dug in her heels as Kukulcon pushed her. She whipped her foot around his ankle, pulling him off balance, and his primordial scream echoed as they fell together.

Imogene heard Professor Schneider's distant voice.

"Imogene, I'll count down from five to one. At one you will awaken, feeling relaxed and happy. Five, four, three…"

She winced as she opened her eyes. The professor's face was close to hers and she could see her reflection in his wire-rimmed glasses.

"I saw you in my dream, professor. And I saw Ezekiel, the lawyer who murdered me. It was so real it scared me!"

He stood and helped her off the couch. "Don't worry, my child. A bad dream can't hurt you."

Nicola, the professor's assistant, walked her to the waiting room door and opened it. Her father, Doctor Pembroke, rose from his seat.

"We're finished for today," she said. "You may return to the ward."

Dr. Pembroke pushed past them, into the office. "Professor Schneider, I have patients to attend to. When can we go home?"

The professor touched her father's shoulder. "The authorities have the final say, not me. I'll ask the Home Office when I deliver my report."

Imogene clasped her father's hand. "Daddy, let's go back to the ward. Mommy and Aunt Sybil will worry."

Her father took her hand, turned, and without another word led her down the stark corridor.

Inspector Grant studied the Prime Minister and the Home Secretary as they entered his office. The Prime Minister's almost-too-perfect features were marred only by a crescent shaped scar on his forehead. A polo accident, it was rumored, received when he fell and his horse kicked him. His dark hair framed an almost frail complexion, hinting that he suffered from asthma. His ready smile and friendly manner had led to an election landslide. The Home Secretary was an old friend, an ex-royal navy commander he respected and understood. Alex's straight backed stance matched his own.

"This way please."

Inspector Grant looked around Swindon Constabulary's packed incident room, and saw everyone was present. He rapped the table with his pointer.

"Welcome. I'd like to introduce The Prime Minister, Frank Carrington, and Home Secretary, Alexander Brittan. The prime minister wants to be brought up to date on the details of the Stonehenge bombing and massacre. Detective McCullage?"

Jim McCullage stood, loosened his collar and opened the file in front of him. "Sirs, first we had two kidnappings in Swindon, then two shopkeepers went missing in Monkton St Michael. It turns out that Ezekiel Yates, a lawyer and leader of a radical Christian cult, had a mission to rid the West Country of 'sinners'. He kidnapped Xantara Pembroke, wife a Monkton St Michael doctor, because he believed she was a witch."

Frank Carrington held up his hand. "Why did they think that?"

"Well, she and seven other women practice an ancient form of healing. The eldest daughters of eight village families have done this for thousands of years. They call themselves 'The Guardians of Avebury Circle', which is a monument similar to Stonehenge but much older."

"So, what did this Yates man do with her?"

"He locked her in the crypt of a local village church."

McCullage glanced again at his folder as he recounted the events, telling how Xantara's seven-year-old daughter Imogene had earlier been crushed by falling rocks on the Isle of Angels. What was assumed to be an accident turned out to be a murder by Ezekiel Yates.

"He wanted to punish her mother," McCullage said. "He also tried to kill her son, by initiating a car accident. The girl's parents removed her body from the morgue and the Guardians performed a healing ceremony at Avebury Circle."

The room became quiet. The prime minister glanced at the home secretary, then back at McCullage.

"And?"

"And—well, she came back to life, as we all saw on the News Broadcast."

The prime minister slapped his hand on the desk. "That isn't possible. It must have been a trick!"

McCullage took a deep breath. "You haven't heard anything yet," he said, softly. "Here goes. As many people witnessed, the daughter also levitated, and delivered a message from the so-called Council of Elders, right in front of a huge crowd and the world's press."

He kept talking, hoping to get his story out and believed, praying these two important people wouldn't simply walk out. He told about Ezekiel and his followers murdering the two shopkeepers, a young gay lad, and an Indian Sikh in the crypt, and how they dragged Xantara through underground tunnels to the island ruin and tried to burn her at the stake.

"Her husband alerted the pastor and me, and we managed to rescue her," he said.

The Prime Minister frowned. "Well, why didn't you arrest them?"

"They fled back through the tunnels. When lightning struck the tower and collapsed the tunnels, we believed them dead."

Inspector Grant's eyes narrowed. "McCullage, tell him about the underground city."

McCullage knew this was getting weirder and weirder. Would these important visitors just throw up their hands and leave?

"Ezekiel's cousin Obadiah used to be in charge of an underground facility near Corsham, built in the fifties to protect dignitaries from nuclear attack. It was decommissioned years ago, and now he uses it as his personal playground. He kidnapped local 'heretics,' held them prisoner and tortured them to 'convert' them. The group stored explosives in the old armory, and used them to blow up Stonehenge at the summer solstice ceremonies."

He sat down and looked at his hands. Hell, he wouldn't have believed such an outlandish story, either.

Inspector Grant nodded to him and turned to Sam Blackbridge. "We'll now hear from the New York CIA agent, Mr. Blackbridge."

Sam blinked and stood. "Jeremiah Yates, Ezekiel's cousin, bungled a bank robbery in New York and fled to Wiltshire. He heads up the Phineas Priesthood, an even more radical religious cult, whose agenda is to eliminate anyone not Christian and white. We believe he's determined to develop Priesthood chapters in Britain, and the Stonehenge massacre was their first major atrocity to cleanse the country of 'sinners.'"

The prime minister wheezed, then cleared his throat. "Do you believe they're planning another terrorist act?"

"Yes, sir, I do. They are true fanatics, convinced of their own superiority and that they are acting within God's will!"

Frank Carrington turned back to McCullage. "Levitation? Detective, do you seriously believe that?"

Damn. There it was. The whole world saw it, and Carrington asks him if he believed it? "No one knows how she did it," he said. "She ordered the world to abandon its selfish ways, but she spoke with a mature woman's voice, and it wasn't an eight-year-old's speech pattern."

"I thought you said she was seven."

"The day of the speech was her birthday, sir."

Frank stood. "Inspector Grant, what's the status of the terrorists, and where is the girl now?"

"We think the terrorists died in the church explosion after a second attempt to kidnap her. We won't know for sure until we clear the tunnels.

Doctor Schneider is evaluating the girl at the Porton Down research facility, as you asked."

Inspector Grant stood stiffly. "Prime Minister, why did you want to keep her at a secret chemical weapon facility?"

"For several reasons. First, it's close to her family home. Second, the complex is secure, and Doctor Schneider is highly qualified. His primary job is to research chemical warfare's psychological effects on the general populace, but he has previous experience with multifaceted childhood issues. He'll use hypnosis and/or drugs to uncover any deceptions."

Ernst Schneider sat at his desk and played the audio of the session he'd just concluded with the Pembroke girl. He called Nicola over. "The child is such a good subject," he said, smiling. "She entered a past life within minutes, and spoke with amazing clarity. I must keep her here, there is so much to learn!"

Nicola sat opposite him, slid her elbows onto the table, and rested her head on her hands. "What happened?"

"She went back to a past life, where she was a human sacrifice to appease a Mayan god. But the remarkable part was that she recognized at least two people from the present day in this past life!"

Nicola frowned. "How could she?"

Schneider tapped his pen against the desk edge as he pondered. "It's collective soul reincarnation," he said, slowly. "The phenomenon is well documented, the most famous case occurred close by in Bath, Avon. A psychiatrist became intrigued when several new patients were plagued with similar bad dreams. The chance of mere coincidence was too great, so he decided to investigate them."

Nicola's eyebrows went up. "What was the collective dream?"

The professor eyed her, unsure of how much to tell her. Finally, he relaxed. "The group experienced being members of the Cathars, a twelfth century religious sect in Southern France. Pope Innocent the Third declared them heretics for their belief in reincarnation, and called for a crusade against them. Thousands were cruelly murdered."

Nicola watched his face closely, as if something troubled her. She leaned back in her chair and crossed her arms. "How did that psychiatrist connect the group?" she asked. "That would seem unlikely."

It was a question he'd asked himself, and researched. The answer was actually quite simple. "He noticed that many of his patients described very similar dreams. After questioning each patient at length, many showed remarkable recall, down to such fixed details as names, family members, and nearby villages. He travelled to France, looked up old records, and dug deep to find the names and locations his patients revealed to him. He couldn't see how such a diverse group could have independently found the information. In any case, they sought help, because the strange dreams disrupted their daily life."

She shook her head. "So, you and I could have experienced past lives together? Do you really believe that?"

"Yes, I believe we could have met before, but relationships might change with each reincarnation. You could be my sister in one life, for example, and my father in another. Each life is designed to work out your Kama. A cruel character in one life becomes the victim next time around. The soul learns their life lesson, or not, then has to repeat the experience."

He paused, thinking. "We have to keep her here until my research is finished," he said, almost to himself.

"How will you arrange that? She has a family, and needs to go to school, lead a normal life."

Schneider formed a steeple with his fingers. "The Prime Minister asked me to evaluate her, and these tests can take a long time. I'll keep her here until I'm sure I have all the information we need. She could reveal new truths to me, and it could prove to be a famous case."

"What about her message and levitation?" Nicola asked. "The authorities will want an explanation for that, it was seen by half the world."

"Of course. I have my methods, and I'll drill into those issues. They mesh nicely into my private research, so I can extend them as long as it takes. Besides, her past lives can connect us with this Council of Elders. I'm convinced they and the Rahmiel personage must live in the spiritual world."

CHAPTER TWO

I n the ward, Imogene switched on the television. "Look, there's Susanne."

Braeden, Xantara and Sybil—her father, mother, and aunt— looked up. Xantara leaned closer in the bright room to see the images on the small screen. Yes, she was right, it was the Channel 5 news anchor seated at the studio's news desk, telling about what had happened at Avebury Circle only three days before.

The TV scene changed, and Imogene pointed at the screen, eyes wide. "Mommy, that's me! How did I float off the ground like that, and whose voice is it?"

Xantara hugged her. "With Rahmiel's help, dear. Yes, it's really something."

"Shush, I want to listen." Imogene's voice from the TV set was low and steady, unfamiliar to Xantara, as she talked to a crowd of hundreds assembled twenty feet below her.

"Did I really say that?" Imogene asked. "How could I know such things?"

"Well, Rahmiel spoke through you, didn't she? She was delivering a message for the whole world."

Xantara watched the rapt attention on her eight-year-old daughter's face, and shuddered. She was so young for this! She pulled her gaze from her daughter and stared at her hands, as her thoughts went back to the day Imogene was killed in a rock fall on the Isle of Angels three weeks ago. She could never have guessed that her work as a healer would lead to her daughter's death, and her own near burning at the stake.

Her eyes filled with tears as she looked at Imogene's upturned innocent face as her daughter watched television. Thank God for her miraculous resurrection by the Light Beings. The malicious Phineas Priesthood led by Jeremiah and Ezekiel Yates hadn't finished with them yet, she was sure.

New voices came from the TV, pulling Xantara from her reverie. She looked up. The TV scene had changed to a plush room, where Susanne the anchorwoman now sat beside a man dressed in a sparkling crimson jacket.

"Who's he, Mommy?"

"I'm not sure. I—I wasn't paying attention."

"She said he's an American evangelist named David Williams," Braeden said. "A bloodsucker, in my opinion."

"Braeden..."

Imogene lost interest and went over to join her Aunt Sybil, who sat with a wet handkerchief in her hand. She touched a corner of it to her red eyes. Imogene grabbed her hand tightly.

"Don't cry, Aunt Sybil, please! Grannie and Bryony live in heaven now. I know! I've been there, and it's wonderful. You'll be with them again when you die. Death isn't something to be frightened of."

Her aunt smiled. "You're such a treasure. I'm not surprised the Council of Elders chose you to deliver their message."

Susanne didn't like the evangelist, the way he smirked as his hangers-on tended to his every need.

"So. Tell me, Mr. Williams, what do you think about Imogene's message?"

His wide grin almost blinded her. "Well, the content is not of God," he said. "This 'Council of Elders' thing certainly isn't biblical. And the message is wrong, totally wrong."

She held her microphone closer to his face. "In what way?'

"She declared the modern world's population to be selfish, because we appreciate good things and don't worry about poverty. God's word tells us that He enriches Christians. He wants His people to live as the King's sons and enjoy his bounty."

Susanne bit her lip. "But what about the babies born without souls? Remember what the girl said about that?" She glanced at her notes. "Here it is." 'Your prejudices have resulted in millions of soulless children. Countless deaths, murders, destruction of people and property, are the consequence. Your present course will destroy the planet if not checked in time. Unless the world addresses these problems, the soulless children will increase. You are creating your own psychopaths, sociopaths, murderers and terrorists. Do any of you want the next generation to be completely soulless?'"

He shook his head, as if to chase the thought away. "Well, isn't the notion simply ridiculous? How can a child be born without a soul?"

She pressed on. "Isn't it true psychopaths have no remorse? Having no soul could be the reason."

David Williams yawned. "In my opinion, the whole incident is a trick. Why would God speak through a child? He would use one of His well-known evangelists, such as me, or perhaps another."

"Thank you for your time, Mr. Williams." She turned to the camera. "This is Susanne Prentice for Channel Five. Keep tuned for more on this mesmerizing story."

 ***

Susanne sat next to her cameraman Hugh as their Boeing 747 taxied along the runway, and pulled her arms in closer to avoid Hugh's bulk as they lifted off. "Cattle class again," she said. "Our bosses can afford to send us first-class, but they're plain mean."

Hugh lowered his tray as the drinks trolley neared. "Williams is a self-important bore. I don't know how you didn't throw up at the interview."

Susanne nodded. "I'll be glad to get back to good old England. We need to find Imogene and her family as soon as possible. They did promise us an exclusive after you saved her life."

He turned to her, his eyelids at half-mast, his two-day-old stubble underlining his lack of sleep. He certainly didn't look like a hero, but he was. He'd used his large frame and strength to rescue Imogene from Hilda that crazy nurse. Camera work involved heavy lifting and his trained eye had spotted her murderous intent straight away. She touched his arm in a quick display of affection.

He ignored it. "You think they'll keep their word? We have to dodge the authorities to do an exclusive, and that damned Official Secrets Act we signed."

"Plus we have to somehow get into that secure government medical facility to talk with them," Susanne said. "Good luck with that."

Hugh sipped his drink, and made a face. "I hate Bacardi and coke in a plastic cup, don't you?" He set it down and wiped his mouth with the little paper napkin that came with it. "I say we go back to Avebury Circle. Film extra footage, and interview the sight-seers."

"Excellent idea." Susanne pulled down her window shade and let her seat back.

Hugh drove the Channel Five van into Avebury village and parked. He collected his gear and followed Susanne into the Circle.

As they neared Imogene's ascension spot Susanne heard a chant and the tinkle of cymbals. An oddly dressed crowd milled around the stone.

Druids! Europe's most ancient recorded pagan religion believed in reincarnation and revered nature.

A man with deer antlers attached to his headwear looked like the leader. Hugh obviously saw Susanne's grip tighten on her microphone, because he hoisted his camera onto his shoulder and adjusted the lens. "Go and get'em!" he said.

Susanne stood in front of the camera. "Susanne, Channel Five - reporting from Avebury Circle in Wiltshire. Many viewers will be more familiar with the Stonehenge monument, especially after the recent terrorist bombing, but the Avebury megalithic stones predate Stonehenge by more than a thousand years, and it is the largest Neolithic circle of its kind in Europe. Avebury village lies in the center of these huge stones."

She signaled to Hugh to pan the camera over the Portal Stones. "This is the exact spot that Imogene Pembroke delivered her message to the world, calling for World leaders to disarm, and help the disenfranchised. This stone is also where according to her parents some power restored their dead child to life, after two weeks in the grave.

Who is this miracle child, and will our leaders accept her message?"

Susanne approached the man with the antlers. "Susanne, Channel Five." She thrust her microphone toward him. "Can you tell me why you're here?"

The Druid smiled. "Sure can. Star Beings have sent the girl to us. She died, and came back to life right here. She's divine, so we must worship her."

Hugh panned a myriad of posies and wreaths laid at the altar base. He zeroed in on fruit offerings in a bowl, then panned back to Susanne. She pushed her mike to within inches of the man's face.

"You say Imogene is a Druid god?"

"Of course! How many people have you seen levitate? And her message? We've tried to deliver a similar one for centuries."

The Druid straightened his top-heavy antler set and looked into the camera. "Imogene is the new prophet, and we're claiming her as our own."

CHAPTER THREE

Bryony, lying with her eyes closed, sensed a presence. Who could it be? And where was she? She pressed her hand to her forehead and tried to sort out in her mind what had happened. Thought fragments bounced around in her skull, trying to form cohesive images. In her mind, she saw the Yates people invade her home, taking her, Sybil and Sabina, Xantara her best friend's mother and aunt. Jeremiah followed with Xantara who held Imogene's hand. She noticed her friend falter as she stepped over Braeden her husband in the kitchen. Did the blow to his head kill him?

The fundamentalist family had targeted Xantara because of her work as a Guardian of the Avebury circle. No doubt she would have been next anyway, she and her fellow Guardians. The scene in the church tunnels made her flinch. Jeremiah cut Sabina's throat without a pause, and now he had abducted her. She tried to resist as he dragged her along the tunnel, but she was no match for the tall albino. Who would have guessed he was Xantara's cousin. Thank God the others got away.

The huge explosion at the Church had sent smoke and flames into the sky, so everyone would believe she'd been killed. As they'd neared their destination, Jeremiah Yates had pressed a rag with chloroform against her face. Where was she now? And why did Jeremiah mention a harem?

She peeked under her lashes, at a figure sitting on the bed wearing a dress. A woman. She relaxed. At least Jeremiah was gone for now. She yawned, then sat up.

The young woman, who had wild red hair and blue eyes, smiled. "How're you feeling?" she asked. "You've been asleep for ages. I'm Sally Lyons. They kidnapped me, too."

Bryony looked around the sparse room, then walked to the window and peeked out. She saw only meadows, then a line of trees, and a mountain range beyond that. She looked down at the courtyard below. Apparently, she was on the house's third floor.

"Where are we?"

Sally flipped her hair back over her shoulders. "The house is called Laird's Hall, I think. And we can't escape. I've tried."

Bryony turned back toward her. "Laird's Hall? You mean we're in Scotland?"

Sally walked to her, and together they looked through the window at the distant mountains. "Yes, Scotland. I've been so lonely, and I'm glad to have company. But I'm sorry at the same time, as I know what'll happen."

Bryony fingered her necklace. "What?"

Sally sat again on her bed. "The Yates family formed a cult called the Phineas Priesthood, and they want to increase their number. You and I are the means to that end."

A chill ran through Bryony's body. She turned to her fellow captive. "So, that's what Jeremiah meant about my joining his harem. He intends us to bear his children, doesn't he?"

Sally gasped, and rubbed her sleeve across her wet eyes. "I think I'm already pregnant," she whispered. "He's horrible, disgusting. And so cold."

Bryony draped an arm around her and led her to the bed. "How old are you, child?"

"Seventeen. They knocked me off my bike as I was riding to work. It was my first job, and I didn't even get the chance to try it. My mom will be frantic."

"You poor child. I'm here now, and we'll find a way to leave. I promise you."

Detective McCullage sat back in his chair opposite the Home Office's Chief Inspector Grant and looked up as a third person with a briefcase came into the room.

"Well, Doctor Schneider. How's the girl?" Inspector Grant asked. The tall thin man, his back like a ramrod pulled his salt and pepper bushy eyebrows together, and looked as if he would stand no nonsense.

Ernst Schneider sat, and pulled a report from his briefcase. He frowned at it, although he obviously knew every word it contained.

"Well, her message appears genuine," he said. "In fact, she repeated it under hypnosis. I need more time with her before I can make a definite diagnosis."

He handed the document to Grant, who dropped it to his desk, unread. "The Prime Minister needs to know who this Rahmiel character is," he said. "He also wants her blood and DNA tested. A medical technician will call this afternoon to extract samples."

"Of course. And I'll keep you informed, naturally. Her father wants to return to his clinic to tend to his patients, as does his wife. She's a midwife."

Grant, now fingering the report, looked up. "Surely they won't leave without their daughter."

"Her great-aunt has offered to stay and care for her."

Inspector Grant stood and held out his hand. "Thank you, doctor. You can release them, but first they must sign the Official Secrets Act."

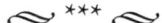

Xantara lay down. "I'll meditate for a while," she said. "Please don't disturb me. I need to unwind, and meditation keeps me sane."

Within moments, she slipped into the space between worlds and relaxed. She repeated her mantra in tune with her breath. All is peace... all is peace...

Her mind drifted to her mother's awful death, and to her best friend Bryony, who obviously had died when the church exploded. How could they both be dead, gone from this earthly plane? All is peace... all is peace... She felt Bryony's life-force. How could that be? Wasn't she dead? She focused on her friend, and the connection grew stronger. Bryony's face swam before her, her thick wavy auburn hair framed her deep green eyes. *Xantara. Help me.*

Bryony's voice echoed through her mind from a great distance. Perhaps she didn't die when the church exploded. The connection faded, then silence.

A door slammed, and she opened her eyes. Inspector Grant and the detective came in. "Sorry to disturb you, Mrs. Pembroke," the Inspector said, "but we need to talk."

She stood from her couch, and joined the others at the table. "May we go home? Our clinic—"

The inspector gave a tight smile. "Well, you and Doctor Pembroke can leave, on two conditions. One, you must both sign the Official Secrets Act, which means you can't discuss Porton Down or what takes place here with anyone. Am I clear?"

Xantara nodded. "Of course. And the second?"

"We must keep your daughter longer. But your aunt can stay and care for her, if she wishes."

"Could we can visit her each day?"

"Of course. I've asked Detective McCullage to be your liaison. He'll collect you both for evening visits."

Xantara turned to Imogene and Sybil. They nodded, and she turned back. "Agreed. I'm sure she'll be safe here."

The inspector and detective stood and moved toward the door. "She'll undergo blood and DNA tests later today. We must learn how she levitates."

Susanne looked up at the Basilica in the Vatican as Hugh filmed her.

"This is Susanne Prentice, Channel Five," she said into her microphone. "Today, we bring you an exclusive interview with Cardinal Ricardo Barzetti, the Pope's aide."

Cardinal Barzetti walked down the marble steps and greeted her. She followed him inside, and they sat in two antique chairs placed near the Cardinal's desk. She waited as Hugh set up his equipment.

"Your eminence, the Imogene Pembroke miracle has caught the public's imagination. The message and levitation amazed everyone. Will you tell me what the Catholic Church's position is?"

Barzetti straightened the ornate cross over his crimson vestment. "If the message is genuine, the Catholic Church doesn't believe it came from God's own lips," he said. "But we do agree with its principal."

"You mean, that babies are being born without souls?"

He frowned, staring at her, then away. "Well, of course not that part. But the increase in greed and violence is undeniable, and sinners must repent and obey God's laws."

Susanne pushed the microphone closer. She felt like a hunting dog, approaching a cornered prey. "What does the Pope think about her comments on retribution? Imogene said mankind faced dire consequences if morality didn't improve."

The Cardinal shifted and stroked his chin. "Well, we don't know how authentic the child is, yet. In my view, corruption and violence brings their own penalties, so in a way her words are prophetic."

"Prophetic? She's a prophet then?"

He glanced up quickly. "I didn't say that. I meant her words were visionary. Sorry, but this interview's over. I enjoyed our talk, but I must go back to my duties."

18

Susanne turned toward the camera, and flicked her platinum blonde hair. "Is the child the Pope's new prophet? This is Susanne Prentice for Channel Five, signing off."

Braeden hugged Imogene. "You'll be okay with Aunt Sybil. We'll visit you every day, I promise."

Imogene smiled. "Of course, Daddy. I know your patients need you."

Xantara hugged them both, then she and Braeden followed McCullage to his car. Twenty-five minutes later they arrived at their clinic in Monkton St Michael. People milled outside, forcing McCullage to drive around the back.

Braeden swiveled around. "Did you see the front? It's covered with flowers, and someone's spray-painted the window."

Xantara frowned. "Did you see the man with the placard? It said 'The End is Near!' How will we see patients with half the population parked on our doorstep?"

McCullage shrugged, and walked them to their back door. "I'll pick you up here tomorrow night," he said. "Meanwhile, I'll post two constables at the entrance. I wish you luck."

Braeden went into the clinic, and the crowd spotted him through the window and shouted. He stepped back into the kitchen. "You'll never believe the words sprayed onto the window," he said. "'The New Messiah!' Will our life ever return to normal?"

Nicola came for Imogene at two o'clock. "The doctor wants to draw blood samples," she said. "It won't hurt. Sybil can come with you."

She led them through a corridor and into an examination room. Sybil sat with her while the technician extracted blood and DNA samples.

Nicola escorted them to Doctor Schneider's office. "A short session this afternoon Imogene," he said, smiling. "Sybil, please wait outside."

Imogene lay on the familiar white couch, and soon was watching the crystal pendant above her swing from side to side. Her eyelids grew heavy, and Doctor Schneider's voice became distant.

Imogene... Imogene... can you hear me?

Aunt Bryony's face swam into focus. Her white skin looked pinched. What was wrong? Are you in Heaven? I miss you.

Imogene, I'm alive. Find me, please rescue me.

Where are you? She tried to hold on to her aunt's essence, but couldn't. Did this mean she'd escaped the church explosion? Her heart soared. Wait until she told her mom.

Bryony concentrated hard, then relaxed. Had Imogene heard her? She would try again later. Dusk descended, and she switched on the bedside lamp.

"Sally, do we get to eat?"

As the words left her mouth, the door opened. A middle-aged woman carried a tray in, and set it on a small table against the wall. Bryony rushed her, but stopped when Jeremiah appeared in the doorway. So, he wasn't taking any chances.

"Eat and rest. I'll be back later," he said. He was smiling, a very strange smile.

Bryony's dry mouth made swallowing difficult, but she was determined to stay healthy. They ate quietly, lost in their own concerns. Boredom finally set in, and since there was no television or books, they talked.

"What did Jeremiah mean when he said he'll be back later?" Bryony asked.

Sally's face flushed. "Well—you know."

Bryony nodded. She flinched as the door opened. Riordan, Jeremiah's nephew, dragged in the frame of a second bed. He set it up and left, and returned moments later dragging its mattress. He threw bedcovers at her. "You can make it."

She made the bed slowly, smoothing out every wrinkle and creating perfect hospital corners with the sheets. She freshened up in the small adjoining bathroom. Thank God, toothpaste. She prided herself on her cleanliness. "We may as well get a few hours' sleep, Sally."

Sally got into her own bed and turned away, pulling the covers almost over her head. "Goodnight."

Much later Bryony heard the door creak open, and stared as a figure entered. The moonlight through the open window highlighted the albino, Jeremiah. She stiffened as the ghost-like apparition walked to her bed. He stood naked beside her, pulled the covers back and clamped his hand over her mouth as he lowered his body against hers.

CHAPTER FOUR

Doctor Schneider drew in a sharp breath. This couldn't be! The letter dropped from his hand as he stared at Nicola. "I fast-tracked Imogene's blood and DNA results, but there must be a mistake. I'll have to run the tests again."

Nicola removed her black rimmed glasses and picked up the letter. "What's wrong with them?"

Ernst retrieved the paper and pointed. "Look at this. Her telomeres are longer and thicker than normal, showing no deterioration. With telomeres like this, she could live forever."

"What do you mean?"

"That's how we age. As the cells replicate, the telomeres at the ends of chromosomes shorten and break down, so we age then die."

He eyed the report, then showed her a picture on page three. "Her DNA is abnormal," he said. "Look at the double helix image. I've never seen a composition like that before. There've found an extra component in Her DNA, and they can't identify it."

Nicola blew out a sharp breath, and stared up at him. "What is she?"

McCullage dashed into the specialist's room, where his wife Nancy waited with the doctor. "Sorry I'm late. He glanced at his wife's drawn face. "Are you okay?"

She nodded and patted the seat next to her. As the doctor opened his file, McCullage saw a fleeting sympathetic expression cross his face.

"What's the prognosis?"

The doctor looked up. "I'm so sorry. Your wife's breast cancer has metastasized, and is now at stage-four. The cancer has spread into her liver, bones and brain. I'm afraid there's nothing we can do." He looked back at the file in his hand. We can only give her treatments that will extend her life for a while."

The detective clasped Nancy's hand, and she squeezed his and looked down. "How long does she have? We've talked about the possibility, and we want to know."

The doctor slowly closed the file. "Three to six months, a year at most. I'm sorry."

As Braeden drove toward Westbury on his afternoon rounds, the famous Westbury White Horse, appeared in the distance. More people than usual gathered on the hilltop to view the chalk monument cut into the hillside. Curious, he drove up the access road to see what was happening.

He parked and walked down the path toward the monument. As he approached the hillcrest, people standing there pointed at something down the other side. A military helicopter roared overhead, so low he ducked. He pushed forward to see what caused the commotion.

He paused at the hilltop and looked down at the wheat field below, to see a complex crop circle. He shrugged. So what was the fuss? They often appeared in this area. The intricate design formed a double helix and appeared three-dimensional. He pulled out his cellphone and photographed it to show Xantara, who knew more about crop circles than he did. Until today, he'd always believed pranksters created them with a board and string, but this circle was so complex, now he wasn't so sure. He wasn't sure about anything.

Imogene watched the pendulum sparkle as Doctor Schneider swung the crystal to and fro. His soft voice lulled her to sleep. "Imogene, you're in a corridor, the corridor of past lives. Each side is lined with doors, choose one now and enter."

She opened the third door on the left, and cringed as an explosion threw up dirt right next to her. Another blast sounded, and she ran and zigzagged to avoid the mortars and threw herself into the ditch beside her comrades. The doctor's voice broke through. "Imogene, look down, what're you wearing?"

"A khaki uniform, I'm a soldier. If I can hang on, I'll be home next week."

"What's the place you're in, and the year?"

"I'm in France, and it's 1918. I don't want to die. I'm nineteen, and I haven't lived yet."

"What's your name?"

"Robert. Robert Clancy."

"Relax Imogene, move on now. Go forward in time. Where are you?"

"It's a school hall, and I'm on a cot. The room's full of soldiers, they've crammed us in, we're sick. Men are dying all around me, I'm scared. It's not fair, to fight for your country and then die of influenza. My chest hurts, I can't breathe, I'm choking. Help me, someone help me!"

"Imogene, listen to me. You will wake up on the count of one. Five...four...three..."

Detective McCullage picked up the Pembrokes to drive them to Porton Down. They made an odd couple, Braeden's blonde hair and icy blue eyes looked almost dark against Xantara's pure white albino skin and hair. Her beautiful opal hued eyes were her saving grace. Braeden tapped his shoulder from the back seat. "Thanks Jim, for the lift."

Jim didn't answer, and they sat in silence for several minutes.

"You appear depressed," Braeden said, finally. "Is something wrong?"

McCullage met the doctor's eyes in the mirror. He wanted to talk, and a doctor would understand. "My wife has cancer. Stage four."

"I'm sorry to hear that. What's the prognosis?"

A lump formed in his throat, and he couldn't speak for a moment. "Three to six months. She waited too long. She felt a swelling two years ago and ignored it, and now the cancer has spread. We celebrated our twenty-fifth wedding anniversary last month, but it'll be our last."

Xantara sat in the front next to him, staring straight ahead. "If Bryony lived, the Guardians would have healed her," she said. "You know, maybe she is alive. Maybe she escaped when the church blew up. I can feel her energy, her life-energy."

McCullage's chest tightened. He hated the Yates family. Were the healings real? After all, Imogene was revived. "We'll know soon enough, the Home Office has ordered the tunnels beneath the church excavated. We need to know for sure Ezekiel and his mob are dead."

He pulled up at Porton Down security gate and showed his ID. The guard waved them through, and he drove toward the north side. Doctor Schneider came out to greet them, then escorted them to his office. They sat in chairs across from his desk.

"I'd like your advice on something," he said. "You're a doctor, Braeden. Look at these test results, and tell me what you think."

Braeden studied the papers, frowning. He looked up. "This is impossible. Will you run the tests again?"

"We already did, and we got the same thing. Your daughter's DNA construction is like none we've ever seen, and her telomeres indicate she could be immortal."

Xantara half rose from her chair. "She must be part Light Being," she said. "That's how she was able to heal Jeremiah."

McCullage turned to her. "She healed Jeremiah? You didn't tell us that."

"I'm sorry, so much happened at the time. Yes, she healed his eyes. He's an albino like me, but he had weak eyesight. He forced Imogene to heal him."

The doctor removed his glasses and rubbed them with a tissue. He replaced them, and stared at Xantara. "This is unbelievable," he said. "She has the power to heal?"

McCullage shrugged. "What else will we learn? We must keep this information top-secret, of course. If word of it got out, thousands would camp at your gates within hours."

Schneider stood. "We've all signed the Official Secrets Act, and this information will stay in this room. But I do have to tell the Prime Minister. Why don't you go and see Imogene and Sybil? I have a lot to think about."

As they walked toward the ward, Braeden turned to the detective. "Have you seen the new crop circle at Westbury White Horse?"

"No, why?"

"The crop circle looked identical to the helix image Schneider just showed us."

"Mommy, Daddy, come play cards with me." Imogene beamed as they sat down, and dealt the pack. "I can play better now," she said. "Aunt Sybil taught me several new tricks." McCullage sat in the corner and picked up a newspaper.

"Mommy, Aunt Bryony talked to me."

Xantara spread out her cards. "In your mind, you mean? I've heard her, too." "Do you think she could be alive?"

26

CHAPTER FIVE

Osahar looked around the chamber beneath the pyramid, and noticed the stars dotting the dark blue vaulted ceiling. "Seth, look at the Sirius constellation," he said, pointing. "The positions match, and the time is at hand. The girl is here, as the Council of Elders foretold."

The High Priest's servant lit the final rush light and looked up. His oiled, hairless body was bathed in the lamplight. "Shall I prepare the mixture?"

"Yes."

Seth moved around the chamber collecting herbs, his feet leaving a trail across the sandy floor as he moved from jar to jar. He bowed and recited a prayer at each small table before he placed each aromatic plant into a small marble basin. He sat at Osahar's feet and poured oil into the brew, then ground it with mortar and pestle into a fine paste. He offered up the bowl.

Osahar received the offering and spooned the narcotic into his mouth. He walked to a stone bench covered with animal skin and lay down. "Go now, Seth. This will take time."

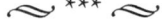

Imogene succumbed to the crystal's movement above her, and Doctor Schneider's voice faded altogether. She was alone. Clouds swirled around her as she floated toward a dim light. The mist dissipated, and a sense of peace replaced her apprehension.

The dark-skinned man lay still before her, his eyes closed. She watched his spirit rise from his body and move toward the tall chair.

"Imogene child, welcome. Please, sit next to me."

She studied the man as she drifted across the chamber. He wore a simple linen skirt with center pleats, and a tall, striped headdress, a snake's head jutting from its front. He smiled, revealing strong white teeth which gleamed in his tanned face. He looked tough, but kind.

"Where am I?" she asked.

"You're in Egypt, my child, in a temple that lies beneath the Great Pyramid. The Council of Elders asked me to assist you. Dark days approach, and your power coupled with mine will herald in humanity's punishment if they ignore the message."

"Have you seen the Elders?"

"Yes. As a child, in the time of Moses. Like you, I died. I drowned in blood-red waters, and my spirit soared to the stars. My mother, a temple priestess, carried my body here. Aten's followers summoned the Light Beings and, as they did with you, they passed through my body and restored me to life. This happened thousands of years ago, and still I live to obey the Council."

"Will people change, as the Elders asked?"

Osahar paused. "They haven't in the past. The Great Flood, the plagues of Egypt, and Europe's black death among other chastisements, failed to change them. The survivors improved for a while, but soon reverted to their old ways. I fear this time the world has deteriorated so much that souls are unwilling to inhabit bodies. Now, the Creator of all has decided that unless they let go of their selfish, evil ways, they will be wiped out. So far humanity has discounted their message, and our instructions are to deliver the final wake-up call."

Imogene felt a cold chill. "What's my part?"

"We are all part of Universal energy, but you and I are special. Our combined will, with every thought and word, creates change within the cosmos. Now it's time for us to create the world's first punishment. Hold my hands, to combine and focus our powers."

She held out her hands and they touched. Power rushed through her like a raging torrent, taking away her breath. A magnificent light streamed upward from their hands, forming a brilliant beam as far as she could see. As quickly as it formed it blinked out, plunging them into darkness. Imogene collapsed and broke contact with the priest. Her body, completely spent, slumped into the chair.

Osahar stepped back. "We've done our part. Let's hope the people recognize the warning as the Council's work."

Imogene drifted back across the chamber. "Can we choose what happens?"

Osahar didn't answer, as Schneider's voice roused her.

McCullage twisted his wedding band slowly around and around, as Inspector Grant addressed the team in the incident room.

"It seems the Yates family, the Phineas Priesthood, has escaped once again," he said. "We've cleared the tunnels under the church, and there's no sign of them. We have no idea where they've gone."

The detective crossed his arms. "Any sign of Bryony?"

"No, but we did recover Mrs. Pembroke's mother, Sabina's body.."

McCullage shifted in his chair. "They must have taken her with them."

Inspector Grant gave the team their orders and the meeting broke up. The CIA agent, Sam, followed him outside. "Do you want lunch? We can work out our next move."

The Cock-and-Bull was almost empty, so they grabbed the window seat. Sam stood. "I'll get the meal. Ploughman's lunch, okay?"

McCullage watched Sam move to the bar, his dark suit and slick black hair disappearing into the shadows. His attention wandered. He'd left Nancy in bed earlier, her cup of tea untouched on the nightstand. The strong medications caused his wife to sleep for hours, but even in sleep her brow furrowed. The anxiety affected them both. Her thin hair had greyed over the past year, and he knew he hadn't escaped the effect of stress. As he shaved that morning, his reflection was of a man ten years older than his forty-two years.

Sam Blackbridge reminded him of an ex-rugby player as he slopped both pints of beer onto the table. The bartender mopped up the mess and served their lunch. "You look distracted. What's the matter? Is this case getting to you?"

Jim lowered his fork. "Nancy, my wife, has terminal cancer."

Sam paused, his glass in midair. "I'm so sorry, I didn't know. Any hope?"

"The Guardians healed Imogene, and I want them to try to heal Nancy," he said. "I know it sounds far-fetched, but I have to try. We need to find Bryony, because the ceremony won't work without her."

Sam looked incredulous. "You're joking." He sipped his drink slowly, then set it down. "I'm sorry. Anything's worth a try, right?"

Bryony lay curled up into a ball, and Sally sat beside her and stroked her hair. "I know, Jeremiah's disgusting! Did he hurt you?"

Bryony didn't move as she drew comfort from the young woman's caresses. "Is this to be our life? We live in this room and endure that man raping us every night? I can't bear it!"

Sally moved away, and Bryony drifted in and out of sleep. She concentrated hard to reach Xantara and Imogene with her telepathic ability. They were their only chance. Contact with Imogene seemed easier, and she tried again. A faint response echoed in her mind. Success! Imogene could hear her. She tried to project an image of Scotland, but

Imogene had never been there, and perhaps she wouldn't recognize the heather-rich mountains. The connection faded, and she wept.

McCullage knocked on Helen's door and stood back. He must be mad, to consult the medium. But recent events had stretched his belief systems, and his situation called for desperate measures.

The pleasantly plump clairvoyant opened the door. Her purple dress and multi-colored shawl made her look bohemian. "Come in, detective, this way."

She led him into her small parlor. She had already drawn the red velvet curtains and lit the candles. "Sit down and tell me how I can help you."

Jim sat across from her, a pack of Tarot cards between them. "I've heard mediums can find people," he said. "That they even help the police at times."

"That's true. Clairvoyance isn't an exact science, but I have known instances where they have helped. Who are you looking for?"

"Bryony, Xantara's friend. The Stonehenge terrorists abducted her."

Helen handed the Tarot pack to him. "Let's try with the cards. Please shuffle the pack and cut it, three times."

Jim handed the cards back and waited while she dealt a Celtic cross on the table. She turned the first card, and frowned.

"The Wheel of Fortune reversed. Circumstances are making you feel out of control." She turned another card, the Moon. "Great fear, anxiety... you're out of your depth and lost, aren't you?"

He didn't answer, focused on the unturned cards.

"The five of cups means despair and regret, and the three of swords—you poor man!"

He glanced up quickly. "What's wrong?"

31

"It means heartbreak, desperation. Is a loved one close to death?"

"Yes, my wife. She has cancer."

Helen turned over the last card. "The nine of wands. Good. This card encourages you to have faith. Don't give up, all's not lost." She paused, thinking. "Nothing about Bryony, I'm afraid, but I could try my dowsing rod."

She ambled over to her sideboard, drew a map and a small split rod from a drawer, returning to the table. She spread out a United Kingdom map, held the rod loosely in both hands, and moved the pointer over the map.

"She's not in the west country, that's for sure." As she moved further north, the rod quivered. "Getting closer," she said.

The rod twitched down violently as she reached Scotland. "There! They've taken her to Scotland. I can't give you the exact spot, but it's certainly somewhere over the border. I'm afraid that's all I can tell you."

McCullage stood. "How much do I owe you?" he asked.

She touched his arm. "Not a penny, detective. I want you to catch them as much as you do."

As Braeden and Xantara got in his car, McCullage glanced at his watch. They'd be at Porton Down in half an hour. He shifted and pulled into the street.

"Bryony's body wasn't in the tunnels," he said. He briefly recounted his visit with the medium.

Xantara clapped her hands. "I told you she's alive! So Helen thinks she's in Scotland? Makes sense, they've taken her as far from Wiltshire as possible without needing a passport. We have to find her."

McCullage stared at the road ahead. "Scotland's a big area. We don't have much time until Nancy…"

"Don't worry, Jim. Imogene and I will work together to establish telepathic contact. She'll give us clues to her whereabouts, and we'll track her down."

They entered the ward at Porton Down, and Xantara and Imogene drew the drapes around the corner bed, sat together, and held hands. Their minds met as they sent out telepathic messages to Bryony. Images flooded back, and they concentrated hard to decipher them. At last they broke apart.

Xantara opened the curtains. "Imogene, what did you get?"

Imogene held a finger to her chin, frowning. "She's in a big house, an old house," she said, softly. "I saw mountains and fields outside. The field was spotted with color—white, pink and yellow. Aunty Bryony is locked in a room, and she's unhappy and scared."

Xantara hugged her daughter. "We'll find her. I saw the same thing. An isolated house, and—I saw a high, jagged peak behind it."

Her daughter smiled, revealing her first half-grown adult tooth. "Mommy, I could find her if we go to Scotland. Her life energy is strong, and I think I can follow it."

McCullage groaned. "The government won't let her out, even if it means tracking the terrorists."

CHAPTER SIX

Frank Carrington scanned Doctor Schneider's report again, then paged the Home Secretary. He tapped the polished mahogany desk as he looked out on to the cloudless London skyline, waiting. The heavy paneled door clicked open, and Alexander Brittan entered.

"Yes, Prime Minister?"

"This report from Schneider worries me. How can I give it to the President?"

Alex ran his fingers across his head. "He's a top guy, sir. Besides, our best geneticists twice independently verified the girl's DNA and blood tests."

"Still, there's something unsettling about the whole thing."

"They're working around the clock to identify the anomalies," Brittan said. "Basically, the girl's DNA carries a genome that's never been seen before."

Frank looked at his limited edition Bremont watch, a gift from his father to celebrate his election, and pulled down the sleeve of his navy pinstriped suit. "The other report from the Home Office says the terrorists escaped, and your team hasn't a clue where they've gone. Is that still the case?"

Brittan reddened and cleared his throat. "I'm afraid so, sir. They're still searching, but—well, no luck. Oh—the President wants an update as soon as possible."

"Thank you, Alex. Please call him now, and listen in. We'll discuss the terrorists later."

Frank straightened his Gucci tie. "Mr. President, good afternoon. How are you?"

The president's deep voice hesitated. "…Well, fine, thank you. Can you update me?"

Frank drew a deep breath. "The blast didn't kill the terrorists. They escaped, and our best men are hunting them down as we speak. We hope to have them in custody before too long."

"Good. And the girl?"

Frank paused. "There's something strange about her. Her DNA and blood makeup don't fit into any normal pattern."

"In what way?"

"Normal DNA has four chemical elements, and they decide who you are, the color of your skin, eyes, hair, and so on. Her DNA has five elements, and our scientists can't identify the extra one, or its effect. And that's not all. Her telomeres are perfect. They tell me this structure has never been seen before, and that it points to a long life—in fact, possibly an immortal life. Plus they think she may have developed the ability to heal, by touch."

The President uttered an odd sound. "If I'd heard that from anyone else, I'd have sent them to a psych ward," he said. "Does this mean her performance and message could be real?"

Frank exchanged a glance with Alex, who perched on his desk edge. "She's an eight-year-old child. Why would a supreme being use her as an envoy?"

"I don't know. Anyway, what she suggests is absurd. No country will disarm unless they're sure their enemies will, too. And how likely is that?"

Frank finished the conversation, clicked off the phone, and turned to Alex. "We need to get the entire Phineas Priesthood behind bars. How can I face the press, when I don't know the truth myself?"

Alex nodded, tidied the reports, slipped them into the manila folder, and crossed the rich Wilton carpet to the door. "The Cabinet demands an emergency meeting sir, as soon as possible. What can I tell them?"

Frank crossed his arms. "Not yet, Alex. We need to gather more information. Tell them anything to keep them happy for now."

Jeremiah sat on a stool in front of dark indigo curtains, watching Obadiah rig up a spotlight of sorts he'd found in the garage. Lighting in position, he faced the tripod mounted camera. Thank God he'd forced Imogene to heal his weak vision. He liked his new look, the opalescence of turquoise eyes looked startling against his pure white Albino skin and hair. He took a deep breath, glanced at his nephew Riordan sitting to the side, then stared at the camera. Obadiah clicked the record switch and stood back.

"I speak for the Phineas Priesthood, a brotherhood blessed by God," Jeremiah said. "He has assigned us to rid the world of sinful people and immoral practices. We were responsible for the bombing at Stonehenge. The gathering was a Pagan ceremony, attended by sinners, people of the occult, and idol worshippers. We, God's faithful, have carried out His judgment. Don't mourn the dark souls who perished, but rejoice for a purer, cleaner world. This attack is the first of many we will carry out in God's Name. Sinners, beware!"

Jeremiah coughed, sipped soda water, then took a deep breath. "The girl you've seen on television recently purports to be the messenger of a 'Council of Elders.' She is really the devil's ambassador, and her message is a deception. We will track her down and destroy her and her entire family."

He paused and glared into the camera. "Imogene Pembroke, take notice. We are coming for you."

He paused again and nodded to Obadiah, who turned the camera off. Riordan clapped. "Well said, Uncle. We must avenge my brother's death." He pulled a handkerchief from his pocket and wiped his sweaty face.

Jeremiah took out the camera's memory card. "We have to upload to YouTube without the authorities tracing it," he said. "I'll find an Internet café in town and email the film to an American contact who's a computer whiz. He'll know what to do." He turned to Riordan, who sat frowning at the floor. "You don't look well," he said. "Do you feel all right?"

Riordan wiped his face again. "I guess it's the flu," he said. "I'll find a couple of aspirins and go to bed."

Jeremiah watched him stumble through the door, his face chalk-white.

 ***

Detective McCullage loosened his tie as he faced the incident board, littered with post-it notes and photographs. How could he broach the subject? He knew he had to, for Nancy's sake.

"Inspector Grant, I've reason to believe the terrorists have fled to Scotland."

Grant frowned and became still, glaring at his subordinate. "And how did you come to that conclusion? Am I missing something?"

McCullage swallowed. "The girl and her mother receive images—mind pictures—from Bryony that suggest a Scottish landscape. I know it's unusual, but everything with this case has been extraordinary."

Grant shook his head slowly. "Detective, I deal in facts, not nonsense."

McCullage shifted in his chair as a tic developed near his right eye. "I also consulted a clairvoyant." He might as well get it all out in the open. He held his breath, as a loud harrumph filled the room.

"Wait, hear me out. Police have used them in the past with some success. Unlikely, I agree, but she also suggested Scotland."

Sam stood straight and faced the inspector. "Sir, the country and the press want answers, and we have no idea where to begin. Isn't it true we've blocked the ports and airports so they couldn't have escaped the country? Scotland's a logical hide-out, remote and wild."

Inspector Grant lowered his stick and glanced at McCullage from under his bushy brows, then at Blackbridge, then back at McCullage. "What do you suggest?"

McCullage let out a long sigh. "Imogene says she feels Bryony's energy, and could lead us to her."

The Inspector raised his eyebrows. "Oh, no. No way! The Prime Minister will never agree to her leaving Porton Down, not for a long time."

"Well, we could try her mother instead. She feels the energy, too. Not so strongly, but it's worth a shot."

The inspector nodded. "I can't spare the Special Armed Services for a wild-goose chase, but you and Sam can try if you want."

Coroner Anne Wilson sat in her cramped office catching up on her day's work, when the phone rang. She glanced at the clock and picked up. "Hi, Julie, what's up in Milton Keyes?"

Her friend sounded anxious. "Our morgue has received an influx of young men who died with flu symptoms," she said. "The illness progresses quickly, and some are gone in less than twenty-four hours."

Anne twisted the grubby government phone cord around her fingers, and pushed her mousey brown hair behind one ear. "Flu? What kind?"

Her friend groaned. "The pathologist's report suggests it's similar to the 1918 pandemic that struck down several million across the world.

The younger adults died, but the children and elderly recovered. But this strain apparently has mutated into a new, deadlier form."

Anne pressed her lips together. "I'll check this out and call you back."

Anne pulled up the most recent local mortuary reports on her screen, scrolled down them, and a cold shiver traveled down her spine. She checked reports from other districts within the London area, and saw a similar trend.

She hesitated, then picked up the phone. "The Health Minister, please." She tapped the table as she waited. "Minister, we have a problem. London morgues have been inundated with young men who have all died suddenly of a new flu strain. The strange thing is, they're all nineteen years old, and share the same birthdate."

 ***

Susanne anchored the Chanel Five morning news. "Good morning, Great Britain. Breaking news, a flu pandemic has swept the nation overnight. Our morgues are full of young men, the cream of our country, all dead within less than twenty-four hours from a lethal virus."

The camera panned to a grief-stricken woman seated next to Susanne. "Mrs. Anderson, I'm so sorry for your loss. Could you share with us what happened?"

The woman looked up, her sodden handkerchief pressed to her nose. "John was a star athlete, strong, healthy," she said. "How could this happen?" She wept, and Susanne passed her a bunch of tissues. "Nineteen, that's no age at all, in fact, he'd celebrated his birthday, last month."

The camera switched to Susanne as she looked into the camera. "What's his birthdate?" she asked.

The mother pushed her hair back. "June. June the eighth. It's the girl, I tell you. The freak who levitated, she's responsible for this."

The woman banged the table and shrieked. The camera crew covered their ears as the sharp sound reverberated around the studio. Her husband helped her off the set. The camera focused on their retreat, then moved back to Susanne.

Susanne looked off the set until the couple moved out of sight, then leaned forward and almost whispered. "That's the mystery here, folks. All the young men who died of this flu virus were born on the same day."

She paused. "Could it be true? Is Imogene Pembroke the harbinger of this disease? Is this part of 'The Consequences' she promised in her speech?"

The station went to a commercial, and she sat back in her plush office chair. "Hugh, what do you think?" she asked. "Is the girl responsible?"

Malachi Yates turned away from the television set and wiped a smear of egg yolk from his chin. "My God!"

His family, all sitting in the breakfast room nook, stared at him. He stood. "Riordan's nineteen, and that's his birthday! Why hasn't he come down for breakfast?"

Malachi's chair hit the floor and he raced toward the door and pounded upstairs. He pushed open his son's bedroom door. Riordan lay on his back on his bed, his open eyes sightless in his blood-drained face.

Malachi knelt beside the bed and stretched his arms over Riordan's cold corpse, then threw his head back and yelled. "It can't be true! Two sons, my boys, dead in less than a week. Why, God, why?"

Tears streamed down his face and he made no effort to stem them. "First, Imogene's brother bludgeoned Seth to death, and now this. That girl and her family will pay. It'll be a pleasure to torture every Pembroke family member slowly to death."

40

CHAPTER SEVEN

T he evening sun cast strange, long shadows across the Porton Down parking lot as Detective McCullage followed Xantara and Braeden to his car. He realized the shadows were from communication antennas sprouting from several buildings, and knew Imogene would be safe there. The guard waved them through the electronic gates, and McCullage half-turned to Xantara.

"How's Imogene coping?"

"She looks well, and enjoys time with my aunt," she said, "but intense sessions twice a day seem too much for an eight-year-old."

He shrugged. "I guess they consider her government property. She does cope surprisingly well, though." He fell silent until they reached Braeden's clinic in Monkton St Michael. "May I come in? I have a problem to discuss with you."

Braeden unlocked the clinic door. "Yes, come in. I'll brew some coffee."

Jim sat at the kitchen table, a mug of coffee steaming in front of him. "I want to thank you guys for your support," he said. "Talking about my wife's illness with someone who understands means a lot to me."

Xantara offered him a biscuit. "How is Nancy?"

Jim sprinkled sugar, bit by bit, into his drink. "Not well, not well at all. The treatments upset her. I guess they prolong her life, but they also drain her. That's why I need your help."

Braeden touched the detective's shoulder. "Of course, we'll help."

McCullage brushed crumbs off his shirt. "I've been a skeptic all my life, but I can't deny what's happened over the past weeks. I think Nancy's only chance to live lies with the Light Beings, at Avebury circle."

Xantara grimaced. "But, we need…"

His chest felt hollow. "Bryony. Yes, I know. Would you go to Scotland with Sam Blackbridge and me to look for her?"

"Do you know where she is?"

"No, but I hope you can find her telepathically. Imogene believed she could, but they won't release her from Porton Down."

Xantara sucked in her lower lip. "Perhaps we could try. I have a stronger connection to my daughter than to Bryony. Perhaps she can pick up Bryony's thoughts and send them to me."

Jim smiled. "Thank you. Let's fly up to Scotland tomorrow. We'll need all the manpower we can get, if we're to find her."

Azazel's red eyes glowed as the dark entity faced his master. The three-horned creature blasted foul air into his minion's face. "If the girl doesn't die, you will be chained forever in the Pit of Despair."

Azazel's long, twisted fingernails scraped the floor as he bowed. "Master, I'll need help. The child's closely guarded. We'll have to take possession of several guards to get near her."

His master picked at an oozing sore on his arm. "You have a legion at your disposal. Don't disappoint me." He paused, thinking, and looked up. "There's another mission," he said, "one that will keep Ezekiel and his family occupied and frustrate the Elders' plans."

"Yes, master?"

"They're holding her at a plant that produces chemical weapons. Among them is a new compound a scientist called Michael Blevins is working on. He calls it 'Zentronia.' I think it can be very useful to us, and I want you to get a sample of it. A large sample."

Azazel backed away between the sulfur pools, and his dark form vanished into mankind's realm.

Malachi placed a last shovel of dirt onto his son's makeshift grave as his family stood close by, watching. His clear green Irish eyes, which matched those of his dead child, watered. "I want revenge, Ezekiel," he said, throwing the shovel to the ground. "Both my boys are gone. How can this be God's will?"

Ezekiel drew him away from the burial site. "God's punishing us because we failed to remove the girl," he said. "Let's return to Wiltshire tomorrow. She'll be in Porton Down for sure, there's nowhere else suitable. The Good Lord will create a way for us to reach her."

Jeremiah walked behind them. "What about the women?"

"Hamish can take care of them. That's what caretakers do. They've both given up hope, I'd say. They won't know we've gone, and he's old but capable."

Jeremiah shook his head. "I'm taking no chances. Before we go, I'll chain their ankles together. It'll be hard to escape like that."

McCullage drove his rental car from Glasgow Airport toward Loch Lomond, with Sam next to him and Braeden and Xantara in the back. He pointed out the bars on the shop windows as he drove past them. "There's a high crime rate in Glasgow," he said. "I blame the long, dark winters."

He parked near the Loch's shoreline and turned to Xantara. "Would you try to contact her to give us directions?"

Xantara got out and walked alone along the shore. Bryony's energy eluded her, so she tried to contact Imogene. She smiled at the instant

43

connection with her daughter. Mommy, remember the mountains, draw the shape. Fool, she should have thought of that.

She returned to the car and asked for a pen and paper. She recalled the unique shape clearly and, as the group drove on, she sketched it out. They stopped at a small wayside inn, where the ruddy-faced landlord welcomed them.

McCullage ordered snacks and drinks, then showed him the sketch. The landlord beamed and pointed toward a weather-beaten old man who sat near the window. "Jock there will know for sure," he said. "He's climbed them all."

The four carried their drinks over to Jock and sat around him, and McCullage offered him a drink. He placed the mountain sketch in front of him. "Sir, do you know of a mountain shaped like this?"

The kilted old-timer studied the picture. "As a youngster, my hobby was Munroe-Bagging."

Sam leaned forward. "What's that?"

"There are two hundred and eighty-four. Munroe's that is. They call them that after Sir Hugh Munro, who attempted to climb them all, but failed. They are Scottish mountains which are over three thousand feet, and I've bagged every single one."

Sam pushed the paper closer. "You've climbed all two hundred and eighty four, you mean?"

"Och aye! I sure have."

"Jock, did you ever climb one shaped like this?"

The old man frowned at the sketch. "Sure I have. Looks like Mount Fuji, like a volcano. It's Mount Schiehallion, without a doubt."

McCullage drew in a sharp breath. "Where's Schiehallion?"

"Why, it's right in Scotland's heart, near Loch Rannoch."

The detective downed his drink, paid the landlord, and the four piled back into the rental car. He drove for hours before they reached Kinloch Rannoch and parked in its main square. Xantara yawned. "Day's closing in. Shall we find a hotel for the night?"

A local directed them to Macdonald Loch Rannoch Hotel, which offered spectacular views over the loch. They rented a room, and Xantara turned as she moved toward the staircase. "I need peace and quiet to contact Bryony," she said. "I should have a better idea where she is tomorrow. Goodnight."

Once in their room, Braeden peered through the window. "Sheep country, grassy slopes dotted with quartzite boulders…the whole area must freeze over in winter. I wonder how close Bryony is, and if we'll find her?"

Doctor Ernst Schneider checked his watch. "Nicola, since her parents won't be here tonight, I'll try a different tack."

Nicola smiled. "What do you have in mind?"

He tapped the desk base with his foot. "Drugs. I want to heighten the hypnotic trance, delve deeper. I want her secrets. Please fetch her, and not a word to her great-aunt."

The doctor's hands trembled as he filled the syringe with sodium thiopental, the so-called truth serum, then squirted some out to clear the air bubbles.

Imogene watched from the door. "What's that?"

He rolled his shoulders. "A small injection, child, to relax you. It won't hurt. Please lay on the couch." He leaned over her and inserted the needle into her arm, depressed the plunger, and watched.

Within minutes the girl looked drunk, her lids half-shut. He moved the pendulum closer. Blood drained from her face as her eyes closed. He hoped he hadn't overestimated the dose!

Imogene pushed against the crowds pressing about her. She must cross back over the Randolph Street Bridge to save her little brother. Flames leapt from the wooden buildings and the air filled with acrid smoke. She coughed and struggled against the tide, and was knocked over time and again.

Schneider's insistent voice interrupted her. "Look down, Imogene. Where are you?"

"On a bridge, the city's aflame. Luke's on the other side."

"Listen to me, child, what city? And what's the date?"

"Chicago. I have to reach Luke."

"The year, Imogene, the year."

"It's 1871, October. The city's on fire, and my home's burnt to ashes." She was silent a moment, then gasped. "No! I tripped, and people are trampling me as they run from the fire! Luke, Luke, where are you?"

She raised her arm in her brother's direction, and looked up as a hobnail boot crushed her head. "Sorry, Luke, too late…"

Osahar stepped forward, and took Imogene's hand.

"Shush, child. You're safe in the temple." He led her to his chair and sat her down. His dark-skinned servant held a goblet of water to her lips.

"Be calm, child. You're here, with me." He waited for her to settle and re-orientate herself. "It's time to carry out the Council of Elders' wishes."

He clasped her hands and, together, they released the power. The universal energy would restore her mind and initiate the next consequence. Such a sweet child. He hated to use her like this.

Ernst Schneider's brow beaded with sweat. He'd lost control. Perhaps the drug was too strong. He watched Imogene's eyes roll as she twisted from side to side.

"Imogene, relax! Listen! You're safe now." He wiped his forehead as she became still. Maybe he could still delve into her mind, and find the answers he sought.

"Imogene, let your soul travel to the space between lives. What do you see?"

She smiled, and her eyes darted beneath her lids. "It's wonderful! The trees, the river— everything is so beautiful."

"Are you alone?"

"No, my spirit guide is with me. We're deciding my next life. I can choose my parents, and we're watching them through a portal."

"Imogene, return to the moment of death and tell me what happens."

"My guide is there, and she's taking me through the vortex of light. I see the life I've left. I see everything, every word, every deed. I feel other people's emotions. I'm sad, my words had hurt many during that incarnation. She shows me the good I did in that life, and I feel better."

"And next?"

"We're going into the hall of learning…"

Her body trembled, and she convulsed. He had to break the trance, he'd gone too far. "Imogene, listen! When you hear the number 'one' you will awaken. Five, four, three…"

Xantara stood on the balcony, watching a lone piper below playing his haunting lament as he marched along the hotel terrace. "How beautiful! Wouldn't life be grand if this were a holiday?"

Braeden joined her, and breathed in the fresh mountain air. "Did you contact Bryony?"

"Not yet. Perhaps I'll sense her energy as we drive around the mountain."

The four met after breakfast, and as they walked to the car, Xantara explained her plan. McCullage unlocked the car doors. "Sit in front, Xantara, and see if you can guide me."

As he drove through the rocky landscape, the mist lifted as the sun rose over the horizon. Xantara sat in silence.

"Anything?" he asked.

Xantara tilted her head to one side. "Maybe."

He swerved as an old army Land Rover bowled around the corner on the wrong side. "Idiot, you could have killed us." His words hung in empty air, the car long gone.

Xantara gripped the dash. "Yes, we're close. Drive to the hilltop and I'll see if I can sense the direction."

The detective parked at a lookout cut into the roadside. They scrambled out, and surveyed the sheep-dotted landscape that rolled out beneath them. McCullage drew out a miniature pair of binoculars and scanned the hills.

"No sign of civilization. Wait—there's a large house, down the valley. A gravel road leads to it, must be two miles long."

Xantara borrowed the binoculars. "Yes, that could be it. It feels similar to the house Bryony showed me. The landscape looks right. There's the mountain, beyond the house."

Sam drew his heavy brows together and slicked down his jet black hair. "We need a plan," he said. "If she's there, we could run into danger. Maybe we should wait for the Special Service guys."

McCullage slapped his palm against the car roof. "No! We could be too late. We need to approach the house tonight, under the cover of darkness."

CHAPTER EIGHT

As Susanne waited for the World Health Organization representative to appear, she turned to her cameraman. "Hugh, isn't Geneva great? I'd love to explore the rest of Switzerland. Fly in, fly out—that's all we ever do."

Andrea Geisert, a small, middle-aged woman, stepped onto the lobby podium as Hugh adjusted his camera. Natural light streamed through the ultra-modern building's high windows, yet lights from the myriad of cameras flashed nonstop. A hush fell as she held her hand high, and everyone focused on her.

"Our committee has met to discuss the recent flu deaths," she said. "The strain is similar to the 2009 pandemic, known as the swine flu, and that strain derived from the 1918 flu pandemic that killed thousands."

The room was silent, yet Susanne leaned forward to catch every word.

"We believe this outbreak is confined to a particular age group. There's no cause for alarm, however. The outbreak has run its course."

The crowd buzzed, then bombarded the woman with questions. Andrea held up her hand, and stepped even closer.

"Is it true that all the victims were nineteen-old males, all born on June the eighth?"

"It appears so."

"Does the disease affect many countries?"

Andrea frowned, glancing down at her notes. "The outbreak—and the deaths—seems to have occurred in every country, worldwide."

Susanne pressed even closer, aware of the whir of Hugh's camera behind her. Camera flashes sporadically lit up the podium.

"Can you give us numbers?"

The speaker paused and coughed. "The statisticians tell us that around 130,000 young men died."

The press went wild, and Hugh turned his camera on Susanne.

"Susanne Prentice, Channel Five, at the World Health Organization headquarters in Geneva," she said. "As you have heard, the pandemic appears to be over. There's no scientific basis for the narrow band of victims, but many people blame the young girl—Imogene Pembroke— for the deaths. Just over a week ago she predicted the world would suffer consequences if people didn't change. Could this be the first catastrophe of many?"

Azazel hovered over Kevin Blockhouse, Porton Down's head guard. He probed the man's mind, smiled, and turned to his minion Gressil. "The man's a chronic thief, naughty boy. He also has access to the whole complex."

He addressed the legion of dark entities behind him. "Examine each soul. When you find an opening caused by malice, deceit or profane anger, enter. Soon we'll control our own troops within the heart of Porton Down. We must work fast, the Phineas priesthood will soon be here."

Azazel slipped into Kevin Blockhouse's soul and explored. His human host stole drugs, among other crimes. A nice earner, it seemed. He believes the government doesn't pay him what he's worth, and in his mind that justifies the thefts.

The entity observed the man's daily routine. He compelled the guard to walk around the complex searching, until at last he saw a white-coated young woman with glasses leading Imogene along a corridor. He smiled. This would be easier than he'd imagined. This time, he would succeed.

He must. The eternal pit frightened even him.

As he drifted away he remembered the scientist, and made his way to the lab. He hovered near the ceiling watching scientists mixing and boiling various liquids. One man, whose name tag said he was M. Blevins, stood out as he held up a flask of pink liquid. Azazel smiled. It was Zetronia, he was sure of it.

Azazel entered the man's mind. To his disappointment it was fairly clean, but the man was an absolute atheist, a blank slate. Quickly he programmed his instructions into the man's mind. He would never know why he left the concoction in the unlocked fridge.

McCullage, Sam, Braeden, and Xantara crept towards the large house, in a quiet, dark valley that stretched into the distance. They'd risked hiking along the dirt road, ready to dive into the bushes should a car approach. As they neared the house, McCullage stopped. A light shone through the third-floor window, but no cars were parked outside. They crept around to the back and saw a light in a downstairs room.

The detective signaled the others to wait, and sneaked closer to peek into a window. It was the kitchen, and he saw an old man and a large, plain woman eating supper. Was this the right place? The Yates people were nowhere in sight. A dog barked, and the old man looked up. It was time to move.

He returned to the others and whispered instructions, and they walked stealthily to the back door. At McCullage's nod, he and Sam busted the door open and rushed the couple. They didn't resist as he handcuffed them. Braeden and Xantara stepped through the door, and stopped.

"Who are you?" McCullage asked as he flashed his identity badge.

The old man trembled. "I'm Hamish, the caretaker, and this is the housekeeper, Abigail. We've done nothing wrong. Ezekiel forced us to look after the women."

"Where is the Yates family?"

Hamish shrugged. "I have no idea. They told us this morning to watch the women, and took off." He leaned back against the table, and stared at the floor. "We was planning to call the police, but never got the chance."

McCullage jabbed the man's shoulder. "Where are the women?"

Hamish glanced up. "Upstairs, in an attic room."

The detective turned to Braeden. "Watch them." He crooked his finger for Sam to follow, went to the stairs, and climbed two flights. They tried the doors until they found one locked. He knocked on it.

"Anyone in here?"

He paused, then knocked again.

"Please save us!" a voice inside said.

McCullage tried the lock again, then stepped back and nodded to Sam, who kicked against the door lock. Its frame splintered as it crashed open.

Inside, two women lay under blankets on their beds, each with one leg chained to the other. The detective picked the lock and the chains dropped to the floor. Bryony jerked up onto her elbows. "Detective, thank God!" She swung her legs around and stood, grabbing the bed for support. McCullage looked at the red-haired girl. "Who are you?"

"Sally Lyons, they kidnapped me weeks ago, in Aberdeen."

"Don't worry, we'll soon have you both home."

Xantara brushed past him and hugged her friend. "Thank God you're okay."

McCullage called the local police to arrest the caretaker and housekeeper, then dialed Inspector Grant. "Sir, we have Bryony and another girl, but the Phineas Priesthood members have left."

"Well done, McCullage, at least you've rescued the women. Tell me where you are, and I'll send the Special Forces team to examine the house. We'll find them."

Susanne watched the news on her IPad as she and Hugh flew back to London. She sat straighter and glanced at him, pointing at the IPad's screen. "Look, Hugh, crop circles all over the West Country. The Westbury circle appeared first, a double helix. I've never seen one like that, have you?"

Hugh stared at the new patterns on her IPad, watching the newscaster show field after field, each design more intricate than the last.

"No. In fact, all the designs appear similar. What can they mean?"

They listened as the newscaster interviewed an expert from the local UFO society. The man, dressed in a crumpled tweed jacket, spoke in a loud voice and looked directly into the camera.

"I believe the current circles represent constellations," he said. "Perhaps they were made by star people, or maybe the Council of Elders the young girl talked about. Viewers can expect an increase in UFO sightings soon. That's the norm when a new crop circle appears."

Susanne closed the cover and adjusted her seat. "Let's go back to Wiltshire. If Imogene's parents are home, maybe we can interview them."

As Ezekiel's cousin Jeremiah drove the Land Rover down a bumpy road, Ezekiel awoke from his nap in the front passenger seat. He folded his arms and eyed the surrounding fields. In the back seat, his cousins Obadiah and Malachi were mumbling about some inane thing. They'd been arguing about something for the past hour.

Ezekiel swigged from his water bottle. Just ahead was the farm he owned, near the Tetricus Science Park section of Porton Down where authorities were housing Imogene. He leaned back and smiled. They'd hole up there and wait for the Lord's instructions.

The Land Rover pulled up outside the Elizabethan farmhouse, set back from the road. As they stepped out of the car, the farmer's wife opened the farmhouse door, wiping her hands on a flowery apron.

"Mr. Yates, sir, we haven't seen you for a long time. Would you please come in?" She stepped aside, head bowed, to let the four men inside.

Ezekiel smiled. "Where's your good husband?"

She glanced nervously outside. "He's in the cowshed. He shouldn't be long. Meanwhile, can I offer you a drink?"

"Certainly."

As she turned toward the kitchen, Jeremiah stepped behind her and expertly twisted her neck. She fell without a sound.

"Hide her before the husband comes in," Ezekiel said. Jeremiah dragged her into a cupboard under the stairs, then waited at the door.

Her husband came through the door. "Whose Land rover is outside?"

Before he could take in the visitors, Jeremiah jumped him and slit his throat, then stashed him with his wife under the stairs.

Ezekiel yawned, and rubbed his chin stubble. "I'll have another nap," he said. "It's been such a long journey, and I need to sleep before I consult the Lord." He climbed the stairs, winced as his gout plagued every step, found the couple's bedroom, and slept.

Jeremiah sat with his brothers around the kitchen table, a gleam in his eye. "I've read up on Porton Down, and I've come up with a plan."

Obadiah sipped his tea, replaced the cup, and licked his lips. "And what's that?"

"I learned they opened the facility in 1916 to research chemical weapons for the First World War," he said. "They supposedly still have stockpiles of Sarin and the Black Plague virus. If we could get our hands on them…"

Obadiah whooped. "The authorities daren't touch us. They couldn't risk a chemical release. Why, we'd be in control. If we were ever cornered, we'd hold the ultimate bargaining chip."

Jeremiah rubbed his hands. "Yes! There's anthrax and CS gas, too. If we can find the cache of chemicals, we would command the world's attention."

CHAPTER NINE

In Chicago, the Sears floor supervisor frowned and shook her head as the young clerk rushed out of the elevator and dashed around the lingerie counter, holding her side.

"Sorry I'm late," she said. "The kids acted up, and I got stuck in traffic. The mayor swore to improve traffic flow, but it's just another broken promise."

The grey-haired woman with bright red lips sighed. "This is one time too many…"

The young woman's eyes filled with tears. "Please! My husband left me, and my twelve-year-old daughter's rebelled. Last week her friends styled her beautiful hair into a Mohawk, then this morning I saw a tattoo on her arm. I'm afraid I lost it and slapped her. Then her little brother kicked me, and I lashed out at him. I feel terrible leaving them without making it up."

The supervisor touched her arm. "I do understand, but I have to answer to my boss. He's received other complaints."

Her assistant hung her head and swallowed. "I'm so sorry. I won't be late again."

"I'll see what I can do. What about your children?"

The mother pressed her hand to her heart. "I'll make it up to them. Tonight I'll give them a treat. Maybe a movie, cuddle up on the settee, and show them how much I love them."

∼ *** ∼

Bill Jackson filled the fuel tanker, waved to his fellow drivers, and set off on his route in the downtown traffic. Why did he have to service these gas stations in the busiest parts of the city? Grid-lock after grid-lock, and then the manager bitched when he was late.

As he passed through a green light, a truck loaded with steel girders ran the red light. Its driver braked at the last moment, but it was too late. The truck hit Jackson's tanker, and its steel beams became projectiles. One crashed through Jackson's windscreen, narrowly missing him. God, that was close.

Thuds echoed through his cabin. My God, the girders are hitting the tanker! He killed the ignition, jumped out, and ran. Fifty yards on he stopped to catch a breath and looked back. No explosion, thank God. His tanker looked like a porcupine, metal rods sprouted all over it.

Jackson pulled out his cell phone and called 911. "Fire department, quick. I'm at the Corner of Cross and Kings, and my tanker's leaking gas." He walked back, a little closer. The petrol ran down the tanker's sides and pooled over several drain covers. The other truck driver stared from across the street. Jackson's face flushed, and he shook his fist. "You mad bastard! Look what you've done!"

The fire truck arrived, and four yellow-suited men jumped out, unrolling their hoses on the run. He relaxed as the professionals gave the porcupine a bubble bath of foam, hoping the stuff worked.

A firefighter called him over. "How much escaped?"

Jackson checked the meter and slapped his forehead. "Damn, the tank's almost empty. It was full!"

The fireman called his chief. "Tom, a full gas tanker leaked its whole load into the drainage system. What should we do?"

"Flood the system with foam," a voice said over the speaker. "And hope it smothers the gas before it ignites!"

The fireman stared at the sewer covers, where gas swirled as if down a bathtub drain. "Where do the sewers run from here?"

"Downtown. Pump foam into the drains, and I'll advise the Department of Water Management."

The panhandler sat on the sidewalk, next to a handmade sign that read "Out of work. Family to feed." He held out his grubby cap to each passer-by, but most ignored him. He looked into his hat. Only a few cents. Well, wait until they fell on hard times.

He craved a joint, and pulled out his stash of weed and papers with his free hand. Over the years he'd perfected the one-hand roll. The match lit as he scraped it against the stone flags, and he held the flame to his joint. He blew out a puff of smoke and relaxed.

He jumped as a police officer walked around the corner, and instinctively threw his hot cigarette butt down a nearby flood drain. The overweight officer strolled on.

Damn, waste of a joint.

***

The young mother glanced at her watch, then at her supervisor.

"Go on, eat lunch, but be back five minutes early, mind."

"Thank you."

She took the elevator down to the employees' cafeteria, and got into line. She sat at a table and looked at the food on her tray, and her stomach cramped. How could she have slapped Colleen? She hoped her daughter would forgive her.

She ate half the burger and a few fries, then pushed her plate away. Time to get back to work, but first a restroom break. Someone held the powder room door for her, and she stepped inside. She gasped as flames shot up from each stall and rolled across the ceiling. A hot blast of air threw her back. She looked down and screamed as her dress caught fire. My kids. Oh God, no! I'll never see them again.

In London, Frank Carrington watched the afternoon news. He sat up straight and his left eyebrow lifted as an inferno filled the screen. Scenes of downtown Chicago, filmed from a helicopter, flashed across his view.

The camera zoomed in on Chicago's Sears building "The entire building's burning," the voice-over said. "At least fifteen other iconic landmarks are burning around it, and fire crews can't get near them. There must be a hundred thousand people in the affected area."

Frank buzzed the Home Secretary. "Alex, come in and see this."

Alex rushed into the Prime minister's office and they focused on the TV screen. The announcer said the Chicago fire chief had linked the blaze to a gas tanker accident. Its petrol entered the storm drain system and had run underground flooding the whole area.

They watched until the advertisement break, then Frank clicked the set off. "The last big Chicago fire was in the eighteen seventies" he said. "A cow kicked over a barn lantern, I believe. I wonder if we can help, somehow." He clicked off the TV. "By the way—anything happening on the terrorist matter?"

"We just got a lead," Alex said. "They went to a central Scotland estate, but have since left. Detective McCullage tracked them down and rescued two kidnapped women."

Frank eyed him. "And just what was their sin?"

"None, apparently. Incredibly, they intended to use them to breed new Phineas Priesthood members. Our men are headed there now."

Frank rubbed his chin. "Well, a little progress, I suppose. Keep me posted."

Bryony lay in bed, eyes open. Would he find her here? Thank God Xantara offered her a room. That horrible man had traumatized her, had damaged her physically and emotionally. A soak in the bath hadn't removed the filth. Her skin still crawled.

Xantara came in and opened the curtains. "Come on, sleepy-head, I've made breakfast."

Bryony donned a borrowed housecoat and followed her best friend downstairs. She stared at the dish of bacon, scrambled eggs and hash browns, her favorite. "I'm not hungry, but the meal looks delicious." Jeremiah had ruined yet another aspect of her life.

"Well, you must eat. Let's have coffee on the veranda."

Bryony rubbed her arms and stared at the floor. "I'm scared."

Her friend stroked her back. "It's over now. You're safe, and can stay with us as long as you like."

Bryony closed her eyes and sighed. "Detective McCullage wants us to heal his wife, but I'm so tired."

Xantara rubbed her friend's back again. "She'll be fine for a few more days. You must recover first."

"Xan, I don't think it's over. Not for me, anyway." Bryony picked at the housecoat belt. "Jeremiah couldn't have raped me at a worse time, the middle of my menstrual cycle. What if I'm already pregnant?"

Doctor Schneider listened to the audio again, and turned to his assistant, Nicola. "Imogene's a great subject," he said. "She enters her past lives with ease. Just think how much we could learn about history, stories lost for centuries!" He leant back in his chair and locked his hands behind his head. "I need her here for at least another six months."

Nicola dropped into the chair opposite him, her smile wavering. "Professor, did you hear the news?"

"No, why?"

His assistant removed her glasses and polished them with the corner of her white lab coat. "Downtown Chicago's on fire. I mean every building. Thousands have died, and the firemen can't get close."

Schneider let his chair down and unclasped his hands. "Well, I'm sorry to hear that, of course. But it doesn't affect us."

She stared at him as she replaced her glasses. "Professor, what was Imogene's past life about?"

Schneider's body felt heavy, and his chest tightened. "The Chicago fire, in 1871. She tried to save her brother, but the crowd trampled her to death."

"And the life before?"

"She was a soldier in World War One, and died from the flu."

She snorted. "She—no, he—was nineteen, just like the boys that just died. Why don't you look him up and check his birthdate?"

He frowned a moment, then his fingers flew over his computer keyboard as he searched for "Robert Clancy." The clicks filled the quiet office, like a ticking time-bomb. "Here he is. Robert Clancy, born June 8!" He stared up at her. "My God, it's got to be a coincidence. Doesn't it?"

Nicola stood and shook her head. "What if another of her past lives re-enacts in the present?"

The doctor stood and backed away. "No. I promise you, the events are coincidental. They have to be." He stared at her for a long moment. "Not a word about this. Not to anybody, understand?"

CHAPTER TEN

Imogene paused at Doctor Schneider's open door, and turned to Nicola. "I don't want to visit the past again. It's sad, and I feel tired for hours afterwards."

"I'm afraid you must, my dear."

The doctor smiled and pushed up his sleeves as he walked toward her, and Nicola left. "Imogene! Today we'll just talk. You can tell me about your family. Be a dear, and lie on the couch."

He swept his hand toward the couch, and she lay down and searched his face. "You promise?"

He went to his desk and returned with a syringe. "Of course! But before we start, you look so pale. You're not getting enough sunlight. These vitamins will bring color to your cheeks."

He poked her with the syringe needle, and she winced. "Ouch, you hurt me."

He sat, crossed his legs and positioned his microphone. "Have you heard from Rahmiel recently?"

She clutched her stomach as a wave of sickness flowed over her. "I can sense her presence, but she hasn't spoken. When can I go home?"

"Not long now. The more you co-operate, the sooner I can release you."

Imogene lifted a hand to her brow. "I feel dizzy. Doctor help me, I'm not well, what's wrong with me?" Her eyes closed, and he began to direct her.

~ *** ~

Ten-year-old Joel Geldersheim stood in line with his parents and his identical twin brother, Jory. His small suitcase contained his metal construction kit, a kite, his beloved toy dog, and other treasured possessions. A man in a pale grey- and black-striped suit snatched it from him and he yelled, but his mother touched his head to silence him.

Joel scowled as he watched the man go along the line removing everyone's luggage. "Mom, why did he steal my case? I want my toys back."

His mother watched the snow-covered train pull away, its wheels squealing, and pulled her scarf tighter. "Be quiet, now. We'll get through this."

The boy looked back at the row of grey, black, and brown coats of the others from the train. Why did they all have a yellow Star of David on them? He turned to a man with a twisted leg, shuffled behind him. "Excuse me sir. Where are we?"

The man's wrinkled, care-worn face formed a grimace. "Auschwitz, child, the labor camp. We'll have to work hard for our keep."

Joel again glanced at the soldier at the front, and focused on the row of medals on his uniform. His long leather coat lay open. He held a riding crop and, as each person reached him, pointed with it, left or right. Mainly the men went right, and the women, children, and crippled men went left. Joel slipped his hand from his mother's grasp and grabbed Jory's. They'd better not separate him from his twin.

His family reached the officer. His father went right and looked back at them, and a soldier prodded him with a rifle.

"Mom, where's Dad going?"

His mother pulled them close.

"Twins?" the officer asked, pointing.

His mother trembled, and held him tighter. "Yes, identical twins."

The officer beckoned to a prisoner. "Take the boys to Mengele's barracks."

Joel clasped his mother's hand harder and kicked out at the man, who at once clouted his ear.

"Please, let me stay with my boys!" His mother pleaded.

Another soldier swung his rifle butt into her stomach and she doubled up, then stumbled to the left. As the man dragged Joel and his brother away, Joel tried to reach for his crying mother. They trudged through the snow to a low wooden building, and the man opened the door and threw them in.

"We'll be all right," he whispered to Jory. He was the oldest, by five minutes, and was supposed to care for him.

He looked around at the long, bleak room. It was full of boys, twin boys, lying on planked platforms. One of the older boys directed them to one, and helped them up. Two filthy blankets were bundled near the back, and he pulled one around Jory.

Jory wrinkled his nose. "It stinks."

Joel sat close to him, huddled under his own blanket. "Never mind, we need to stay warm. The cold can kill us."

Late that afternoon, an overweight soldier ordered them to the room's center. His assistant pulled off their pullovers and shirts, and told Joel to lie on a wooden bench. As he tattooed something above on Joel's arm, Jory cried. In moments he was also tattooed with the number 1528792.

"It's okay Jory. It hurts a little, that's all."

The assistant measured their height and weight, and wrote something on a piece of paper with printing on it. At last he let them go, and they climbed back onto their dark platform and lay down.

The next morning, a soldier forced the boys into a line outside the barracks. Joel whispered to the boy next to him. "What will they do?"

"They line us up every morning for a roll-call, then give us a small bowl of porridge and a cup of water." He pressed a finger to his lips as a guard walked by.

The next day a slight, smartly dressed officer entered the room. "Good morning, boys." He threw candy on the floor, and the boys scrabbled for a piece. He turned to Joel and Jory.

"What have we here?"

A soldier behind him shoved the boys in line, side by side. "A new pair of identical twins, sir."

The first soldier caught Jory's chin between his fingers and inspected him. "Good, good! Bring them to the laboratory after lunch."

When the men left, Joel turned to his neighbor. "What will they do with us?" he asked. "What's a laboratory?"

The boy's head sank to his chest. "That's Mengele, Joseph Mengele. He's a doctor who works on us."

"What do you mean, he works on us?"

The boy pointed down the room. "See the boy swaying over there? The doctor tied him in a chair and hammered his head for hours, and he went mad." He pointed to a pair of boys opposite them. "He poured chemicals into their eyes, trying to turn them from brown to blue. They're both blind now."

"What did he do to you?"

"He's drawn blood, pints of it. I'm tired all the time." He held out his arms. "Look at the scars. He did the same to my twin, but he died."

Joel moved away and covered his ears. What would happen to him and his brother?

Imogene's eyes rolled. Her breath grew shallow, and she convulsed violently.

Schneider jumped up, ran across the room, and pulled out a phial and syringe from the corner cabinet. A dose of Felbatol should work. He plunged the needle into her arm, and vowed to reduce the dose next time. The convulsions abated.

He needed to learn more. He put his lips close to her ear. "Imogene, relax. Go back through the door to your past life in Auschwitz." He stroked her hand. "It's only a dream, Imogene. The journey can't hurt you."

He watched as her eyes darted beneath her lids. Good. She was back.

Joel heard a truck pull up outside, and hugged his brother. "Don't worry, we'll be okay. Stay close."

They joined the other twins on the truck bed. Joel noticed a few cried, but most wore a vacant stare. His knees trembled, his head swam, and the hair on his arms and the back of his head rose. He jammed his hands under his armpits as they passed gaunt men with shaved heads. Not one glanced up at him.

The white-coated assistants made the children undress and lie next to one another on their backs. Several people examined every inch of their bodies, then drew blood and ordered them to turn over.

Joel screamed as the large needle entered the base of his spine. Two men held him down, and the third extracted the spinal fluid. Joel's brother shook uncontrollably next to him. As his brother screamed, a murderous rage flooded Joel's body. He struggled to help, but couldn't break free.

"Line up!" someone yelled. The twins helped one another up and formed a queue. A man walked down the line, injecting one twin of each pair in the arm. Joel prayed he would bypass Jory and inject him, but he didn't. He looked behind him. Tables held smoking glass flasks which sprouted tubes. What were they for? His body stiffened, and he whimpered.

As the truck carried them back to the barracks, he sat next to the same boy. "When will our parents fetch us?"

The boy touched his shoulder. "You don't know what happens here, do you? They gassed your mother, then burnt her in the ovens. They'll work your father for a few weeks before taking him to the gas chambers. Come here."

The boy led him through the near darkness to a dirty window, and pointed. "See the smoke coming from that tall chimney? That's where they gassed and burnt my parents and three sisters." He sobbed and turned away. "They told me," he said. "The guards told me."

Joel gasped. He couldn't believe it. He studied the young boy's face and sobbed himself.

The boy, white-faced, touched his arm. "You can smell it," he said. "You see the fire, and then smell it. And that's not all. We've seen things you wouldn't believe."

"What?"

"Well, people clubbed to death, carts loaded with dead bodies. This isn't a labor camp, this is a death camp."

As the night closed in Joel hugged his brother, and they cried for their parents. Joel kissed him. "I'm sorry, Jory. I'll always love you, whatever happens."

Imogene awoke, and opened her eyes. Schneider smiled. "Are you all right, my dear?"

She shrank back and slipped off the far side of the couch. "You monster, you were Mengele! He looked different, but his spirit matched yours. Don't touch me, ever again!"

Schneider sat back in his chair. "Perhaps I was," he said, slowly. "We don't remember our past lives, but we work through our karma. At least I'm in a new body now." A flush spread across his cheeks, and he stood.

Imogene rushed around the couch and pummeled his chest. "I hate you! You're not taking me back there. I'll tell my mom and dad."

Schneider shrugged. "Sorry, my dear, I've had to suspend their visits. You're not well."

She stepped back, and her shoulders dropped. "I'll tell my aunt."

"My staff has already escorted your Aunt Sybil home. We told them you may have a contagious disease and we need to monitor you in isolation. Behave yourself, and Nicola will walk you back to the ward."

Imogene sat on a bed and looked around the empty ward. It was true, Aunty Sybil has gone. How could she leave? She sighed and lay back, sniffed loudly, and hugged herself.

"Rahmiel, I need you."

A pin-point of spectral light appeared beside her bed, then shimmered and grew. She heard soft music, and knew the angel lady would help her. Rahmiel's figure sharpened, and she smiled.

"Imogene, my love. This is difficult for you, but necessary. I'm sorry, but the Council of Elders needs you to explore your past lives. They use the energy released to create events that shape people's direction."

Imogene shook her head slowly. "Those poor twins. How can I see their pain again? I don't want to know what happens to them—happened to me, my past self. Isn't there another way?"

Rahmiel floated above her. "I'm sorry, but you're a strong child. The council chose you because you have a resilient spirit. This work will help all people, including your parents. Please, do it for them."

The woman vanished, and Imogene closed her eyes. She was so tired. Did she have the strength? When would she see her parents again?

CHAPTER ELEVEN

Azazel loomed behind Ezekiel unobserved, as his charge knelt beside the bed.

"Lord what would you have me do?" Ezekiel asked.

The evil entity's fingers reached into the lawyer's skull. "Fetch the girl, and kill her at Avebury Circle. The head guard will help you, but first you must create a diversion."

"Yes, Lord."

"My angels will control the guards and a certain scientist. I will arrange for the scientist to leave a flask of toxic chemical in a small unlocked fridge in the corner. You are to take it from the lab."

Ezekiel rested his head on his arms. "Yes, Lord. I'm your faithful servant."

Ezekiel stood and smiled. Again, he'd heard the Lord's voice, talking directly to him. He went downstairs, almost floating in his warm feelings for God, and joined his three cousins.

"The Lord has spoken," he said. "It's time to finish the Pembroke girl off, for good. And we are to steal a chemical weapon. The Lord told me so, in my prayers."

"We need a diversion." Obadiah thought a moment, then slapped his fist into his hand. "I know! Tomorrow night there's a race meet at Salisbury racecourse. The grandstand is two levels high, and holds maybe a couple hundred people. If we had explosives, we could set a bomb and cause a diversion."

Jeremiah sat straight. "No problem. An accelerant and a match will do the trick. Obadiah, see to that, while we get the girl. We'll do God's work at Porton Down, and burn a few sinful gamblers at Salisbury. What could be better than that?"

Malachi spooned sugar into his coffee. "You mentioned the head guard. Who is he?"

"The Lord gave me a name," Ezekiel said. "Kevin Blockhouse. Jeremiah, check Facebook. Maybe we can find a photo."

Jeremiah opened his laptop. "Porton Down will have tight security. What if we're caught?"

Ezekiel touched his arm. "Don't worry. The Lord has the whole operation under control."

Jeremiah stopped his Land Rover and studied the Porton Down base through his high-powered binoculars. There he was. Mr. Blockhouse was leaving in his car.

He shifted into drive and followed the guard's car for three miles, until it turned left into a small housing estate. Jeremiah parked behind his car, waited perhaps ten minutes, then knocked on his front door. When Mr. Blockhouse answered it, Jeremiah opened a bag filled with fifty pound notes. The man's eyes widened.

"For you, if you can help me."

Without a word, the guard ushered him inside.

Jeremiah glanced about. The dingy room was furnished with a torn maroon faux leather couch and a coffee table, both from the sixties. He sat and waited, the open moneybag between his feet. The man's gaze didn't leave the bag for an instant.

"What do you want me to do?" he asked, finally.

Jeremiah shut the case and stashed it behind his knees. "Have you seen a young girl at Porton?"

"Yes, Doctor Schneider's treating her. Why?"

"Because her detention is illegal. We want to return her to her home."

Blockhouse leaned back into the couch, resting on its arm. His fingers rapped it slowly as he frowned. "But the government is holding her, not thugs. Besides, you'd never get away with it."

"That's not your concern. Do you have a pass key?"

The guard felt his front pocket. "Yes, but I don't want any trouble."

"Don't worry. All I want are three guard's uniforms, the key, and directions to the girl. No one will connect you to this, I promise. You'll be here, at home."

Keith Blockhouse rubbed his chin and looked at the moneybag that poked out behind Jeremiah legs. "How much?"

"Thirty thousand pounds in cash. Unmarked notes."

His eyes narrowed. "Well, if you say they're holding her illegally…"

Susanne and Hugh booked the twin rooms at Monkton St Michael's Inn, then walked down the quiet High Street. The clinic closed at five, so the news anchor banged on the glass. Braeden poked his head around the clinic door, she waved, and he let them in. He led them through his office into the kitchen.

"Please have a seat," he said.

"Thank you." As they did, Xantara and Bryony came down the stairs.

Susanne's eyes widened. "Bryony, you're alive! How did you get here?"

Xantara shook her head. "I wish I could tell you, but everything's classified. Can I get you two a drink?"

"No, thanks. Are they still holding Imogene at Porton Down?"

"I'm sorry…"

Bryony reached across the table and tapped Susanne's arm. "I haven't signed any secrecy papers, so I can tell you. The authorities said she had a communicable disease, and suspended all visits. But we don't believe a word of it."

Susanne glanced at Hugh, then back. "Maybe we can help. If we say on TV that they're holding her hostage, maybe public pressure would get her released." She turned to Bryony. "We thought you'd died in the church explosion. Where have you been, and how did you get here? Wait—could I interview you on camera?"

"I don't know. If those people find out where I am, they may come after me."

"Don't worry. We'll keep the location secret."

Bryony looked down at her own hands. She flexed her fingers slowly, then looked up. "Okay. If it would help free Imogene, I'll do it."

"Good! Hugh, why don't you get your equipment?"

Susanne twisted a strand of hair with one finger, watching him leave. "Xantara, what do you know about crop circles?"

Xantara smiled. "I've seen the news reports. Well, my ancestors have noted them for centuries. In fact, they've seen them appear."

"So—you're saying they're not made by two men using a plank?"

"Have you seen how complex they are?"

Susanne nodded. "Well, how are they created, then?"

"Light beams. They come straight down from the heavens. The intricate shapes appear in minutes, so few people have seen them form."

"Do you know who's responsible?"

"I think Light Beings create them," Xantara said. "These mystical forms help us heal at Avebury. That's only my opinion, but I think it's as close to the truth as you'll find."

Hugh returned with his arms full. He clicked open a simple backdrop screen and set up two floodlights, then placed a kitchen chair before it. Bryony checked her hair in the mirror, settled in the chair, and Susanne sat facing her.

"Just be natural, and relax."

Bryony smoothed her skirt and looked up, frowning. "Will you promise not to push me for answers? I don't want to get the detective who rescued me into trouble."

"Of course. We won't broadcast anything you're uncomfortable with." Susanne nodded to Hugh, who flipped on his camera.

"Bryony, people thought you died when terrorists blew up St Michael's church. Would you please tell us what really happened?"

"The Yates family came to my house and knocked Braeden out, then kidnapped us."

"Us? Who is 'us?'"

"Myself, Imogene, her mother Xantara, her grandmother Sabina, and grandmother's twin sister Sybil. They took us into the church's catacombs to hide out before taking Imogene to Avebury Circle."

"Why would they do that?"

Bryony stiffened, and looked up. "To kill her! I don't know why, but the monument is the only place she can die, and stay dead."

Bryony glanced at Xantara, who nodded. She entwined her fingers and looked up into the camera.

"The detective found Braeden unconscious," she said. "They searched the church and couldn't find us, but did find Xantara's necklace. Later Braeden and his son Alistair returned and found the catacomb's entrance, then you and Hugh arrived."

To the point. Vivid detail after detail. The woman must have relived the scene a hundred times in her mind. "Tell us. Who killed Sabina?"

"Jeremiah Yates. He'd just learned Sybil was his mother. She'd been raped and left the resulting child—him—at a home for unwed mothers. That animal slit his aunt's throat for revenge." Bryony's eyes teared. "You wouldn't believe it—" She turned away.

Susanne leaned towards her and touched her cheek. "I believe you, Bryony. Of course, I believe you."

Bryony turned back. She dabbed her eyes, then took a deep breath.

"The Light Beings came," she said, softly. She peered into Susanne's face, and apparently realized she just might believe her, as she said. She grasped Susanne's knee and squeezed it tightly. "Then the dark entities came. I've never seen anything like that battle between them. Jeremiah and the others dragged me down a side tunnel. It's all like a dream, Susanne. I barely remember that horrible car ride to Scotland. And then that young woman—"

She sobbed again, and Susanne turned to Hugh. "Shut it down," she said. "Bryony...?"

"No!" Bryony jumped up. "We have to do this. Perhaps a glass of water, and I'll be fine."

Xantara brought her water from the kitchen tap, and she slipped it slowly. Finally, she set it down and resumed her seat. Hugh, who had indeed turned his camera off, switched it back on.

"Now, where were we?" Bryony asked.

"You said something about going to Scotland, and about a young woman. Who was she?"

"Ezekiel owned a Scottish manor," Bryony said. "The young woman was there when we arrived. Sally Lyons, her name was. They planned to breed us both to birth new priesthood members. Thank God those two detectives rescued us."

Susanne leaned back. "That is unbelievable," she whispered. "Oh, I believe you! But it's such an outrageous thing to happen."

"I know."

"Where's Imogene Pembroke now?"

"The government is evaluating her at Porton Down, and won't let her parents visit. They're distraught, as you can imagine. Their murdered daughter, miraculously restored to them, was stolen by the government."

Susanne turned to Hugh, and he turned the camera on her. "Who is Imogene Pembroke?" she asked. "What has she become? Should the government return her home? We believe so. We also believe the government should tell the public about the terrorists, and the child's test results. We want to know if her message is true, and what the consequences in that message are. This is Susanne Prentice, signing off for Channel Five."

Jim McCullage stood at his wife's bedside as the doctor listened to her heart. Her face still showed a tinge of blue, but she relaxed after an injection.

"Why couldn't she breathe?" he asked. "Will she be okay?"

The doctor motioned him outside and led him downstairs. "Her heart's weaker. I'd hoped for a few months, but…"

The detective closed the front door after the doctor and went back upstairs. Nancy tried to reach her water glass, but fell back against the pillow. He sat beside her and lifted her head to drink.

"Are you comfortable/?" he asked.

She gasped. "Honey, please pass me my medication. I need to sleep."

He kicked off his shoes and lay next to her, and cradled her frail body. The lump in her breast had gotten larger over the past few days, and now pressed against her diaphragm. She closed her eyes and smiled.

"I love you, and always will," she whispered. "Let me go."

"I can't!" He caught himself, realizing he was showing his own panic. "I'll arrange the healing with Bryony and Xantara immediately. Hang on, love, it will work. Believe me."

He watched the shallow rise and fall of her chest. Her face smoothed as sleep relaxed her muscles. His throat hurt, as he stroked her hair. She must survive until the healing ceremony. He kissed her forehead and watched her sleep. He couldn't bear her cruel disease's rapid progression.

Only one person loved him, and she lay on the brink of death. If the ceremony came too late, who would he confide in? Share a joke with? Look forward to coming home to? Would he be in time? Bryony had to arrange the healing ceremony right away. The rites must happen tomorrow night, but would she last until then?

CHAPTER TWELVE

"Ouch!"

Imogene clutched her stinging arm, as Dr. Schneider removed the syringe. She lay back on the white leather couch as he wiped the needle clean.

"Sorry, child." He laid the syringe on the table. "You're quiet today. Have you decided to cooperate?"

She stared up at him. "I don't want to go back to Auschwitz," she said. "I don't want to be Joel again, in that horrible place. I want to go home."

He smiled. "And you shall, my dear. I promise. My tests should be done in three or four weeks, then you can see your family. Now, watch the pendulum and relax."

Joel helped his brother onto the truck bed. On this trip he counted six sets of twins, all trembling. His brother huddled against him as he chewed his lip until he tasted blood. What would Mengele do to them today?

The soldiers prodded them into the lab and lined them up. Doctor Mengele tapped his riding crop across his palm as he sauntered along the row, inspecting each boy. Joel held his breath as he stopped opposite Jory, who hyperventilated and shrank back. The man pointed the whip at him.

"Take him into the surgery."

Joel's fists tightened. "Leave my brother alone!" He sprang at the doctor, knocking him to the floor. A guard struck his head and he fell, dizzy. Another soldier raised a rifle butt and he shielded his face.

"No, stop! Take me instead."

Mengele scrambled to his feet and pushed the rifle away. "I've a better idea." He signaled two soldiers to hold him. "Bring them both."

The soldiers dragged both boys into the surgery room, stripped them naked, and manacled them side by side on the operating table. Joel flinched as Mengele, smiling, injected them both. "So, you want to stay with your twin brother? Today I'll fulfill your wish. There's no closer relationship than Siamese twins."

Joel's body relaxed against his will. He couldn't move a muscle. What had the monster injected them with? Through half-open eyes he watched the doctor hold a scalpel high, then plunge it into him. An unimaginable pain shot through his side. His inner screams became a single tumult of terror until he blacked out.

Joel came to in the truck, his body racked with pain. He looked down and discovered, in the near darkness, that they'd stitched Jory to him from his underarm down to his hip.

"Jory…"

His brother didn't answer. The truck rumbled past a street light, and he gasped. Jory's face was gone. Only his eyes remained, floating in a mess of bloody sinew and bone.

He moaned. What had they done to him? Was he dead? Bile rose into his throat. He coughed and turned his head so he wouldn't choke.

The truck jerked to a stop, sending a fresh wave of pain through his body, and soldiers carried them into a building and dumped them on its cold concrete floor. The door slammed shut and a crowd of people, all naked, loomed over them.

"Joel?"

His heart soared. He'd never expected to hear that voice again.

"Dad? Dad!"

His father knelt beside him and Jory, and shed tears onto his face as he kissed him.

"Son, I'm here. We'll go to heaven together."

Joel squeezed him tightly. "Mom and Jory are already there,' he said. "Hold me."

His father's chin trembled. "What did they do to you?"

Joel flinched as he studied his brother. "Don't look at him, Dad! Cover his face."

"Son, there's nothing to cover him with. Everyone's naked, for the showers."

As Joel pressed hard into his father's body, several thuds sounded outside. A noxious odor enveloped him, and he and the others coughed and fought for breath. His father's body slumped on top of him, and he welcomed the pain. His dad's chest heaved as he sighed, and his lungs rattled.

The Reich had murdered his entire family. He was alone. His head spun, and a sour taste filled his mouth. He wanted to die, and prayed God would take him quickly.

Imogene's spirit left the scene, and she found herself once more in Osahar's Egyptian temple. The priest held a sweet-smelling bowl under her nose, and she relaxed.

"You look shocked, child."

She shuddered. "Those poor boys! Why do monsters walk the Earth? Why do I have to go through these horrible experiences?"

He moved closer, his stance strong. "I understand your pain, but you have a greater purpose here. Your actions will help rid humanity of such monsters. Come, hold my hands."

This time Imogene was ready for the rush of energy, and used the moment to revitalize her soul. Her body strengthened. Yes, she could carry out the tasks Rahmiel requested.

But just what event were she and Osahar creating?

McCullage watched the eight Guardians prepare for the ceremony, and glanced about. Avebury Circle wore a mysterious air at midnight, as if miracles could happen. He shifted from one foot to the other and checked his luminous dial. The women, in identical white robes, moved among the stones placing lighted candles and burning herbs. His heart pounded, and he tingled all over. At last Xantara nodded to him as they joined hands and formed a circle. Their soft chant filled the night air as he returned to his car.

Nancy lay on the back seat, covered with a tartan rug. He looked at her, his mouth set. "Not long now, my darling." He picked her up easily. Her weight had plummeted over the last few months, as her sickness progressed. He could barely feel her heartbeat against his chest as he carried her past the portal stones. "Hold on, my love. The Light Beings will help you!"

Her lids fluttered as he laid her on the altar rock and covered her with the rug. Please God, heal her, I beg you. I'll promise anything. Have mercy! He swallowed rapidly and stepped back as the Guardians formed a circle around his wife.

A faint pulsating glow appeared from behind the portal stones, then a Light Being emerged. Thank God, thank God. The Guardians swayed and raised their arms as their chant grew louder. The stars looked brighter in the indigo sky, but the new moon's thin sliver cast little light. The surreal sight made his head swim, and he clasped his hands together. Please God, heal her! Heal Nancy and I'll never ask for another favor.

More Light Beings streamed towards his wife. She looked deathly pale as they passed through her body, again and again. He felt himself stiffen, and tried to relax his shoulders. Did the ritual work? Was she healed? Finally, the spectral forms drifted back to the portal stones, faded, and disappeared. The women's arms dropped, and they beckoned him.

He ran forward and examined Nancy's face. She tried to sit, but fell back. "I'm so tired. Please take me home."

His heart dropped. Would she recover?

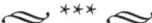

Susanne, hiding behind a monolith stone at the circle's edge, high-fived Hugh. They'd done it. What a scoop! She beamed and punched the air.

"Well done, Hugh," she whispered. "What a brilliant idea to follow them here. We got the whole ceremony on film, without a soul noticing. Do you think those creatures healed the woman? The boss will be ecstatic! Of course, we'd better not tell him until we find out."

Jim and Nancy returned home and he helped her to bed. She didn't look different, and as tired as ever.

He dropped into the easy chair next to her bed and watched her as she slept, conjuring up scenes from their life together. The wedding held at the registry office, because neither had relatives. Italy was the perfect country to honeymoon. He pictured the scene now, the moonlit dinner overlooking a beautiful bay. They'd spent the day exploring ancient white-washed hilltop towns, and enjoying the sweet scent from the glorious lavender fields. This house remained a joint effort, even though his work interfered at times. Together they'd decided on its décor and picked out the comfortable furniture they both loved.

Was their life together over?

He dreamt of her as he slept. Her wavy hazelnut hair swept back, framing her silvery gray eyes and soft pink lips. They laughed as they walked through the woods one spring day, and enjoyed a wonderful picnic spread out amid the trees. He grasped her hands and they rose together up to the heavens, and danced among the stars. How he loved her.

The sun shining on his face startled him awake, a new day already. He looked across the room to an empty bed. Where was she? Nancy stepped through the doorway, holding two cups of tea.

"Come on sleepy-head, time to get going. I've cooked your favorite breakfast. From now on I'll be caring for you."

Jim grinned, then reached out and took the cups. He picked her up and swung her round and round, released her, and dropped to his knees. "It worked. You're better! Thank you, God. Thank you!"

CHAPTER THIRTEEN

Doctor Schneider set up his laptop on a stainless steel desk in the small basement safe room, adjusted it so its web cam had a good view of the bunk before him, and called Nicola in. "Prepare the bed for Imogene," he said, pointing to it.

Nicola glanced around the small room, then at him. "Why the bunker?"

He adjusted his wire-rimmed glasses. "The guards don't have access to this room, so they won't bother us on their rounds."

Nicola made the narrow bunk up with a crisp white sheet and a gray army-issue blanket, then looked at him, eyebrows raised.

"I need a longer session with the child," he said. "I want to record details of two pre-birth events. I want to find out what happens between reincarnations, and go back in time to the soul's origin."

She stood a metal chair beside the bed and patted the pillow. "How long will you keep her under?"

"All night, I expect, if her body doesn't collapse. So many questions remain unanswered. I want to find out why souls undertake so many past lives."

Nicola left the room to get Imogene, and Schneider prepared the injection. He needed a breakthrough. His heart quickened and thumped in his chest. The girl held the key to human consciousness and to age-old questions, and success in this cutting-edge research would prove to be a godsend for his career.

The Porton Down gate guard carefully examined Jeremiah, Ezekiel and Malachi's passes, and waved their Land Rover through. They parked and walked into the security headquarters building where two guards, their eyes glazed over, ignored them. Jeremiah glanced at the sketch Keith Blockhouse had drawn, and crooked his finger at his brother and cousin. "This way."

Ten minutes later, they entered her ward. It was empty. Ezekiel walked through into the kitchen. "Where the devil is she?"

Jeremiah picked a child's storybook off the central table. "This is the right ward," he said, flipping through it. "Maybe she's with the psychiatrist. Let's check his office." He consulted the map and set off at a brisk pace, Ezekiel and Malachi trailing behind.

Doctor Schneider smiled as Nicola brought Imogene into the safe room. He was thankful for the thick walls, which he knew were soundproof.

"Welcome. Please lie down, Imogene."

She did so, and lay with her arms straight along her sides. She looked at the object in his hands.

"Sorry, a small injection. But I'll be careful."

Imogene lay passively as he injected her. He extracted the crystal pendulum from his lab coat and held it above her face. "Relax, now. Imagine you're walking down a flight of stairs, one step at a time. Twenty … step down … nineteen … doubly relaxed … eighteen…"

He checked her pulse and watched her eyes dull as she relaxed. "Imogene, move down the hallway of past lives. Find the door marked 'between lives,' and enter. Tell me everything you see and experience."

She curled her fingers, and thrashed about. "My guide's here. How wonderful to see her! We drift into the temple and sit near the mist, and when it clears I see myself as a child. We talk about my past life, good times and bad. I wasn't kind to my younger sister, but I made up with her before she passed on."

She became still, and frowned. "My life flashes forward. I'm an old woman, now. I don't want to die, and I shout at the people who care for me. My guide says I still need to show patience and empathy. She leads me to visit the Council of Elders, so they can see if I've learned the lessons they gave me before my re-incarnation."

The doctor leaned in closer. "Look around, and describe the scene."

"We walk through the Grecian colonnades into a temple, where the Council sits around a marble table. My guide asks me to sit on a stone chair. They decide I need rest and healing before I choose my next family."

Schneider pressed a button on his iPod, and the room filled with soft music. "Imogene, move forward in time to the rest area, and describe everything you see."

The young girl laughed. "There's my friend! He finished his incarnation before me. We walk through the meadows, where flowers glow with brilliant colors only found here. There's a swing hanging from a beautiful oak tree, and we sit in it and talk about other soul group members."

"Do souls choose their group, or do the spirit guides arrange that?"

"In my group we share a similar soul level. When a soul improves, it joins a more advanced class."

"How does a soul improve?"

"By learning life's lessons. But all souls repeat lives. It takes many lifetimes to learn one lesson, such as compassion."

Schneider touched Imogene's head gently, and she quieted. "Rest a while, child. Later we'll travel to the time of your soul's origin."

He heard Nicola gasp, and turned to her. She had her hand to her opened mouth.

"My God, I don't believe it!"

He followed her gaze, to where Imogene's spirit hovered two feet above her body.

"See the cord?" Nicola whispered. "I read somewhere that our spirits are attached to our bodies by a silver cord. It's true!"

He moved around the desk and stepped toward the girl, and Nicola grabbed his white coat to hold him back. "No, don't go near her! Her spirit could separate, and she could die."

Imogene turned her head, and her icy gaze bored into him. He shivered as his blood ran cold.

Jeremiah burst into the psychiatrist's office. "She's not here." He shuffled through files on the doctor's desk and grabbed one marked 'Imogene Pembroke.' "They've moved her," he said, tucking it under his jacket. He consulted his map. "The chemical store is two buildings over. We'd better move on."

He crossed the courtyard and paused, looking out over the plain. "Look at the horizon, a faint glow," he said, smiling. "Obadiah's done his job at the racecourse."

They entered the low-set block building and he swiped the pass key and stepped in. Squinting in the low light, he saw the long room held three rows of lab tables, perhaps forty feet long. At its other end was a single door made of shiny metal. He walked to it and saw it was solid steel, which certainly made sense. He tried the key card.

"What's wrong?"

He kicked at the door. "It won't open!" He peered at the locking mechanism. "Damn. It has a palm print system."

Jeremiah and Ezekiel searched among the chemical paraphernalia and he spotted the corner fridge. It was unlocked, as the Lord foretold. He reached in and extracted a single flask full of pink liquid.

He smiled. "Let's go."

Ernst Schneider sipped his coffee as he watched Imogene, her spirit now back in her body. It was incredible. Now he had proof of the soul's existence. He'd actually seen one, first-hand. It was indisputable! What secrets did this child hold, and how could he answer the question that's plagued mankind for millennium? Does the soul live forever?

He whispered close to her ear. "Imogene, leave your friend and move further back in time. How many lives have you lived?"

Imogene stirred, and her eyelids fluttered. "Many. I've experienced thousands of reincarnations, mostly on earth."

Schneider stiffened. "You've lived in other worlds?"

"We can pick from many worlds, planets in other solar systems. The Council sends us to these worlds to recuperate. Earth's the best planet to learn life's lessons, as humanity remains primitive, violent and debased, ideal conditions to test souls."

"Imogene, listen closely. Where did you begin? Did you always exist, or did someone—something—create your soul? Can you travel back to before your first life?"

The room was silent a moment. Finally Imogene mumbled something, and he leaned in yet even closer to listen.

"Bubbles, I'm in a bubble cocoon. The bubble bursts and I'm free, a new soul. They nurture and teach me for many years before they send me to earth. Times have changed, how awful." Tears trickled down her cheeks.

"What's wrong, child?"

"The cocoons lie empty. There are no new souls waiting."

"Why not? Where are they?"

"The energy of love has gone, and souls need that. I see now why Rahmiel and the Council of Elders are afraid. Babies still come, but they have no souls!" She cried, a long wail, and the doctor stepped back. "Those poor babies, born without a soul—they'll become evil monsters. The future looks so scary."

"Imogene, move forward in time to today, and beyond. Can you tell the future?"

"We're not allowed."

"How often do you reincarnate?"

"We used to wait for years, even a century, before entering a new body. But now they send us back almost immediately, to raise positive vibrations."

"How do you keep contact with the other side?"

"A part of our spirit stays there, and when we die our soul becomes whole. Most of us forget our past lives, but—well, our talents—art, music, things like that—develop and mature over several lifetimes."

Imogene's face drained, and she trembled. He would have to end the session, in case she was permanently damaged, but he still had many questions. Why did souls choose less-than-perfect bodies? And what happened when incarnations were fully completed? Did souls become guides or …? He shook off his thoughts. Maybe tomorrow he'd learn more.

 *****

As the four priesthood members sprawled in the farmhouse lounge, Jeremiah eyed the stolen flask on the sideboard, and frowned. "The Lord said to steal a flask holding a new deadly chemical," he said, slowly. "But how can we know we got the right one?"

Ezekiel looked up at him sharply. "Wasn't it the only flask there?"

"Well, I think so, but…"

Ezekiel re-filled his whisky tumbler. "We'll have to make sure. Maybe contaminate some food, and get someone to eat it."

"I'm disappointed we couldn't find the girl. But if the chemical works, the effort was worthwhile."

Obadiah turned on the TV to check the late night news, and grinned as his face flickered with its bright light. "Look! The racecourse stand was engulfed in flames, and burned up in minutes. Why, there must be two-hundred casualties! Jeremiah, you must claim the deaths for the Phineas Priesthood on You Tube."

Ezekiel watched the small yellow Volkswagen Beetle pull up outside the farmhouse. A Miss Marple look-alike eased out of the driver's seat and made her way to the door. He opened it before she could knock.

"Good morning, madam. Can I help you?"

The elderly woman fiddled with the string of pearls around her emaciated neck. "Where's the farmer's wife? I've come to pick up some fresh eggs."

Ezekiel held the door wide. "Come in and wait. She's in the henhouse, collecting them right now."

She stepped in and he shut the door behind her. "I've brewed a fresh pot of tea, would you like a cup?"

"So kind, don't mind if I do."

CHAPTER FOURTEEN

McCullage grinned as he joined the Home office team in the incident room. Sam looked up, and frowned. "What's happened?"

Jim sat next to him and gave him a thumbs up. "The ceremony worked. Nancy's healed."

Sam slowly shook his head. "I can't believe it. Are you sure?"

"She made breakfast this morning, and this afternoon she'll visit her doctor. You should see her, Sam. The color in her cheeks, the spring in her step—it's a miracle."

Inspector Grant entered and rapped the table. "The Phineas Priesthood has claimed responsibility for the lives lost at Salisbury racecourse," he said. "That's not all, watch this." He nodded to a team member, who tapped his computer.

Jeremiah's face filled the large screen. The camera pulled away, to show the tall Albino standing stiffly against a blank wall, holding a pink flask.

"God doesn't like gamblers, and it's the priesthood's pleasure to rid the world of one hundred and sixty-six sinners," he said. "Our next target will be faggots. Dirty faggots, beware! It's the Lord's will for us to end your disgusting practices." Jeremiah grinned as he held the flask up before him.

Inspector Grant's jaw clenched as he tapped the screen. "That's a deliberate taunt. See the flask? We could be facing a chemical attack. McCullage and Blackbridge, go and interview the Porton Down scientists. See if they can identify the pink liquid." He banged the table. "Well, what are you waiting for? We may not have much time."

Jim entered the Porton Down lab, accompanied by Sam and a guard, and counted seven white-coated scientists scattered around the room. Tubes and flasks covered the tables, and bottles bubbled away over Bunsen burners. Jim picked up a flask, pulled a picture of the suspect flask from his coat pocket, and compared them. They appeared identical.

Jim examined each scientist's face in turn, then his gaze locked with that of a dark, curly-headed, slightly built man. He waved him over. The man walked hesitantly to him, saw the picture, and stopped, his face turning white. Jim's lips pressed together.

"You know about the flask, don't you?"

The scientist studied the photograph, then his gaze darted around the room, as if searching for support from his colleagues. Sweat ran down his face, and he fought for breath. Jim pulled out a chair. "Please have a seat and tell me what you know."

He gave the man a moment to collect himself. "What is it, we need to identify it quickly," he said, tapping the photo, "and how terrorists were able to remove the chemical from a high-security site."

The scientist slumped in his chair. . "I should have placed it in the secure store, but I was running late and put it in the fridge," he said." It dawned on me as I drove home that I hadn't locked the fridge." He looked up at Dan. "But no one's ever broken into Porton Down, they wouldn't dare! Please believe me, I can't imagine how they got in to take it."

Jim folded his arms. "What's the pink liquid?"

The man looked up briefly. "It's an experimental mix, to use in chemical warfare. We call it Zetronia."

Jim raised his eyebrows. "What does it do, exactly?"

"It works in a similar way to sarin gas, but it's a liquid. You can spray it on food, clothing, or people, and it's lethal within thirty seconds. It paralyses muscles, and the victim suffocates. It also enters the bloodstream, poisoning the brain. We've worked for months, but haven't been able to develop an antidote."

Jim snapped his pen and let it fall. "You left it for anyone to pick up? Too much bother, was it? Didn't want miss a night in front of the television? You must try to develop the antidote quickly. There's no knowing how they will use the substance, or when. We need to be ready. You must make it a priority." He turned to the guard. "Show us last night's security footage."

Jim and Sam followed the guard back to his station. The man set three chairs in a row and they sat, watching him fiddle with the computer keys. He pulled up the lab video. In it, three guards entered the lab, and the tallest one tried to open the locked store. He kicked it in disgust. The rotund one picked up the flask.

"Zoom in on their faces."

Sam slapped his knee. "Jeremiah, without a doubt."

"Yes, and the tall fat one is Ezekiel Yates. Malachi's the other man, the cousin from Ireland. I wonder where Obadiah Yates is."

Sam peered at the screen. "Check the time. I'll bet Obadiah was busy being a firebug. It's the exact time the racecourse stand went up in flames."

"Give me that film footage," he told the guard. He turned to the others, "How did they get guard's uniforms and gain access? This won't please the inspector." He paused in the doorway. "We'd better check on Imogene before we go, I'm surprised they didn't try to abduct her."

Susanne Prentice gave a throaty laugh , turned to the camera and Hugh turned the spotlight on her.

"Folks, the film you're about to see will amaze you. It's exclusive film of an authentic healing at Avebury Stone Circle, carried out by the Guardians, a secret sect. As you may recall, this is the sacred site where they raised Imogene Pembroke back to life, and where she delivered her message to mankind."

The camera zeroed in on Xantara's face. "Imogene's mother, Xantara Pembroke, is believed to be the head Guardian." The camera flashed to a man carrying a woman toward the altar stone. "This is Detective Jim McCullage, with his wife Nancy. He's involved in the search for the Stonehenge terrorists. As you'll see, the Guardians performed the ceremony, then the detective carried his wife back to their car."

Spectral beings floated across the screen. "Isn't it amazing? What are these creatures? Can we use them to heal others?"

Susanne sat in her studio chair and shook her finger. "I'm sure you'd all like to see if Nancy benefited from the healing rite. We learned that she had only a few weeks to live. In fact, she lay on the brink of death. But watch this clip."

The scene changed to show Nancy walk to her car, slip inside, and drive away. "Now, does that look like a woman on her death bed?"

Susanne looked straight into the camera. "Folks, we have to accept that the young girl's message could be valid. The resurrection was no trick. I've seen her since with my own eyes. And it's a fact they buried her two weeks before, and now this healing is caught on tape. Are the flu pandemic and other events part of the consequences she promised? What will be next?"

Jim grabbed Sam's arm as they watched the Channel Five footage in the incident room. Inspector Grant's mouth fell open. "Is this true?"

"Yes, sir. The Guardians healed my wife, but I had no idea the media filmed the ceremony."

The inspector dropped into a chair. "Never in my life have I encountered a case with so many supernatural elements. I don't know what to think. But I know for sure we must catch those criminals before they use the chemical. I've set up roadblocks, and I want you two to search house-to-house, radiating out from Porton Down. But first question the guards, and find out how they got hold of the uniforms and pass key."

As they drove to Porton down, Jim called Nancy. "You okay?"

"Yes, love, but I can't go home. Media have surrounded the house."

"What did the specialist say?"

"The MRI shows the cancer's gone, but he's taken blood tests to check for sure."

"Nancy, go to the clinic in Monkton St Michael, park at the rear, and knock the back door. I'll call the doctor and his wife and let them know you're on your way. Sam and I have to go to Porton, and I don't know when I'll get back."

Jeremiah grinned as he switched off the computer. "This video will give the authorities the horrors. The old woman who called for her eggs died thirty seconds after sipping her tea. If a tiny drop like that can work so fast, we have the ideal substance for our work. The hate preacher in America, the one with the placards, he fascinates me, and he's given me an idea."

Obadiah smiled. "I know, the church that pickets soldiers' funerals, and the signs they carry talk about faggots, and say that God killed the soldiers because of America's sins."

"Yes, he's the one. The Lesbian and Gay Mardi Gras function is in Cardiff in Wales, next week. Faggots galore, in fact, hundreds of them. Now, that would be an event the authorities couldn't ignore."

94

Ezekiel coughed. "Perfect. We need to get away from here, anyhow. I have a cottage in Porthcawl on the coast, nineteen miles from Cardiff. It's right on the beach at Sker Point. The boatshed houses a launch, which could be handy."

"Praise the Lord, amen?"

"Amen."

CHAPTER FIFTEEN

"Hey Bud, move over. You're blocking my shot."

David's son threw him an insolent stare, but did move. David shook his head. His grandfather wouldn't have understood modern youth, after spending his own childhood years in this accursed place. He panned the prison's fence, then raised his camera to video the famous words: "Arbeit macht frei" – "Work sets you free."

For years, his grandfather had told him tales of his time here in Auschwitz. His great-uncle Moses, his grandfather's twin brother, had died after the infamous Doctor Mengele experimented on him. Menashe mourned his brother, his parents and three young sisters until the day he died.

David turned to his son. Thank God Menashe survived. If he hadn't, neither of them would ever have been born. He stared at Bud's clothing, which included a baseball jersey and cap. They didn't look right here, in this place. A wave of annoyance passed through him. "Bud, show respect. Lose the gum."

Bud spat his gum onto the ground. "Do we have to look around this dump? I want to go back to the hotel and play a video game. This vacation's so dumb."

David sighed. His grandfather survived to produce a great-grandson like this? He loved the boy, for sure, but he didn't like his behavior.

They followed the tour guide into the camp and David studied the wooden buildings. He tried to imagine Menashe as a young boy, but found it difficult. He passed a low building and peeked inside. The rows of platforms were exactly as his grandfather described.

"Look son, maybe my grandfather slept right here."

The chubby youth glanced inside. "You wouldn't catch me sleeping there."

David moved on. What had he brought into the world? He'd tried so hard with the lad, but Bud remained insensitive, even cruel. He'd caught him once burning ants with a magnifying glass. The boy didn't have a shred of empathy.

The tour guide called them, and they followed him to block four. The man pointed out the room filled with hair piled behind the glass.

"They shaved off people's hair before sending them to the showers," he said. "Thousands upon thousands, black, brown, blonde, even a few redheads. They sometimes used the hair to stuff mattresses for submarines, because human hair doesn't mold or get waterlogged."

David turned away, then back. What if his great-uncle's hair lay hidden in that pile? His own DNA could be there. Thank God his grandfather had passed on. He would have been terribly upset to see this macabre site.

His son peered through the large glass showcase in block five. "Dad, what's that load of junk?"

"Artificial limbs. They removed them before sending their owners to the gas chambers."

The guide hurried them along. "Block six is dedicated to the camp children," he said.

Bud shuffled from foot to foot. "How much longer, Dad?"

"Son, look at this row of children's photographs. Why, one could be my grandfather. My God, the clothes, the tiny shoes! Man's inhumanity never fails to astound me." He followed his son outside and gulped in the fresh air.

Bud pointed to the sky. "Dad, look!"

He looked up and jumped back as a bird fell at his feet. More birds thudded hard into the ground all around them. Thousands of starlings fell from the sky as they and the tour group sought shelter.

The boy looked through the doorway. "What's happening, Dad?"

"I don't know…" He glanced around, as if seeking an answer. "Look! It's not just the starlings. Sparrows, blackbirds you name it—all the birds appear affected."

The fall rate slowed and finally stopped, and they followed the tour group back to the bus. He searched the sky, and saw a huge dark cloud forming overhead. It looked strange, dark with a greenish tinge. The eerie round mass, which floated directly over the camp, was unlike any he'd seen before. The cloud's edges expanded so fast dusk fell early.

"Quickly! Everyone back on the bus!" The driver waved frantically, herding them like so many cattle. When they were all in, he switched on the interior lights.

"Look, folks, the weather's closing in. I think it's best we return to the hotel." The passengers were silent, staring out the windows. He drove along a gravel road and joined the main route.

The sky darkened as the cloud dropped lower, and David felt the bus speed up as the driver attempted to outrun the menacing mass. The bus reached the autobahn and the driver pressed the accelerator hard, pushing the passengers back in their seats.

Bud looked scared. "It's okay son, a little bad weather, that's all. We'll be back at the hotel soon."

The cloud dropped, and the driver pulled over as the swirling dark-green blanket surrounded the bus, closing off all visibility. Wisps of mist infiltrated through cracks in ill-fitting doors and windows, and filled the bus. The Dutch woman in front coughed and collapsed, then her husband. Horrified, David watched as each head disappeared below the high seat backs. He breathed in …

"Let's do it, then."

Susanne reluctantly walked onto the news set, as the crew scurried about. Her make-up artist hurried forward and powdered her nose, and she turned to face the camera. The light turned green. Time to roll.

"Good evening. Susanne Prentice, Channel Five, with breaking news. A strange cloud has appeared over Europe. Reports tell us the cloud first formed over the village of Auschwitz, near the infamous Nazi camp, and rapidly spread. Satellite views and sonar confirm it now covers the three capital cities of Berlin, Warsaw and Prague, and every town and village in between."

She paused as she silently read the next paragraph on her prompter. Brushing away a stray tear she read on.

"As the cloud dispersed, it revealed thousands of bodies. People, animals and birds littered the ground. This satellite view shows the utter devastation. Armageddon is the precise word to describe this tragedy. The estimated deaths are between six and eight million people, and there were apparently no survivors in the affected area."

The camera panned to the man who sat beside her. "I would like to introduce Sir Thomas Wilson, renowned astral physicist, and expert on space cloud formation. Mr. Wilson, can you explain this extraordinary event?"

The physicist's face looked drawn, his eyes mere pinpricks in his sunken face. "This incident is unprecedented in modern times, but may have occurred several times in past centuries," he said. "The Earth's magnetic field shifts on occasion, and flips. The poles literally change places, leading up to today's literal Holocaust."

Susanne poured water and handed the glass to him. "So, the magnetic shift has caused a toxic cloud? I'm confused, please explain."

The camera zeroed in on the scientist's face. Susanne could see every pore and line on her monitor and motioned Hugh to pull back. Mr. Wilson blinked and rubbed his upper lip.

"As the magnetic shift occurred, a comet, its gravity dragging a gas cloud behind, neared our atmosphere. The protective magnetic field ripped, just fraction of a second, at exactly the right time to allow the gas to enter our atmosphere. As the comet passed, the heat generated by its brush with the atmosphere blasted out jets of hydrogen cyanide, which is heavier than air. The cloud formed and sank to ground level."

Susanne gasped. "Could this happen again?"

The man nodded. "Any time. We're at risk from various types of deadly space clouds. Several regularly rain down radiation, but this one contained cyanide. I estimate the concentrated level killed in under a minute. Birds would have been affected first. That's the first sign. In recent times, several countries have experienced whole flocks of birds drop from the sky. The air contamination level in those cases was enough to kill birds, but not humans."

"But this time?"

"They call this cloud type 'noctilucent.' Normally, earth's magnetic field would protect us. The advent of the magnetic shift coupled with the comet produced the disaster. I would like to reassure the viewers that the chances of another event of this magnitude happening again over the next million years are very remote."

"Thank you, Sir Wilson." She faced the second camera. "Throughout the night and tomorrow we will update you each hour. If you have relatives from these cities, please call the number on your screen for advice."

Susanne dropped her head into her arms, and Hugh walked over and touched her shoulder. "Are you all right?"

She looked up and stared sightlessly into the distance. "Should we connect these deaths with the message? Another unimaginable consequence. It couldn't be, could it?"

Nicola heard a strange, strangled cry from behind the doctor's door, and stepped closer and listened. She knocked, pushed the door open and froze.

Schneider sat there, tears pouring down his face. Muffled sobs came from behind the handkerchief he pressed to his mouth. He stared at his laptop and sobbed louder.

She shook her head slowly. What could be wrong? He wasn't given to emotional outpouring like this. "What's the matter?"

His reddened eyes met hers. "My family, my entire family lives in Berlin. The toxic cloud killed them all, every one." He twisted the computer around, revealing a satellite image of the city. "Look at this! Not a living soul left, and it's my fault." He jabbed at the screen. "A gaseous cloud formed over Auschwitz and spread for over a thousand miles. Berlin, Warsaw and Prague—millions are dead, and I launched the whole event. You were right, Nicola, I should have realized the connection earlier. I don't know how, but Imogene is using the past life regressions to cause the consequences she promised."

Nicola sat opposite and leaned across to touch his arm. "I said it seemed there were coincidences, but I never expected anything like this. It's not your fault. If she is responsible, I'm sure she would have found another way to bring it about. What shall we do?"

Ernst Schneider clenched his fists and stared into space. He looked lost, and her heart ached. "I'll...I'll have to tell the authorities. But will they even believe me? I'm not convinced myself."

Frank Carrington looked up from the official report of the Schneider interview. "What do you think, Alex?"

The Home Secretary scratched his temple and grimaced. "Hard, isn't it? Schneider's tied three events together, each worse than the last. The flu pandemic—now that's odd. One could even say, impossible. Every dead person was a young man born on a certain day. The odds must be astronomical."

The Prime Minister tilted his head and pursed his lips. "The Chicago fire appears to be a definite tie-in to Imogene's past life recollection."

"Um…we can't deny the toxic cloud formed over Auschwitz before spreading. The people were gassed, like the death camp inmates seventy-odd years ago. The death count coincides with the Holocaust deaths and the World War Two soldier's deaths combined. Six to eight million, has to be close, doesn't it?"

Frank's mind raced, searching for answers. "To be honest, I don't know what to think."

"There are two common factors. One, Imogene Pembroke. Two, all the events have a supernatural component."

Frank tapped his finger against his lower lip. "Do we tell the world about this? I don't know if they would believe us anyway. I have to alert the US President and the House, then see where it goes from there."

"We do, I'm not sure what the President will think, but another viewpoint might clarify our own thoughts."

"True, but what do we do with Doctor Schneider? Should we allow him to continue to regress her, and risk more catastrophes?"

Alex looked out the office window, then back. "Here's another idea to consider. The child could reveal the next target, and give us time to prepare or prevent an event."

Frank pulled out his inhaler and puffed. "The terrorists, the girl—what a nightmare! Let's think about her message again. This Council of Elders wants the world to reduce violence and set up programs for the disenfranchised. Obey the Council, and the consequences end."

"Good luck with that. The Council's right. The world has worsened, and continues to slide further day by day."

A sense of calm infused Frank. "I've got an idea! We could use Imogene to contact this Council of Elders. Ask them to be more specific, and suggest they stop these atrocities and give us time to comply."

Alex gave a half-smile. "We'd still have to persuade the whole world to co-operate. That could take centuries!"

CHAPTER SIXTEEN

Frank Carrington tapped the back of the seat, and glanced at Alex next to him. "What's the holdup? I've never seen the traffic this bad along here." He signaled to the driver. "Switch on the news, and see if there's been an accident."

The driver fiddled for the local station. Thank God they'd chosen to go to Porton Down in an unmarked car. Other cars pressed them on every side, and he didn't want to be recognized. He relaxed back in his seat. The odor of fresh leather reminded him of his first brand-new car, back when he'd won the Stafford election. How full of ideals he'd been, and how quickly they were knocked out of him. The public had no idea of government trickeries, the deals done under the table, compromises made. But often it was the only way to get a law passed, Even then, of course, the law often ended up diluted.

The broadcast interrupted his reverie.

"...thousands of cars head for Avebury Circle, in response to last night's Channel Five broadcast. The police estimate over one hundred thousand hopeful families have already overrun the village and the monumental stones. Local police can't control them, and alarmed conservationists fear damage to the ancient site. Wheelchairs battle with one another to get closer, and cripples use their crutches as weapons. Several parents are carrying their sick children into the circle on homemade stretchers. The whole scene is chaotic, and more people arrive every hour hoping for a miracle..."

Frank banged the seat back again, this time harder. "That stupid reporter. Didn't she realize that showing that Avebury Circle thing would cause this? All she's interested in is a scoop, and these soon-to-be disappointed families—"

Alex leaned forward and asked the driver to turn off the radio. "Let's take the long way around. The road across Salisbury Plain is clogged up."

Frank sighed. "Call Inspector Grant, and tell him to clear the people before they hurt one another." He lay back and closed his eyes, just a moment, and turned his attention back to the road. Could a little girl really cause people to die with just her mind? He turned again to Alex. "I'm worried, you know? My son Julian's birthday is June 8th. What if he'd been born a year earlier?"

He hadn't really expected to become Prime Minister. He truly wanted to make a difference, but that seemed nearly impossible. There was always someone telling him why he couldn't do this, couldn't change that, for fear of upsetting this group or another. With recent events, disaster on disaster, people living in fear, mobs out of control and now a lethal chemical in terrorist's hands, he might have to declare martial law.

As McCullage and Blackbridge drove along the tree-lined farmhouse drive, Jim peered ahead. "That's the nearest semi-isolated house to Porton Down," he said, pointing. "It's our best bet."

They parked alongside a yellow Volkswagen. "Call the number plate in," Sam said. "Let's collect all the information we can before going in. The chemical's lethal, and we don't want to come in contact with it."

Jim looked for signs of life in the house as he waited for the policewoman to trace the license number. He stashed his iPhone and turned to Sam. "It belongs to a woman who went missing yesterday," he said. He glanced back at the house, hoping she was all right. "We should call in scientists in hazard suits from the base, just in case."

They did so. While they waited, Jim wondered how Nancy was feeling. He pictured her in the bedroom doorway, tray in hand. Her cheeks glowed, and the soft smile had returned. He'd missed that whimsical look and the personality behind it.

An hour later a soldier drove up in a large black van, and two men wearing orange hazard suits got out. McCullage recognized one; the idiot who'd left the flask out.

"Any spare suits?" he asked.

The scientist pointed to the van's back seat, and the soldier pulled two suits out. Jim and Sam struggled into them, and the soldier helped them with the oxygen tanks. McCullage found it hard to breathe. The smell of rubber and a slight case of claustrophobia made him want to shuck the suit, but he controlled his panic and led the other three to the front door. They entered the hallway and looked around. Sam pointed to the stair bottom, where a pool of blood ran from under a small storage door onto well-worn oaken floor boards.

Jim opened the low door, and an arm flopped out. He jumped back. He saw three bodies, stuffed inside. The face of the old woman on top looked beaten.

"Those bluish marks are chemical damage," the scientist said. "And look at her arms—the swollen veins and purple marks tinged with yellow."

Jim led the group out of the house. They struggled out of the suits and tossed them into the van.

Sam caught Jim's arm. "Retrieving these bodies is a case for the specialists," he said. "We'll come back when they give the all-clear." He frowned. "Did you notice the younger woman's throat? Jeremiah's work, for sure. The other two are probably the farmer and his wife. Let's walk around back."

A deathly quiet surrounded the house and land. They entered a dark barn and found a single piebald horse, assorted tackle, and a red tractor. Clucking drew them to the henhouse, where all the hens looked unaffected. "As usual they've gone and we're no nearer to finding them."

They returned to the car, and McCullage shifted into drive. "I'm tempted to re-visit the medium," he said. "She helped find Bryony, so maybe she can help us find them."

Doctor Schneider watched the cars park outside the medical block. The two-man escort stationed themselves to guard the doorway. He held the door as the Prime Minister and Home Secretary stepped out of their black SUV. "This way, please, sirs," he said.

They followed him into his minimalistic office, and the Prime Minister eyed the white leather couch. "Is this where you hypnotize the child?" he asked.

The doctor sat at his desk and looked into his drawer. "Yes, I'll get her file, the details are all there." He rummaged about, blood rushing to his head. Where was it? He would have a nervous breakdown any minute now. He could feel the pressure, his entire career was about to implode. The girl was a curse. What did his research matter now? Because of her, his whole family had paid the ultimate price.

Carrington tapped his foot. "Is the file's missing?"

Schneider wiped his hands on his handkerchief. "I'm sorry. The intruders must have it, but I can rewrite it! I recorded the sessions, and they're etched in my memory. The information I sent to you told everything of importance."

Schneider shrank and wished he could disappear. Would they send him to jail?

Carrington looked the psychiatrist straight in the eye. "That means the intruders have top secret information. I need to know exactly what the file contains and why the girl is so important to the Phineas Priesthood. Is there any chance the three regressions and the events that followed were coincidental?"

The doctor tried, unsuccessfully, to swallow the enormous lump in his throat. "That's up for interpretation, of course, but I do believe the girl somehow triggered all three events. With this Council of Elders' help, of course. After each past-life event she talks about an Egyptian priest called Osahar. They join hands and release a kind of power surge. Perhaps that's the trigger."

"If you're right, can you hypnotize her to give us contact with the Council?"

Schneider held his palms out. "I can try, but I can't give any guarantees."

Carrington pursed his lips. "I would like to meet her, but not here in your office."

Schneider led the two men to the ward and unlocked the door. The Prime Minister blocked the way and held up his hand. "I'll go in alone, if you don't mind. Meanwhile, brief the Home Secretary. Try to recall every detail from your report. Even minor facts could be important."

Frank shut the door behind him. The ward was as sparse as the doctor's office. The eight beds were covered with plain white bedspreads. White blinds hung half way down the frosted windows, the space's sterility unrelieved by the white and polished chrome table in the center. Imogene sat on one of the beds, her knees pulled up under her chin, staring into space.

"Imogene, my name's Frank. I'd like to have a chat, do you mind?"

The young child, who looked like an angel, a sad angel, didn't turn as he perched on the bed's edge. "I have a daughter a little older than you. You'd like her."

The girl turned to him. "What's her name?"

"Elizabeth. She's ten, and the youngest of my four children. Julian's the eldest, and Lizzy is my baby. You remind me of her."

Imogene's face flushed. She grinned, and her eyes sparkled. The change startled him for a moment, as if a real angel had touched him with a magic wand.

"Can I meet her? Would she play with me?"

Frank's heart sank. He would hate for Lizzy to be in her situation. How cruel to keep her locked up! But there seemed to be no choice.

"One day, perhaps. For now, we need your help. Will you work with us?"

She bent forward and rested her head on her knees. "I have to, anyway. Rahmiel told me to. She said the doctor's sessions would help my parents, and everyone else. But I miss my mom and dad, and the doctor's stopped them visiting me. Can I see them?"

A quiver ran through his soul as he touched her arm. "I don't see why not. I'd like to meet them, myself. I'll be around here for a few days."

Bryony held the test strip high, and shivered. It had turned pink. My God, she was pregnant!

She sat on the guest bed, hand to her aching head. A baby. She'd always longed for this day, but certainly not under these circumstances. Her flat stomach hid a miracle, but her mind swirled, pain mixed with delight.

She went downstairs to the kitchen and held the test strip out for Xantara to see. "In my heart I suspected this would be the outcome," she said. "What shall I do?"

Xantara put her arm around her shoulders and steered her toward the table. "Sit down, dear. I'll brew a pot of tea, and we'll talk it over."

Bryony's knees felt weak, and she shook her head. "That monster's child is alive inside me. What if it inherits his evil genes?"

Xantara set a cup in front of her and poured. "You could terminate it."

Bryony's heart rebelled. "I can't. Abortion is against all my principles. How could I live with myself if I destroyed a new life?"

"I feel the same way, but there's another consideration."

Bryony slopped her tea into the saucer. "What do you mean?"

"If the baby's a girl, she'll be a Guardian, and if she's never born the healings will end with you. Only the first born female can assume the mantle."

Bryony mopped away her mess. "Yes, I hadn't considered that. And Jeremiah's your cousin, which makes this baby part of you, too. I could never destroy anybody, let alone my own flesh."

Xantara took her hand. "Try not to worry. Between us, we'll raise the child to be kind, a good child."

Bryony tried to calm herself. "But how much is nature, and how much nurture? Despite our best efforts, he or she could be a clone of Jeremiah Yates." Unbidden, the memory of his cold, white form pressed against hers caused a shudder through her body and soul.

Braeden startled Bryony when he poked his head into the kitchen. "We've got visitors." He ushered in two smartly dressed men in dark suits. "Frank Carrington, our Prime Minister and Alexander Brittan, the Home Secretary."

Xantara flushed and flew out of her chair. "Please—please, sit down."

They sat at the table. Frank smiled. "Thank you for allowing us into your home," he said. "We'd like to discuss your daughter and the possibility of reinstating visits."

Bryony watched her friend lay her hand over her heart. Thank God. It was about time they let them see Imogene. She stood. "I'll be upstairs if you need me."

Xantara grabbed her arm. "Please stay. You're as much a part of this as we are. Mr. Carrington, this is Bryony, one of the women rescued from the Priesthood, and my best friend."

Frank offered her his hand. "Pleased to meet you."

She took it, and briefly squeezed it tight. If only he knew of the damage she hadn't been able to escape from. "Yes, I'm very grateful to Detective McCullage." At least it was only one baby. It could have been dozens, coming into the world with his evil genes. Her mind drifted to Sally, the young red-headed girl from Aberdeen. Was she pregnant, too? That would mean her baby and this one would be cousins.

Xantara and Braeden blurted out in unison. "How's Imogene?"

"She's well, and would like to see you both. But we must keep her at Porton for the time being. Doctor Schneider has hypnotized her several times, and discovered she has past lives that appear to have predicted recent events. For instance, one involved a soldier who survived the First World War, but returned home to die of influenza. His age and birthdate matched that of the recent flu victims."

Braeden tilted his head. "So you think Imogene created the recent outbreak?"

"We're not sure. But when you consider the next two events, it's a possibility. In the second session he regressed her back to the great fire of Chicago."

Xantara gasped. "And the third?"

"Well, she went back in time to Auschwitz. A young boy's life ended in the gas chamber."

Xantara's voice wavered. "Oh, no. Millions died in the toxic gas cloud. But how can it be connected to my daughter?"

Frank reddened. "Look, we're not certain. But it is an enormous coincidence, don't you agree? Her message from the Council of Elders did threaten consequences if the world didn't change. We want to try to contact the Council through her, and ask them how we can prevent further catastrophes."

Braeden pulled his wife close. "They have to find the truth. We can support her through this, if you'll let us."

"Yes—yes, I'm afraid you're right."

Frank stood and held out his hand. "Thank you both. We'll exercise every care to keep her comfortable, and you can visit her again once a day. I'm sorry, but there really isn't a choice. The world's fate may lie in her hands."

Bryony sighed as the door closed behind the two men. "I wouldn't mind if my fate were in his hands. Such a handsome man! The scar enhances his masculine appeal, don't you think?"

Braeden returned to the kitchen and shook his head. "I can't believe this. Xan, are past lives real?"

Bryony nodded hard, and Xantara smiled. "You and I have been together in numerous lives in many situations," she said, "and will be again. Our spiritual bond is unbreakable and forever."

He ran his fingers through his mop of blonde hair. "And Imogene?"

"Of course. When we see her we'll ask her about the lives she recalls. Snippets of past lives have teased my brain from time to time. Perhaps she can help us recall previous joint lives we've all experienced over the centuries."

Bryony smiled. "Past lives are a reality. Don't forget your son and me. We're part of your soul family, too." She patted her tummy. "And this new child may be an old soul waiting to be re-united with us all."

Braeden's eyes opened wide. "You're pregnant?"

"Yes."

He shook his head, in wonder.

CHAPTER SEVENTEEN

Jeremiah backed the 'Mary Rose' out of the boathouse, frowning at Ezekiel's pride and joy. It was much too conservative for him.

He flexed his long, white fingers and gripped the wheel. His strong hands had served him well, and he itched to use them again. His blood boiled as he recalled Bryony's rescue, which he'd recorded with his hidden security camera, which he had accessed over the internet and replayed over and over. How he wished his hands could be around that detective's neck! But he'd get her back, and use her again. She belonged to him.

He grimaced at the antiquated engine's putt-putt noise. Why would his cousin want a classic fifties wooden boat when he could afford a fast launch? He opened the throttle, and the stench of diesel filled his nostrils. Well, at least the speed was reasonable, and the engine well maintained. The craft would carry him around the headland and into Cardiff harbor, and that's what mattered.

He passed the dam built between Cardiff and Penarth docks and through the locks, and entered the five hundred acre freshwater lake. The sun sank below the horizon as he tied up at Ezekiel's private mooring outside the Cardiff Bay Yacht Club. He pulled his cap low, and hailed a taxi.

The Pakistani driver dropped him off on Dumballs Road, where the "Mardi Gras" parade gathered before moving along St Mary Street, then into the High Street. He decided to follow the procession's route all the way to Bute Park at Coopers Field, where they held the main attractions.

He paced along the faggot's course, deep in thought. How could he introduce the lethal chemical into the food chain? Ice cream sellers? No, too difficult. He glanced about him. The row of bare frames standing stark against the shop-lit windows would be tomorrow's well-laden food stalls. But how would he poison the food without being seen? He studied the brightly lit High Street. The quiet road, lifeless at nine at night, would change when the pubs closed. He should move on.

Flashes from a storefront caught his eye, and he froze as he looked at the window display of televisions. His muscles grew rigid, and he clenched his jaw. Each screen showed the identical images; him, Ezekiel, Obadiah, and Malachi. A ticker tape crawled across the screen's bottom. Stonehenge terrorists identified... dangerous to approach... call your local police station... Why had they waited so long to send out an all-points bulletin? Now they must exercise more caution. He snorted. No matter. God was on their side, so they needn't fear man.

Thank the Lord Ezekiel had prepared for this day! He'd put all his properties and bank accounts under pseudonyms, and they were untraceable. But now their faces were broadcast! He grimaced at his colorless, slightly reddened eyes on the screen, and wished the photograph showed his new, colored eyes. Still, in this situation, those hideous things would help protect his identity.

He slipped into a late-night pharmacy and browsed the shelves of hair-care products. Ebony seemed an appropriate color to match his black clothing. As he set the hair dye, eyebrow and lash color onto the counter, he noticed the chemist watching a small television set below, and stiffened.

"I'd like to pay for these."

He kept his face down but, the man stared at him, fear in his eyes. "Yes, I need—I need to get bags. Won't be a minute."

The pharmacist ducked into the back room, and Jeremiah rushed after him. The small, packed storeroom slowed the man as he picked his way down the aisle. Jeremiah snatched a blood pressure monitor off a shelf, unwound the long red rubber tube, and approached the man from behind.

~ *** ~

McCullage knocked on the Pembroke's back door. Nancy opened it right away, and fell into his arms. "Thank God you're back," she said.

He half carried her into the kitchen, where Xantara was stirring a large pot. He sniffed the air, enjoying the delicious aroma. He couldn't recall the last time he'd eaten. Or slept, for that matter.

Xantara waved her wooden spatula. "Why don't you two sit in the lounge? I'll call you when dinner's ready."

Jim sat on the comfortable sofa and leaned back. He pulled Nancy close and tenderly kissed her forehead. "You okay?"

She smiled, and squeezed his hand. "I'm more than okay. I got my blood test results today. All clear, not a trace of cancer. My specialist watched the Avebury film and still couldn't believe it. He mumbled something about remission, but I don't care. I'm cured, one hundred percent!"

Jim bowed his head. "Thank God. I can hardly believe myself that the Light Beings healed you."

Nancy cleared her throat and waited. "You haven't noticed."

"Noticed what?"

His wife lifted a lock of deep auburn hair. "Xantara insisted, and colored it for me this afternoon. Not a single grey strand. Do you like it?"

"Honey, your hair's beautiful, and frames your gorgeous eyes."

She dropped a kiss onto his lips. "You look exhausted. Shall we go home after tea?"

"I suppose we could. Inspector Grant saw the film and understands our position. If the press returns, I'm sure he'll allocate a couple officers for door duty."

Nancy frowned. "Any luck with the terrorist search?"

He shook his head. "No sign, and all the paper trails remain cold. Perhaps I should consult the medium again." He paused, thinking. "The Phineas Priesthood must have unlimited resources. As soon as we get close, they melt into thin air. Now they've threatened an attack on, in their words, 'faggots.'"

"Why are they against gays and lesbians?"

He shrugged. "They've done nothing wrong. Luck of the draw at birth, I suppose."

Nancy tilted her head. "They'd want to find a crowd for maximum impact, wouldn't they? I think I can guess where. Our next door neighbor's son always visits the Welsh Mardi Gras in Cardiff. The parade's tomorrow."

He kissed her hard. "You're brilliant. Sorry, love. It's two hours' drive to Cardiff, and I'll have to pick up Sam on the way."

"Your dinner…"

Jeremiah patted his pocket, and felt the small spray bottle holding the chemical. Last night was a waste of time, but today he would find a way. Bloody faggots!

He watched the marshals coaxing the diverse crowd gathered into line, but the people milled about and broke ranks. The leaders waved rainbow-striped flags and pro-gay banners. Transvestites mixed with other people of undetermined sex, their outrageous outfits vying with the marchers who wore barely any clothes at all.

He'd dyed his hair and brows a dark black, and had just completed his outfit with a rainbow-colored scarf he'd bought from a young vendor. As he tied it, he smiled. He looked the part. Well, almost. At least the police gave him no notice.

Jeremiah hurried toward the food stalls that lined the High Street. As he mingled in the crowd, a youth smiled and lifted an eyebrow at him.

The evil look he returned made the boy shrink back and turn away. A bloody faggot, how dare he?

With black leather gloves, he held the spray bottle close to his leg, half-covered by his jacket. The first stall holder strained to watch the parade as it appeared at the junction. Jeremiah covered his face with his hand and sprayed. Good, he didn't notice. Too easy!

He forced himself to contain his excitement as he held his breath and sprayed God's wrath over the exposed food, a variety of fresh pastries, burgers, and sandwiches. He smiled inwardly as he watched the fine mist settle, forming an invisible toxic veneer. At the street's end he turned and made his way down the other side.

A hand clamped on his shoulder.

"What do you think you're doing?"

The stallholder wore a short leather jerkin. Through the gap, Jeremiah glimpsed a respectable six pack on his otherwise naked stomach. He stashed the bottle in his pocket.

"Oh, I'm sorry. My inhaler, I'm asthmatic."

The man didn't look convinced, but released him. "Be more careful in the future."

"I will. Sorry, my mistake."

He strode down a side street and hailed a taxi.

McCullage and Blackbridge scanned each face as they walked alongside the rowdy crowd chanting pro-gay songs and waving rainbow flags. Two half-dressed women embraced each other as they walked along. A six-foot tall man tottered past in high heels, the highest Jim had ever seen. How on earth could he walk? And how long had it taken to apply the plastered-on make-up? It was difficult to recognize individual faces, since most looked like circus clowns. Anyone could be a Priesthood member in disguise. Jim focused instead on body language. People couldn't easily cover up their gestures and the way they walked.

As the crowd reached the High Street the stallholders shouted out for customers, tempting them with food samples on plastic trays. Jim's mouth watered. He still hadn't eaten since last night's missed dinner.

Sam reached for his wallet. "Would you like a pie?"

"Keep your eyes peeled, we'll eat later."

The crowd laughed and joked as they drank beers and ate burgers, pies, and cakes. A commotion sounded from the parade ahead, and Jim turned, and gasped. All around him people choked and fell, bowling over like nine pins down the line. He stared and held his breath. "What's happening?"

Sam rushed forward and knocked a burger from a young man's hand.

The man stepped back. "Hey, mate, careful!"

"That food's poisoned!"

Others overheard him, and threw down their food. Jim jogged down the left of the street, and Sam down the right. "Don't eat anything!" They shouted in unison. Jim realized their caution was too late for a lot of visitors. Bodies littered the street and pavements, their faces black and blue with corded veins. Exactly like the old woman. Police officers and parade officials lay among the dead. No one directed the crowd that wailed and screamed around him.

One teen grabbed his boyfriend's arm, and within seconds he, too, fell to the ground. Stunned, Jim's mind raced. That was it! He shouted across the road to Sam. "Don't let them touch bare skin. I think the pores absorb the chemical!" Jim drew his crime-scene purple silicone gloves from his pocket and continued down the street, warning the few people left.

Young and old alike slumped against shop windows and cried. Some of the women acted with aggression, some men acted like swooning southern belles. Jim tried to make sense of this topsy-turvy scene as he directed survivors away from the dead.

McCullage helped where he could, then found a quiet corner to call Inspector Grant. "Sir, they've used the chemical here in Cardiff. Four, five hundred people are dead. Send a clean-up team right away, but warn them not to touch the bodies with their bare hands."

Grant cursed. "Bloody psychopaths! We have to find them. They've got to be close. Keep me informed."

Jim signed the register for them both. The waterfront hotel stood well away from the High Street, and they needed rest. He sat at the bar and nursed a brandy, his haggard features reflected in the polished steel counter.

"We can't do much until they clear the contamination," he said. "Where do you think they'd hide out?"

Sam's hollow face and the dark shadows around his eyes made him look sinister. "Could be anywhere, but I know I need food and sleep."

McCullage sighed. "I agree. But I'll find it hard to sleep. What if they have more Zetronia?"

CHAPTER EIGHTEEN

Frank Carrington sat beside Dr. Schneider's white leather couch, watching him extract a phial and needle from the glass cabinet. He filled the needle and squirted the injection into the air, apparently to remove bubbles.

"Why the shot?"

The doctor half turned and smiled. "It's a truth drug. It will relax her and help keep her hypnotized for longer."

Poor kid. Frank hated his role in her ordeals. "Is the stuff safe?"

"Yes. I've reduced the dose to account for her age and body weight."

The door opened, and Nicola led Imogene into the room. The young girls face lit up, and Frank grinned. "Frank, did you bring Elizabeth to play with me?"

"Sorry, but she lives a long way from here, in London. But I promise. One day you'll meet her."

He noticed she wore a different outfit. "What a pretty dress."

Imogene held out her skirt and twirled around. "Mommy gave it to me last night. Pink and purple are my favorite colors."

As Nicola helped her lie down, he marveled at her composure. Lizzie would be scared to death by now. Her smile dropped as she eyed the needle, but she held out her arm. Frank shivered as a wave of guilt passed through him.

Schneider swung a bright crystal attached to a silver chain above her face. "Relax, and picture the staircase, the one with twenty steps. Now, step down the first stair. Nineteen…eighteen…seventeen…

Frank also watched the crystal, swinging back and forth, back and forth… Concentrate on the matter in hand. The Council would have to listen, and give him more time. He shuffled his feet, and Schneider placed a finger to his lips.

The doctor leaned closer. "Imogene, find Rahmiel and the Council. We have questions. Describe all you see and hear."

The girl eyes darted under her lids. "I'm in the Egyptian temple, and Osahar is here. He doesn't want me to speak to the Elders."

"Listen to me, Imogene. Leave the priest, and find the Council."

Frank jotted a note and handed it to Schneider. The words read, "Find out if Osahar lives now."

The doctor nodded. "Imogene, ask the priest if he's alive at this time."

Her voice was low, but clear. "Yes. He has lived for over two thousand years."

"Is that because his DNA and telomeres are like yours?"

"The Light Beings brought him back to life, like they did me. Since then he's lived here, serving the Council."

"Where's the temple?"

"In Egypt. Deep under the Great Pyramid, he says, well hidden."

Dr. Schneider worked his lips. "Ask him if we can negotiate with the Council of Elders. We need more time."

Frank sat straight. Could this be for real? Did a priest named Osahar live inside a pyramid, or was that simply a young girl's imagination? Why did these weird events have to happen now, during his term as Prime Minister?

The girl's pale face worried him, but Schneider looked unconcerned. Her lips moved without a sound, as if she conversed with an unknown entity. Well, he supposed she was, wasn't she?

A deep male voice filled the room, and his stomach churned.

"You dregs of humanity! Have you ever listened to reason? Do you think more time will change anything? Corruption is endemic among world leaders. Your own greed won't allow you to work together for the greater good, and it disgusts me. But the Elders have the wisdom, and I will ask."

Imogene's head dropped to one side, and she curled up into a ball and slept.

Frank clenched his hands and reached for his inhaler. He didn't like this Osahar. True, one couldn't trust many heads of state, even his own cabinet, but he remained an idealist. He rose and moved toward the door, then turned. "Schneider, didn't you say you controlled her? I wanted to speak with the Council. Will she wake soon?"

Schneider's voice thickened, his German accent strong. "Hypnosis is not an exact science, and my research has just begun. Still, it looks as if Osahar is our contact point. We shall see at the next session, but I'm afraid this one is over."

"When can we have another one?"

"Tomorrow. That will give the child rest, and Osahar time to consult with the Council."

"I agree. Time is short, but we can't risk harming the child."

McCullage and Sam walked to the taxi stand, and showed the four fugitive's photos to each driver. A middle-aged Pakistani jabbed at Jeremiah's picture. "That's him, I'm sure. He had white skin and hair, but I don't remember his eyes being so pale and red. I've never seen such a man before."

Jim and Sam exchanged a look. "When and where did you pick him up?"

The man rubbed his hooked nose. "Near the wharf, outside Cardiff Bay Yacht Club. Just after eight thirty."

"Do you remember anything else? Anything at all?"

"Well, I dropped him off at Dumballs Road, and he paid cash."

They thanked the man and moved away. Sam grinned. "He came by boat. Let's head down to the water."

 ***

The yacht club manager didn't look pleased.

"I don't want trouble. We have a reputation to uphold, and some of our members are powerful people."

McCullage touched the man's arm. "All we need is security footage from last night. Not inside the club, but outside."

"Come with me, you can talk to Edward."

He led them to a small room at the club's rear. A ruddy-faced mariner, who wore a navy sweater and sported an anchor tattoo on his forearm, stood and greeted them.

"Edward will find the film. Please use the rear exit on your way out."

Edward gave a mock salute as the manager let the door bang behind him.

The three men reviewed the tape, and soon spotted their target. They watched Jeremiah come into view from the left. The taxi pulled over, and he got in. Sam raised an eyebrow. "Where did he come from?"

"He must have cruised in," the mariner said. "That path leads to private moorings. And before you ask, there's no security camera down there."

McCullage's familiar facial tic sprang into life. Why couldn't they get a real break? He picked a couple a chewable aspirins from his pocket and tossed them into his mouth. His head ached, and he wanted to go home to Nancy.

"How many private moorings are there?" he asked.

"Eighteen. Two guys live on their boats, maybe they saw something."

Sam thanked the man, and they walked toward the quay. Small runabouts filled half the berths, but he noticed a few grander vessels. The

122

smell of barbecued meat led them to a man aboard a larger yacht, busy flipping a steak. Jim showed him the pictures.

"Well, the white-haired man could be the one who moored here last night. Beautiful vessel, polished wood and brass, meticulously restored to original condition. I noticed because I hadn't seen it for more than a year. He left again late this afternoon."

"What time did he come?"

"Around eight, I think."

"Do you know who owns it?"

"Sorry, I don't. He's rich, though. That boat's worth a mint."

Frank walked slowly to Schneider's office, hoping he'd get answers today, but knowing the girl shouldn't have this burden thrust upon her. The doctor removed the syringe from the cabinet as he entered.

"All set, doctor?"

Imogene grabbed his arm. "I'm glad you're here. I feel safe with you."

Her words sliced through him. What was he doing? "I hope you can go home soon, Imogene. And thank you for your help."

She smiled and held out her hand. His broad palm engulfed it, and he saw that his touch soothed her. "You'll be fine. Relax. I'm right here."

"Rahmiel! I've missed you." She loved her wispy gown and wished she had one exactly like it. "They want to talk to the Elders."

Rahmiel floated around her. "Yes, they've agreed to send another message. Come, I'll escort you."

The Council Elders around the large marble table once again made room for her to join them. Kabshiel, the chief elder, nodded to her. "Osahar has made your leader's requests to us, and we've considered our position," he said. "Imogene, brave child, we've decided to communicate through you to your leader. Please drink this."

Imogene drank the honey-like liquid and lay down.

 ***

Frank shuddered as Imogene's mouth opened, and a deep voice boomed out. "Leader, the Council of Elders agree to converse with you. What's your question?"

He felt like a fish as he gasped for air. "Hum...I...need time." Her lips had moved in sync with the voice, like in a scene from The Exorcist!

"Time for what?"

"Please, have patience with us. Did you cause the flu virus deaths? The city fire, and the toxic cloud? Are they the promised consequences?"

"Indeed. What did you expect? Your heads of state continue to ignore us."

Frank shifted in his chair. "Please, give us time and specific directions."

"Time is short. Even without our involvement, you're attracting more and more calamities. Meanwhile, the soulless children multiply, and grow into what? Psychopaths, murderers, and manipulators, with empty bodies—all ripe for possession. Evil entities wait for the chance to live in human form, and their strength grows daily. You're creating your own penalties with your refusal to change."

Frank blew out a series of rapid breaths. "Please! Tell me what to do, and I'll consult with the United Nations. But I need time to convince them to act as one."

"I sense a good spirit in you, and that pleases me. Very well. We will allow you one year to convince mankind to destroy their weapons, to redistribute wealth to relieve the poor, and relearn the basics of compassion, faith, and charity. But I warn you. Your chances remain slim, as history habitually repeats itself. But this time there's no leeway. If you fail, the earth's population will cease to exist."

CHAPTER NINETEEN

F our months later...

The nurse smeared clear gel on her Bryony's stomach, and she shivered. She watched the nurse's hand move the ultrasound scanner back and forth, and tilted her head to look at the screen.

The image morphed into a baby shape, the tiny body floating like an astronaut in space. The nurse moved the scanner again, and she saw the small heart beating. Her own heart pounded as she witnessed her little miracle.

The nurse frowned and moved the scanner around to her left side. "What have we here, a second heartbeat? Twins!"

She manipulated Bryony's stomach and moved the front baby aside to reveal the second. She clicked the scanner several times, and peered at the black-and-white images. "I'll give you a photo to take home. Do you want to know the sex?"

"Yes, please." Bryony wrinkled her nose as she struggled to see the images. "Why's the second baby so much smaller than the first?"

The nurse ignored the question. "They're identical twins. See, they share the placenta. Girls. You're pregnant with twin girls."

A feeling of weightlessness bathed Byrony. Twins, like Sabina and Sybil. And one of them would be the next Guardian. Her eyes filled with tears. She couldn't wait to cuddle them. She would love them, despite how they were conceived. Despite their father's genes.

The nurse completed the babies' measurements, smiled, and patted Bryony's tummy. "Wait a moment, while I get the pediatrician. We have to be extra careful with multiples." She left, and returned in a moment with an earnest young man in a white coat.

"Bryony, I'm Doctor Applewhite. How are you?"

"Fine, thank you. Is there a problem?"

"Let's have a look."

The doctor's face was intense as he scanned and measured. She tensed and tried to decipher the babies' features. "One baby is smaller than the other."

Doctor Applewhite ignored her comment. At last he asked the nurse to clean off the gel. "Can I see you in my office, when you've finished here please, Bryony?"

Bryony knocked on the doctor's door, and entered. The windowless office looked cramped, medical journals jostled with untidy file stacks on every surface. She cleared her throat and waited.

Doctor Applegate studied the ultra-sound images. "Congratulations, you have twin girls," he said. "But there's an issue, I'm afraid, as you can see by their relative sizes."

Bryony stared at the scan. "What?"

"The babies have TTTS. The term stands for 'twin-to-twin transfusion syndrome.' It's a rare condition, and only occurs with identical twins."

"What are the implications?"

"In simple terms, the dominant twin feeds off the smaller one. She's taking more than her fair share of the blood supply. The smaller twin could die if we don't do something about it."

A cold chill went through Byrony's body. "What can we do?"

"We can operate, but the placenta's placement complicates matters. I'll have to work around it." He paused, frowning. "The placenta has three main blood vessels. We can adjust their blood supplies with a laser, to make them more even."

"Will the smaller twin catch up in size?"

"Not fully, but it should catch up sufficiently by the time they're born. Be prepared for an early labor."

Bryony relaxed back in her bed. Twins! She'd never considered that possibility. She held the photo scan up to the light and sighed. They were so sweet, tiny and vulnerable. Well, she would be a devoted mother, and the evil albino would never lay eyes or hands on them.

McCullage loosened his collar as he watched Helen turn the tarot cards over, one by one. The single candle on the table cast an eerie light in the familiar dimly lit room, making the cards glow against the ruby tablecloth. He cut the pack three times.

Helen's gold charm bracelet jangled as she jabbed at the first card. "Magician reversed. This card tells me there are undercurrents and deception. Think about synchronicities, unrelated events which could connect. Search for small signs, look at the overall picture, and link them to discover the whole."

Jim shook his head. What on earth did she mean?

The second card flew out of her hand, and the hairs on the back of his neck stiffened.

Helen's long cerise fingernails tapped the card. "This is the so-called Death card. It means significant events will occur, and soon. You can't stop them, but you can try to adapt to them. The evil forces grow stronger, and to prevail you must first let go of preconceived beliefs."

Helen's hand quivered as she dropped the next card. "Dear, oh dear, the Devil's card. This means you'll face great trickery and deceit. Beware! Unseen spiritual battles rage around you, so you must protect your soul from the evil forces. Imagine a powerful white light surrounding you for protection."

McCullage tensed. Where was the good news? He watched, mesmerized, as her nails played a tattoo on the table. She revealed the next card. "The world. That's better. You carry the weight of the world on your shoulders, but relief is close. Take heart, you will triumph."

She wrapped the cards into a silk cloth and switched on the lamp. Jim felt his face grow warm. "Can we consult the map again?" he asked. "Do you mind? We think the terrorists are in Wales, but I'd like to confirm it."

"Of course, wait one moment." She removed the map and dousing rod from the sideboard drawer and set them out. She moved the rod's tip over the Welsh border, and it twitched. "Yes, South Wales, as you expected."

"Can you add any more information?"

She closed her eyes, swayed a little, then nodded. "They're close to the South Wales coastline," she said. "My spirit guide shows me a typical Welsh stone cottage with a boathouse in a small bay. That's all I can tell you, I'm sorry."

As he drove away, he called Sam. "They're still on the Welsh coast. We'll have to do a house-to-house search from Cardiff, east to west."

Bryony showed the ultrasound photographs to Xantara, and let out a deep sigh. "I hope they'll both be okay."

Her friend grinned. "Of course they will be, and you don't have to wait to find out."

"What do you mean?"

"Think, girl. You're a Guardian. Tonight we can call on the Light Beings."

Bryony nibbled at a hangnail. "You're forgetting. Since half the population descended on Avebury Circle, the army guards it. No one's allowed near the monument." She shook her head. "Those unfortunate people looked so desperate. I wish we could heal them all."

"Let's see if Detective McCullage can help us." Xantara pressed the buttons on her cell phone.

Frank Carrington twiddled his thumbs, and turned to Alex. "Time's marching on, and I can't convince anyone the world's in danger. What should I do?"

Alex paced across the office to the window, paused, and stared out at the wintry landscape. His white military haircut merged with the snow-laden sky. "Christmas already, people's memories are so short. Look at them, shopping for gifts, the lost lives forgotten." He turned back and resumed his seat. "You have to convince at least one influential leader. Use all your persuasive powers. Show every scrap of evidence we have that the message is genuine." He eyed Frank, frowning. "You and the American President are friends, and he can influence the other heads of state. Get him on your side, and the rest will follow."

Frank clicked his empty stapler several times and sighed. "The truth sounds impossible, by any sane person's standard. The Council of Elders will begin the punishments again in only eight months, and I'm sure they'll be even worse this time than before."

Alex laid his hands flat on the table and looked directly at him. "Go to America and talk to him, face to face. Show him the videos, and let him hear the recordings of Imogene's regressions. Europe's still in turmoil. The German, Czech Republic and Polish governments all perished when the toxic space cloud covered their capital cities, and the newly elected members haven't gotten their act together. Convincing the American President is the only option left."

"You're right, of course. I'll call him."

130

McCullage and Blackbridge walked onto the shingle beach and looked back at the bleak grey Welsh stone cottage. It sat under the cliff, its drawn curtains blanking the small windows. Jim pointed left. "Let's check the boathouse first."

The stiff, frost-covered door opened with the second push, and McCullage saw waves lapping against the stone-lined walls in the dim interior. Sam clapped his hands together to warm them.

"Empty. Let's examine the house. It could be a vacation home, shut up for the winter. But if so, a boat should be here."

"Wait, look at this." Jim pointed out a small framed black-and-white photo hanging at an angle on the back wall. "That's a fifties launch, I'm sure. Look at the wooden band around the rail and the cabin. This could be the boat."

They approached the cottage, and Sam went around back while Jim rapped the front door. The house remained silent. Jim peered up at the granite cliff face that towered behind.

"Sam, there's no one here, let's go in. I have a feeling the Yates were here."

He broke open the front door, and they entered. Sam held his gun at the ready as he walked ahead. His ankle touched something taut and he heard a click.

"Run!" He pushed Jim out the door, and they both ran toward the sea.

The massive boom hurt Jim's ears, and he clasped his head. The explosion impacted the cliff face, and its surface crumbled. Jim pulled Sam into the icy sea as rocks rained down. They both ducked under water.

Jim burst through the surface and gasped. He shivered as the chilly water turned to ice and his clothes stiffened against his skin. He heard

Sam's teeth clatter as he helped him scramble ashore. "We need to find a warm room to dry out in, before we freeze to death."

Sam steadied himself on Jim's arm and turned toward the cottage. "Nothing left but a pile of rubble," he said, slowly. "Any clues we could have gleaned are gone."

Jim threw down his ruined cell phone and scanned the beach, and spotted a gap along the rock-strewn path. They scrambled over the smaller stones and made their way along the steep trail.

Water squished over the car seats and Jim turned the heater on full blast. He gunned the engine and headed for Cardiff. All he wanted was to get back to Nancy, and that possibility seemed even further away. Where had the bastards gone?

CHAPTER TWENTY

Imogene peered through the thick snowflakes melting on the windowpane, and finally saw it. The detective's car. Her stomach churned as her parents, Aunt Sybil, and Bryony walked toward the entrance carrying armfuls of brightly wrapped gifts.

The detective waved to her. She waved back and watched him drive away, then rushed to the door and hugged each family member in turn.

"Can I open my presents, Mom?"

Her mother laughed. "Let us get in first, and Merry Christmas."

Her father picked her up and she snuggled into his shoulder. "Who gave you the Christmas tree?" he asked.

"Doctor Schneider brought it, and a box of ornaments. He told me about his holidays as a little boy in Germany, and helped me decorate it. Do you like the fairy on top?"

"She's gorgeous, but not as gorgeous as my beautiful daughter." He set her down and handed her a gift. "Hope you like it."

She ripped off the Christmas wrap and squealed. "An iPad, my best present ever! Thank you daddy, I love you."

Her father glanced around the room. "You need more stimulation in here. Maybe they'll let me Skype you, but I wouldn't bank on it."

Imogene opened several presents. She sat in a sea of discarded Christmas wrap and opened yet another, this one from Bryony. "Oh, twin babies with matching cots! Thank you, Aunty Bryony."

Her aunt Sybil smiled and touched her arm. "Great news, Imogene. The authorities have agreed to let me stay with you again."

She whooped, jumped up, and threw both arms around her. "I've been so bored. Can you stay right now?"

"There's my suitcase."

After a fancy Christmas dinner kindly provided by Doctor Schneider, her parents and Sybil settled down to watch the Queen's speech. Aunty Bryony called her over. "Come and have a cuddle," she said. "I want to tell you something."

Bryony drew the bed curtains back, and Imogene snuggled next to her. "I have good news. I'm expecting, twins—identical baby girls."

"Wow! Can I help you bathe and dress them?"

"Of course you can, and change their diapers."

"Ugh, maybe you can do that job."

Aunty Bryony sighed. "There's one small problem. One twin is bigger, and she's drawing more than her fair share of blood. The doctor can operate but that's risky. Your mom suggested we have a healing ceremony at Avebury Circle, but no one's allowed there now."

Imogene frowned, then perked up. "Maybe I can heal the baby. I healed Jeremiah's eyes, didn't I?"

"Would you try?"

Imogene knelt next to Aunty Bryony's tummy and laid her hands on her bare skin. She grinned. "I feel the babies move. When will they be born?"

"They're due in May."

Imogene closed her eyes and tuned into the twins' energy. A sweet vibration reached her from the smaller twin. The larger twin's energy avoided her, and she sensed darkness—no, a nothingness about the baby. She explored with her mind, found the blood vessels, and directed her energy toward them. Again she tested the tiny baby's vibration. The energy felt stronger, and she sensed the child's spirit thank her.

Imogene sat back. "I've done it. I felt the change in energy. The babies are fine now."

134

Her aunt hugged her hard. "You're my angel. Thank you from me, and thank you from them."

"Have you named them yet?"

"Not yet. Would you like to help me choose?"

"I'd love to."

The Prime Minister tensed as his chauffeur-driven limousine glided through Catoctin Mountain Park toward Camp David. How could he convince the United States President they faced a real threat? He scarcely glanced at the picturesque Blue Ridge Mountains as he leaned forward to catch a glimpse of Camp David proper.

They passed through three rings of fences, his driver showing his security pass to the Marine Guards at each check-point. Still nervous, Frank patted his briefcase as he passed the famous Camp David sign. Hastily he lifted his Ventolin puffer and inhaled. The limousine drew alongside the substantial home, and the President opened its door to greet him.

"Frank, welcome to Camp David. Come in out of the cold."

A huge log fire crackled in the main foyer, and as Frank removed his coat the cozy interior's warmth enveloped him. He paused, collecting his thoughts.

"Did you and your family have a good Christmas?" he asked.

The President passed him a glass of mulled wine. "Come with me," he said. "The butler will deal with your luggage. A great Christmas with the family, thank you, but the round of tedious formal events..."

"I know what you mean."

After the family dinner, the President excused them and suggested they go to the library. Decanter in hand, he held up a glass. "Bourbon?"

Frank settled in a comfortable chair near an open fire. "Yes, please."

The generous tumbler loaded with ice tinkled as the President set the drink at his side. "You must have important business to discuss, to travel so far."

Frank picked up his glass and swirled the contents. "I have, but I'm not sure where to begin. I hope you'll believe an incredible story."

"Sounds intriguing. Try me."

He reached for his briefcase. "I'd like you to watch three short videos first, then listen to several transcriptions. The girl who levitated— Imogene Pembroke—is central to my story."

The President nodded, and waited in silence as he set up his laptop. First he showed the young girl's levitation and communication at Avebury Circle, then the healing filmed by Channel Five. The third video was a thirty-second clip taken in the church catacombs, where dim light made the film grainy as strange beings swirled around, appearing to fight one another.

The President laughed. "Unbelievable. The film must be a hoax."

"Wait! Listen to these recordings. Doctor Schneider, the psychiatrist at our Porton Down research facility, uses hypnosis to regress the child to visit her past lives."

The President looked up. "I don't believe in reincarnation."

Frank's chest tightened. "Please keep an open mind for the moment. As you hear this, think about the recent disasters. The flu pandemic, the Chicago fire, the millions who died in Europe from the toxic space cloud…"

As the final past-life audio finished, the President shook his head. "They have to be co-incidental."

Frank opened a new file on his computer. "Now, listen to this." He played the Council of Elders session agreeing to one year's grace. "That conversation took place four months ago."

The President chuckled. "Well done, you've got me. What a prank!"

Frank stared at him in silence, and the President frowned.

"You can't be serious."

"Deadly. Can you afford to ignore the threat?"

The President shook his head. "Even if what you said is true, the Senate would never understand. Or other world leaders, for that matter. Let me sleep on it, and we'll talk again in the morning."

The next morning, Frank strolled beside the President through the grounds. "Have you reached a conclusion?"

"Frank, we've been friends for a long time, and I respect your judgment. But in this case, I can't get my head around it. Look at the facts. An unusual, but nonetheless plausible, series of events caused the Chicago fire. Scientists explained the gas cloud was dragged into our atmosphere by a magnetic polar shift. The pandemic was just an extraordinary phenomenon. I can't explain why the young men shared their birthdates. Perhaps the virus attacked the men the day of their birth and manifested nineteen years later. There must be a logical explanation, other than a levitating child and indistinct otherworldly beings."

Frank stuck his hands into his pockets, stopped, and turned to the President. "Remember the message? It said babies have been born without souls for many years. The Council said that's why mindless violence increased, and the perpetrators showed no remorse. Isn't it true that mall and school shootings are at an all-time high? In fact, they've recently risen by as much as two hundred percent."

The President turned and walked back toward the house. "Yes, that is true. But it's just a sign of the times, not supernatural."

Frank, head down, kicked at a pile of autumn leaves. He'd been a fool to think the President would believe him. He ground his teeth. What did the Council expect him to do?

Braeden followed Nicola's slender figure down the hallway. She reached the ward and turned. "No Mrs. Pembroke tonight?"

"One of her patients went into premature labor, and she had to stay to monitor her progress." He stepped into the ward and caught Imogene as she flew into his arms.

"Please press the buzzer when you're ready to leave."

He heard the lock drop into its cylinder behind him. "How are you, honey?"

His heart glowed as his daughter's face lit it like a bright summer's day. "What have you done today?"

Her face darkened, as if a dark stormy cloud passed over. "I've had two more sessions with Doctor Schneider. Daddy, I feel so tired afterwards, all I do is sleep."

A cold wave rippled over his skin. "I'll talk to him."

"Where's Mommy?"

"An early birth, honey. Babies are hardly ever on time. What shall we play?"

Sybil walked in from the kitchen. "Hungry?" She set a plate of sandwiches on the table. "It's a shame Xantara couldn't make it, that's the problem with being a midwife. Give her my love, won't you?"

After Imogene ate, her smile returned. "Look daddy, the twin babies Aunty Bryony gave me. It's time for their bath." She fetched a jug of warm water from the kitchen and undressed the dolls.

For the next hour he helped her bathe and dress them, then she hopped into bed and he read her a story. He watched her eyelids droop, and finally close. His little angel's face looked serene, except for the dark smudges beneath her eyes. When would she come home? He kissed the top of her head and dimmed the light.

Sybil sat at the far end of the ward watching a sitcom with the volume turned down. "Bye, Sybil. See you tomorrow."

He pressed the buzzer and the door opened almost immediately. Nicola looked different. Very different. Her hair flowed free, her glossy red lipstick highlighted her full lips, and her glasses and the white coat were gone. A silvery spaghetti-strapped top complimented the short tight black skirt.

"Ready, Doctor?"

Her patent stilettos clicked down the hallway. "Going out tonight?" Braeden asked.

"No, now and then I like to get out of my lab clothes."

"I'd like a word with Schneider."

"Sorry, he's asked not to be disturbed tonight. Why don't you have a drink with me, tell me the problem, and I'll talk to him about it tomorrow? I do have Imogene's best interests at heart. She's a sweet kid."

She led him to a small suite of rooms and poured two vodkas in shot glasses. Braeden tossed his back. "It's nice to relax for a change," he said. "How long have you worked with Doctor Schneider?"

They sat, and her knees almost touched his as she leaned forward. Her deep violet eyes grew larger as she held his gaze. "About four years. We both have an interest in hypnosis, that's how we met. I became one of his research subjects to earn extra money. London's an expensive place to live."

She refilled his glass and he tossed it back, too. God knows he needed to relax, and the alcohol quietened his anxiety. "Are you there when Schneider hypnotizes my daughter?"

"Most times. But sometimes the sessions are so long, and I have other duties."

Her heady perfume filled the room, and he tried to shake off the effect of her nearness. "She complains of tiredness. I'm concerned, and I would like him to cut the sessions short. He could be damaging her health."

Nicola smiled, revealing small even teeth. "I agree. I'll talk to him about it tomorrow."

Braeden picked up his shot glass. Was that the fourth, or fifth? "I must go, my ride will be here soon."

As he tried to rise, she moved closer and leaned over him, put her hands each side of his head, and kissed him passionately. His body went rigid, and he tried ineffectually to push her off. Nicola's tongue explored his mouth and he responded. My God, what was he thinking? He made another half-hearted attempt to push her away, but his body betrayed him.

CHAPTER TWENTY-ONE

"It's madness, I tell you."

Frank cringed as the House of Commons opposition leader thumped the bench. Sweat glistened on the lame man's bald head. Perhaps he was so antagonistic because polio had left his left leg weak. He'd never disliked the man more.

"Prime Minister, you must stand down," a member roared. "You've lost all reason!"

Frank raised a hand until a hush fell over the gathering. "I beg you to consider the evidence," he said. "Can't you see? The girl's clearly generating these events. We have to listen to the Council of Elders and take action, before we're too late."

Derisive laughter filled the chamber. The opposition members drummed the benches in unison. "Shame! Shame!" they chanted. "Out, out, with the lunatic."

The opposition leader's face looked as if he would have an apoplectic fit at any moment. "Good Heavens, man, you intend to take this cock-and-bull fairy-tale to the United Nations? We'd be the laughing stock of the world!"

The Prime Minister sank back in his seat as The Home Secretary tried to restore order. Dear Alex, what a staunch supporter, a faithful friend. His former naval training made him the perfect ally. Relying on Alex made his life easier, that was for sure. Frank touched his arm and indicated they should leave, but Alex shook his head and turned to the Speaker.

"Order!" The Speaker banged his gavel. "Order, or I will clear the house."

Alex stepped forward. "Speaker, please allow me to address the opposition leader." He waited until complete silence descended. "I suggest we form a by-partisan committee to evaluate the Prime Minister's information."

"No, it's absolute poppycock. A ploy to deflect our attention from the fact that you've failed to capture the Stonehenge terrorists."

Alex's lips thinned. "I promise, it's not. The task force is close to apprehending the bombers as I speak."

The opposition leader rolled his eyes. "Humph! I demand the Prime Minister stand down, and I hereby raise a motion to that effect." He turned to face his supporters. "Hear, hear." They stamped and shouted, and interspersed with loud snorts.

The dark- suited opposition members rose off the green leather benches like a pack of enraged wolves. "Out, out!" The rhythmic drumming arose again, and the noise deafened Frank.

"Come on, Alex, let's leave."

The friends moved toward the massive carved doors, followed by derisive shouts. "Cowards! Liars! Run, little rabbits, run!"

Alex shrugged as they entered the quiet corridor. "We'll have to re-group and issue an official statement to the people," he said. "If they don't support your position as Prime Minister, I'm afraid the opposition may succeed in removing you from office."

Frank felt his heart race. "We have only four months! I doubt I can convince anybody in that time. I'll talk with the Council of Elders, maybe they'll help me."

"Good idea. They instigated these problems."

Frank shook his head slowly. "Alex, am I mad? Is this simply a recurring nightmare?"

~ *** ~

Braeden stared into the empty grave. A few short months ago Imogene had lain there, cold and dead. The dark earth lay damp from a recent shower, and flowers scattered the area. He noticed Druid emblems carved into the nearby grass, no doubt in honour of their new prophet, his daughter.

He walked away with a heavy heart, then turned toward the ruined church. The doors and roof were gone, destroyed in the blast. Xantara had lost her mother in the explosion, and now he had let her down. She couldn't take much more. He had to keep his indiscretion quiet.

But would Nicola?

He picked his way through the rubble to the crypt entrance. The stone steps appeared clear enough, so he walked down them, and stood at the bottom. The whole vault remained unchanged. The central altar stone stood as it had for centuries, with traces of blood trapped in its rough cracks. His chest felt hollow as he entered the cell where they'd kept Xantara.

Daylight poured through the open roof and lit up the round stone room. He realized how cold and damp the cell must have been in the dark. Xantara would have been terrified, and his actions had sent her there. He shivered as he recalled the horrors he'd witnessed, both here and on the island. The sight of her tied to the fiery stake filled his mind. Her death had never been closer. What kind of man was he? Never in his wildest imagination would he have believed he could betray her.

She'd forgiven him when he didn't deserve her compassion such a short time ago, and now he'd deceived her again, betrayed her trust, her love. She wouldn't forgive his infidelity, nor should she.

He blamed Nicola. She'd led him on, plied him with alcohol. How dare she? He was a vulnerable man, under incredible stress. She should have known he couldn't resist. A few moments of pleasure, normalcy, that's all. Who could blame him?

Yes, but everyone would, he couldn't deny it.

The unvarnished truth was that he'd succumbed to temptation. The girl must be just out of her teens, and he was a professional in his forties. How could he exercise so little control?

He sat on the abandoned stool and dropped his head into his hands, his elbows pushed hard into his legs. Fatigue weighed him down. How could he have been so stupid, so incredibly irresponsible? What now?

 ***

Bryony cocked her head to one side. Was that a sound? No, there was nothing to worry about, it was just her imagination. She shifted to a more comfortable position, then moved her pillow to better support her developing tummy. As the babies grew she found sleep difficult, especially when they kicked. She closed her eyes and tried to get back to sleep.

What was that?

Her body stiffened, and she strained to hear. She could swear she heard breathing. The hair on her arms lifted and a cold sweat bathed her body. Someone was there.

A wide beam of moonlight filtered through the partly closed curtains. She turned, little by little, and peeped above the bedcovers. A figure sat in the corner chair, the light slanting across his white face. Her adrenaline spiked, then a sharp pain struck her chest. It was him!

She lay as still as a marble statue. What should she do? Her skin crawled and prickled as fear washed over her, a terrible dark shadow.

"Bryony, my dear," he whispered. "How are you? Well, I hope. Are you taking good care of our child?"

His low voice sounded ominous, but silky. He knew she could see him. She turned, hitched herself up, then leaned back against her pillows. She clicked on the bedside lamp with one hand as she fumbled beneath the covers with the other. Her fingers clasped the baseball bat. Good.

"How do you know I'm pregnant?" she asked.

"I've watched you over the last few days, and it's hard to hide the bump."

She glanced across the room at the pair of bassinets she'd bought the week before, their identical mobiles hanging over twin coverlets. She looked back quickly, but too late.

A slow smile spread across his face, and his thin, colorless lips formed a grotesque slash in his pale features. "Twins, how intriguing. What a pity you won't be keeping them. Unless, of course, you decide to live with me."

He rose and moved toward the bed. Her hand gripped the bat, but he pressed her arms to her side. The smell of peppermint hit her full blast as his lips touched hers. Frozen with fear she held her breath, then let it out as he released her. Each baby inside her shook as he tapped them, one by one. The mobiles quivered as the albino passed by.

"I'll be back." He gave a mock bow and left.

Bryony rushed to the window and looked out. His tall, slender frame crossed the back garden and disappeared into the night. She clutched her stomach, heaved, and ran to the bathroom. She barely made the toilet before she vomited. My God, he's back, and he would snatch the babies! She couldn't bear it, but she had no choice. No one could stop him, and he would be merciless. A cold wave made her shiver, and she climbed back into bed and pulled the covers tight around her. Exhausted, she stared into the darkness. Joy and expectation fled, replaced by a deep aching hollowness in her soul.

 ***

Jeremiah thanked God as he made his way to the road. The army cordon around Avebury Circle didn't reach as far as her cottage near Sudbury hill, and no one had seen him. The stolen black sedan purred into the night toward Bodmin Moor.

Several hours later he parked outside the isolated cottage, set deep within a rocky depression. Ezekiel and his brothers were asleep as he switched on an antique lamp.

He sat and nursed a tot of rum. He would be the father of twins, better than he'd ever imagined. They would be a solid foundation for the Phineas Priesthood. It was a shame the current hideout lay so far away, but with half the country hunting them, the cottage seemed the perfect spot to lay low.

Perhaps he'd impregnated the Scottish lass, too? What was her name? Yes, Sally Lyons, that was it. A trip to Scotland was in order. He would ask Ezekiel to go with him. They could use the travel time to work out a new strategy.

Where the devil were they? Jim McCullage stared at the incident board. He reread each note and studied every picture, then turned as the door opened. "Sam, I didn't expect to see you, it's almost midnight."

Sam slouched into the inspector's chair. "Couldn't sleep. Any new leads?"

The detective shook his head. "There has to be a paper trail. Ezekiel prepared well, dozens of aliases, bank accounts and an endless collection of property."

The CIA agent twiddled his thumbs. "My boss wants results. We'd better find them soon, or he'll recall me. Maybe we're approaching the problem from the wrong angle."

"What do you mean?"

Sam picked up the Inspector's cane and pointed it at the map. "The likelihood is their hideout is somewhere remote. Let's pick a few locations, say within two hundred miles, then try to match his aliases to recent property purchases in the area."

"Let's get to it."

Many cups of coffee, tired eyes from staring at the screen, and three hours later, Jim smiled. "This looks promising." He threw the printout over to Sam.

Sam nodded. "Bodmin Moor. You can't get much more remote than that."

"This time we'll mobilize an SAS team. With luck we'll take them by surprise. Tomorrow night, in the early hours."

CHAPTER TWENTY-TWO

TV anchorwoman Susanne Prentice paced the hallway. What could the Prime Minister want with her? Threaten to shut her up, she supposed, or perhaps... She immediately recognized the military-styled man who approached her with a serious expression. It was Alexander Brittan, alias The Home Secretary.

"Miss Prentice, please follow me," he said.

Her steel-tipped stilettos echoed down the tiled hallway. "What's this about?"

"In due time." He opened a door and stood aside. "Please."

The Prime Minister stood from his desk chair and extended his hand. "Thank you for coming, Miss Prentice. Please sit."

She shook his hand and sat down. "Please call me Susanne." She waited. Hadn't she read somewhere successful negotiators never spoke first? His extraordinarily handsome face was perfectly proportioned. She'd read about the Golden Ratio, or Divine Proportioned faces, and here was a textbook example. His features couldn't help but get him elected. Such beauty was wasted on a man, but he was easy on the eye, that was for sure.

Frank Carrington motioned to the Home Secretary. "Coffee, please, Alex. We could be a while." He waited until the door softly closed. "You must be curious about why I asked for this meeting."

"Of course, Prime Minister." She glanced around his office. The thick carpet, antique furniture, and city view impressed her. Her attention returned to him. "How can I help you?"

"You're involved with the girl, Imogene Pembroke, and her family. What do you think about her message?"

"I believe it. I've seen many extraordinary things over the past few months. Impossible, unprecedented events. I'd class them as extreme consequences, as promised."

The man watched her a long moment, then turned to look out the window. She walked around so she could see his face. "The world's in crisis," she said. "I address you now as a world citizen, not as a journalist."

He nodded. "I need your help to save—yes, save—the world from destruction. I might sound melodramatic, but trust me. I'm deadly serious. I need your commitment to do as I say before I disclose details. Will you help?"

Susanne felt the blood drain from her face. He sounded somber. Exactly how bad was his position? No, their position? A battle raged inside her.

"Of course, Prime Minister."

The Home Secretary returned, tray in hand. She noticed a small blue anchor tattoo on his wrist as he set it down and locked the office door.

Two hours later, she stepped into a chauffeured ministerial car. Their words whirled in her mind, tumbling over and over, as she tried to make sense of the government's reaction. Incredible. Could they save the world together? The onus was now on her. She'd have to get people's attention, but could she do it? Could she convince them? The reports would ensure world fame, But without a world…

Xantara studied her husband's profile as they drove away from Porton. Something was wrong, but what? His forehead creases had deepened in the last few days, and he barely spoke to her.

"Imogene's happier with Sybil there," she said. "But how much longer before they let her home?"

He grunted. "Who knows? The government has all but taken away our parental rights."

She was silent over the next few miles. Her intuition had never let her down, and right now her stomach turned somersaults. What could the problem be? They'd both settled back into their work schedule, and as far as she knew no new complications had emerged.

"Did you notice Nicola wears contacts now? And makeup? Perhaps she's dating. An attractive woman, don't you think?"

"Humph."

She fiddled with her wedding band. "Doctor Schneider hasn't been able to lead Imogene into any more past lives. He sounds frustrated."

"Good. Perhaps he'll send her home."

The detective parked outside the clinic.

Braeden unlocked the clinic door. "Doctor Schneider said the Prime Minister will be there tomorrow. We should ask him to let her out."

Xantara shook her head. "We can ask."

Jim and Sam peered over the rocky peak into the valley. "There's a light on," Jim said, pointing to the house below. "Someone's there, but is it them?"

Six SAS men, clad in black, faces camouflaged, and one with a tracker dog, stood behind them. Jim could barely see them. A canopy of brilliant stars hung over the dark moor, but the new moon gave little light. The commander signaled for his men to don night-vision goggles, and passed a pair to him and Sam.

"Wear these and you can follow us in. We'll storm the house, secure the rooms, then signal you."

Sam nudged him. "Did you see that?"

"What?"

"A shadow passed across the window. There's at least one person in there."

He watched the men spread out, then approach the cottage from every side. One advanced toward the front door with a battering ram. He struck at the commander's signal, and the door smashed open. The soldiers stormed in. The back door crashed open, and within seconds all six men entered the property.

Jim pulled Sam's sleeve. "Come on!" They raced down the rocky slope and halted at the front door.

The commander emerged and shook his head. "The building's empty."

"But Sam saw a shadow cross the window."

Jim pushed past him. He searched the house from top to bottom. The small two-bedroomed cottage held little furniture, so there was nowhere to hide.

Sam picked up a book from a side table and flipped through its pages. "Look—Ezekiel's bible, with his name inside the front cover. He's been here."

The commander shouted. "There's a cellar."

They followed his voice and stepped down into a small, dank basement. Jim walked around its perimeter, pulled cardboard boxes away from the wall, not sure what he was looking for. He moved a particularly large one, and felt a cold breeze from behind it. "An escape hole! We should have known."

A soldier brought the dog over. It sniffed around the space, then sat and wagged his tail, flicking coal dust into the air. "He's scented them. Watkins, go through the passage, and we'll meet you outside."

They clattered up the stairs and ran after the dog across the dark moor. Jim and Sam followed, but soon lagged behind. The detective stopped and held his side. "I should be fitter than this."

Sam waited for him. Younger and in tiptop shape, he showed no signs of exertion.

They caught up with the Commander. "Look, here's the exit to their escape hole," Sam said. "Didn't you say the bombers are middle-aged?"

Jim gulped in a deep breath. "Three are. Jeremiah's younger than the others."

"They won't get far. We'll catch them."

"I can't believe they'll escape again. Come on, Sam."

Half a mile farther, Jim's night-vision goggles picked up the other five government men, green shapes standing in a circle. He puffed, tripped over rough grass tufts, and stopped to examine what the men were looking at. Two men lay face down on the ground before them. The soldiers rolled them onto their backs.

Jim grunted. "Obadiah and Malachi. Where are the other two?"

Obadiah's contorted face spat hatred toward the detective. "They're not here, and don't think you'll hold us for long. The Lord will set his followers free."

The soldiers yanked them to their feet and secured their hands behind their backs. Headlights flashed over the moor as an all-terrain vehicle neared to pick them up.

Jim stared hard into the prisoners' faces. "Obadiah and Malachi Yates, you're under arrest for the Stonehenge massacre, plus many other charges. Anything you say will be used in evidence, do you understand?"

Neither man spoke. Jim nodded to the soldiers, who led them up the slope toward the armored car. The two middle-aged men exchanged glances as they traipsed between the soldiers. Jim turned to Sam. "Not your typical terrorists, are they?"

Later he and Sam stepped back inside the house. "Let's search each room," Jim said. "We still have to find Ezekiel and Jeremiah. What a pity we didn't catch them all together."

They found no clues to the whereabouts of the priesthood's absent members. Jim opened the fridge. "There's enough food in here for four people." He pushed a milk container aside and breathed out. "Wow! The chemical flask's here, and partially full. At least we have that. Better call the specialists to remove it."

Sam peered around the fridge door. "Thank God they can't use it to kill again. But is the chemical all there?" The CIA agent tapped a number into his cell phone. "It's a pity you Brits don't have a Guatemano Bay compound. We Yanks would get them to talk."

Bryony's hand trembled as she sipped her coffee, spilling some. "I was terrified. How long had he been in my house?"

Xantara put a paper towel under her friend's cup, and a dark stain spread across it. "We have to tell Detective McCullage. Perhaps he can post a guard."

Bryony shook her head. "That would be pointless. They can't watch me all the time. He'll find a way to snatch the babies, I know it." She pulled a handkerchief from her pocket and dabbed her eyes. "What shall I do?"

"Do you want to move back here? Live with us?"

Bryony smiled. "Thank you, but I miss my home. Besides, I have to return at some stage. I'll have a security firm install locks and cameras."

"Good idea. Be sure to ask for a panic button that alerts their base." She frowned, thinking. "On another matter, I have a problem of my own."

Bryony set her cup down. "How selfish you must think me. What's wrong?"

Xantara sighed. "Braeden has changed the past few days. He seldom talks, and appears to be avoiding me. He even refused to visit Imogene this week. Twice."

"That's serious. He's never missed a chance to see her. Any clues?"

Xantara's fingertip drew imaginary circles on the tablecloth. "I've no idea. Work is fine, at least no dramas I've heard about. Of course Imogene's absence is stressful, but it always has been."

Bryony reached out for her friend's hand. "Stop imagining the worst," she said. "Just ask him."

"You're right. I'll sit him down tonight and demand he tell me what's wrong."

Bryony stood. "I'd better go and organize the security. Call me tomorrow."

Charles Strathfield, opposition leader, settled back in his personal Lear jet. The Bilderberg Group was horrified when he reported on the Prime Minister's speech. What on earth possessed Frank Carrington to push this issue? He'll have to go, and as soon as possible.

His trusty butler brought in a vodka and lime with a snack selection.

"What do you think, Jones?"

"About what, sir?"

"That maniac, the Prime Minister."

"From what you've told me, sir, his story has merit. The evidence leaves no other explanation."

"Merit? Of course, and that's the problem! The Bilderberg Group controls more than half the world's wealth, and they won't allow their money and power to be distributed among the poor."

His butler stood with a starched white napkin over his arm. "Yes, sir. But if what the Prime Minister says is true, there will be no world in which to spend it."

Strathfield downed his drink and held out his glass. "Our members will know what to do. They'll stop this so-called 'Council of Elders.' No one has ever defeated the Bilderbergers."

CHAPTER TWENTY-THREE

There she is!

Jeremiah watched the young woman through his binoculars as she hung out her washing. A radio played softly behind him, where Ezekiel waited in the car.

He rocked back on his heels. Yes! Sally Lyons' silhouette clearly showed she was close to term. She stopped and rubbed her back. By her size, she could be pregnant with twins, too. What should he do? Grab her now? Or wait and take the babies?

An older woman emerged from the house, picked up the clothes basket, and Sally followed her inside. A few minutes later a car revved and a small, red hatchback pulled out of the driveway and turned onto the road. It held one occupant, the older woman.

Jeremiah considered his options. The house stood back from the highway, and the nearest neighbor's house was at least four hundred yards away. He scrambled back up the slope.

"Ezekiel, she's alone. We're going in."

He directed his cousin down the hill, and they pulled into the driveway. As soon as the car stopped he jumped out and ran around behind the house.

Sally looked terrified as he grabbed her. He held her close as he struggled to open the garage door with his other hand, then signaled for Ezekiel to drive in. "Dare scream and you'll suffer," he said.

He pulled the girl into the kitchen, ripped off apron straps, and tied her to a hard-backed chair. "Who's the woman who left? Your mother?"

Wide-eyed, she nodded.

"When's she due back?"

"Soon. She's only gone to buy groceries."

"Good. We'll wait."

He took the tablecloth from the kitchen table, ripped off a strip and gagged her with it, then selected a sharp boning knife from a knife block. Tendons stood out on the young woman's neck, her pulse visible.

"Calm down," he said. "I won't hurt you. All I want is my child."

Ezekiel switched on the kettle, then rummaged in the walk-in pantry. "I'm starving. Care for a cheese and tomato sandwich?"

Jeremiah nodded, and watched his cousin assemble the snack as he listened for the mother's return. Sally shrank back in the chair, making her stomach protrude even more. He loosened the gag.

"When's the baby due?"

She flinched. "Any time, now. Please don't hurt us."

He retightened the gag, cutting off her next words.

He and his cousin sat and wolfed down the sandwiches as they waited. Jeremiah cocked his head as car tires rumbled over the gravel driveway. He hid behind the front door as a key turn in the lock, and the mother struggled in with an armful of bags. He lunged toward her, but she ducked and swung a bag into his crotch. He doubled up and let out a howl. "You're dead!"

He chased her past her daughter and up the stairs. Trapped, she turned and shielded herself with her arms. He stabbed at her, again and again. She picked up the bedside lamp and swung it at him, and its solid base glanced off his temple. He lunged and jabbed the blade up between her ribs, straight into her heart. Her eyes widened, and she dropped.

He returned to the kitchen, and Sally tried to make noises behind the gag. Her eyes were widened as she looked toward the stairs. "Yes, the bitch is dead! She shouldn't have hurt me! Make sure you co-operate or you will join her!"

The sky darkened as night closed in. Sally moaned as he drew the curtains and switched on the overhead light. "I'll remove the gag, if you promise to be quiet."

She nodded, and he dropped the gag. "I'm in labor," she said. "Please, call an ambulance. I won't tell anybody. When the baby's born I'll give it to you. Please, I don't want to die." Beads of sweat spotted her lip and forehead.

Jeremiah's heart raced. His child would arrive any minute now. "Don't worry, I'll look after you. We'll go upstairs, where you'll be more comfortable."

She stumbled up the stairs, stopping every few steps to clutch her stomach. She froze as she saw her mother's body, stiff and still, face up under the windowsill, her eyes open. Tears coursed down Sally's contorted face, and she moaned louder as the men undressed her and lifted her onto the bed. Ezekiel returned downstairs, and Jeremiah sat on the bed's edge and waited.

Sally screamed and drew up her legs. She lifted her head as she pushed and pushed. Her face reddened, and sweat beaded her brow. He watched blood trickle from between her legs. The child's head crowned, an orangey cap covered with crimson blood.

She pushed, and the head emerged. The body soon followed. A boy! He had a son! His son wailed weakly as Sally fell back on the pillow. Blood gushed and soaked the mattress as her eyes rolled back into her head.

Jeremiah fetched a towel from the bathroom and wrapped the child. What now? He searched the bathroom cabinet, and returned with scissors and floss and tied and cut the umbilical cord. His boy's face turned red and he cried louder. He was alive, thank the Lord.

He moved to the stair top. "Ezekiel, the child's a boy. I have a son." He returned to the bedroom and cradled the baby. "Shush, shush, little man."

The baby fell silent and opened his eyes, and father and son regarded each other. The baby's eyes matched his own, a brilliant turquoise blue.

The ginger hair must have come from the woman. Thank God he hadn't inherited the albino gene.

Sally lay motionless, her face white. Blood still poured from between her legs, darkening the mattress. Hemorrhage, it must be. He felt for a pulse. Very weak. As he held her it faltered, then stopped. He smiled. Good, one less complication.

He turned his attention to the boy, who sucked his fist. Milk, he needed milk. He carried him downstairs and held him out for Ezekiel to see. "The Lord has blessed me today. Isn't he perfect?"

"A handsome son, indeed. What will you call him?"

"Gideon. A good name for our newest Phineas Priesthood member. Yes, Gideon."

"Tell me where they are!"

Detective McCullage's throat constricted as he faced Obadiah in the stark interrogation room. The ex-army major's face looked shrunken and grey against the orange jumpsuit.

"Look—I know you're not the main player here. Tell me where to find Ezekiel and Jeremiah, and I'll ask the court for leniency."

A chain rattled as Obadiah raised his hand to attend to an itch in his ear. He stared past the investigator, his lips set in a slight smirk. "Detective, right is on our side. We did the Lord's work. Look at the dead. Idolaters, evildoers, heathens—Druids, for goodness sake. The Phineas Priesthood did the world a favor, clearing out the scum."

McCullage sniffed. "Thousands died, including innocent children. They weren't evil. Do you want to spend the rest of your life in prison? Tell me where they are, and you might get a reduced sentence."

Obadiah held his gaze. "You don't know your Bible, do you? Children are born sinful, each one. Only by accepting Jesus can they be cleansed from sin and saved."

"Tell me where they are! Don't you want to lessen your sentence?"

Obadiah sneered. "You don't understand, detective. I won't be in prison. The Lord will set me free. Malachi, too. You're no match for His power. I'll never go to trial. In fact, I'll be back out there within a month."

McCullage motioned the guard. "Take him back to his cell, and bring in Malachi. Maybe he'll listen to reason."

Sam Blackbridge walked in, and McCullage turned. "A quick word, Jim. I noticed a change in Obadiah through the two-way mirror. Did you see it?"

Jim frowned. "No, what?"

Sam hesitated. "Well, his eyes, his whole demeanor changed."

"I don't understand."

"He has blue eyes, right? They darkened, just like his soul got switched out. Someone else looked through his eyes, I swear. He stared straight at me through the glass, a look of pure hate. A cold chill ran down my spine. Evil, pure evil."

Xantara fried the diced beef and onions, then paused. What caused Braeden's sudden personality change the week before? Her instinct never let her down. Something was wrong, dreadfully wrong.

She tossed vegetables into the casserole dish, seasoned the mixture, and shook her head. Hadn't they been together, all week? What was it?

She crumbled stock cubes into the pot, added a spoonful of herbs, then covered the meat with hot water. Wait. Wasn't it a week ago she attended the breech birth? Braeden visited Imogene alone. Did something happen then?

Beef casserole completed, she reached for a wine bottle. A pleasant Shiraz would be perfect. She uncorked the drink, poured herself a glass, and pictured that night as she walked into the bedroom. She'd returned home after midnight to find him asleep, and as she climbed into bed she smelled alcohol. Yes, he'd been drinking, but it was a weekday. That was unusual for him. A slight chill ran down her spine.

The doorbell tinkled as Braeden's last patient left. Moments later he came in, a scowl on his face.

"Bloody hypochondriacs! Why do they always come in last, then stay until they've covered every imaginary disease?"

Xantara rose. "Sit down, relax. I'll pour you a glass of wine."

She went into the kitchen to get the drink, and the news blared out on the TV as she returned. She gave him the glass and switched off the television. "Braeden, we need to talk."

He picked up the newspaper and opened it, right between them. "I'm tired."

Xantara ripped the paper away. "And I want to talk!"

He stared at her, his eyes wide. "What on earth…okay, let's talk."

She scrutinized his face and touched his knee. "Love, what's wrong? I know there's something, and we're not eating dinner until you tell me."

Braeden yawned and rubbed the back of his neck. "It's nothing. I'm tired, that's all. Tired of patients, tired of Imogene being away. What's life about?"

Chilled, she turned up the gas fire and sat next to him. "It's more than that. I know it, and you know it. What happened when you visited Imogene last week?"

His face reddened and he turned away. She'd hit the mark! So the change occurred then, as she suspected. "You know I'll find out, so you may as well tell me."

Braeden looked down. His shoulders dropped, and sighed again. "Nicola came onto me."

"And?"

"She asked me to her room for a few drinks, and the evening got out of hand."

160

Images flashed through Xantara's head. Nicola. Her heavy glasses replaced with contacts, the fresh makeup, and recently tighter and shorter skirts.

She stood. "Don't lie to me. Guilt's written all over your face. You slept with her, didn't you?"

Braeden didn't answer. She turned on her heel and went upstairs. Tears dripped onto the clothes as she packed an overnight case. After all they'd been through, and now this!

He didn't move as she trundled her case past him.

"Dinner's in the oven. Enjoy!"

An hour later she sobbed into Bryony's arms. "It's over. He's gone too far. There's no excuse. After all we've been through—I've forgiven him for his actions when I was in the cell, although I almost lost my life because of him. But this, I can't—I won't—forgive."

CHAPTER TWENTY-FOUR

Charles Strathfield tugged the neck of the coarse friar's habit. At least the hood covered his bald pate. Plain stupid, to dress up like old hams at the theatre royal, but one played along. The price to pay, he supposed, to be allowed to join the Bilderberg group's inner circle.

He thrust out his chest as he recalled his inauguration into the "Ring of Troth" secret society. Jacques de Sales, a Swiss financier, had explained the group was loosely based on "The Book of Troth," but with a few weird ancient Egyptian rites mixed in. He didn't actually care, but he liked the ideals, and the fact the society was capped at eight members. Jacques had shaken his hand. "Most Bilderberg members don't know we exist," he said. "We vet our new members carefully, to get the best of the best. Welcome."

Charles limped down the dark tunnel and emerged into the sacred hall. A huge backdrop, dominated by an equally huge, extravagantly decorated man/bird figure, hung behind the altar. He stared around, at the walls. The magnificent frescoes must contain enough gold-leaf to buy a super yacht. What did those hieroglyphics mean? Utter baloney, he expected, meaningless nonsense that Jacques dreamed up. The man was a nutcase. An enormously rich nutcase.

Gold watches and diamond rings flashed under the loose sleeves of the seven hooded men who turned to greet him, and he frowned as he joined their circle. Just what were those stupid sacred words he'd had to recite during his inauguration?

Jacques' voice rang out, reverberating against the marble walls. "We are strong, never weak. We are courageous, never cowards. Joy, freedom, and indulgence are our aims. Brotherhood increases wealth, so we pledge to aid our brothers to rule and control all others."

The rites concluded, and Charles trailed behind the sect into a spacious anteroom. He glanced around. The bizarre black and gold symbols adorning the walls reminded him of a Freemason's lodge he'd frequented in his early days. He sat and set his computer atop a dark baronial table. Another member set up a screen and connected his computer.

The men turned as the screen sprang to life. The British government's derisive cries filled the room.

"Sorry, I'll rewind," Charles said quickly. "Here's the Prime Minister's speech."

Frank Carrington's earnest face appeared on the screen. They listened in silence as he explained Imogene's message and his later conversation with the Council of Elders, via the child.

Jacques de Sales grimaced. "Charles, I commend you for bringing this to our attention. We have to act."

One member laughed. "You can't be serious, Jacques. None of this is real."

De Sales sat and stared hard at the man. "Deadly serious, my friend. The minister talks about an ancient Egyptian named Osahar. I know he exists, and he's not alone. Many times I've spoken with a similar entity when in a deep meditative state. A woman, Sakhment. She also mentioned the Council of Elders and their role in our world."

Charles shut his laptop. "Well, I'm not sharing my wealth with the poor. But if we don't, how can we prevent the Council destroying the world?"

Jacques' perfect white teeth flashed. "The girl's the key. Carrington said she must cooperate with the Egyptian priest to trigger these events. We have to bring her here."

Charles' hood slipped off his bare head as waved his fist. "To kill her?"

"No, to use her. If she can interact with Osahar, maybe she can work with our entity too, and create events for us."

"Porton Down would be nigh impossible to breach," Charles said. "It's a chemical weapons facility, and is well guarded. It's a fortress."

Jacques looked at each face in turn. "Leave the details to me. Security won't be a problem. I'll get it organized. "

Bulgarian Lilya Kaminski rolled over, found her phone, and read the text message.

"Mother expects you to visit."

At last, contact. She bounded out of bed and went through her half hour martial arts practice, watching herself in the full-length robe mirror to perfect each move. She smiled at her slim, lithe body as she jabbed and postured.

She flicked her short honey-blonde bob and switched on the shower, washed, and turned the spray to cold. She shivered under the flow as her heartbeat drummed in her chest. Five minutes later she strode back to the bedroom encased in a large, fleecy bathrobe. Her fingers flew over the cell phone keys.

On my way. Will bring flowers."

Susanne smoothed her pencil skirt and faced the camera, nodded to Hugh, and tapped her microphone. "The Prime Minister will now address the nation." She turned toward Frank Carrington. "Prime Minister, recent events have terrorized the country, and we need answers and reassurance. What can you tell us?"

Frank looked straight into the camera, his practiced smile exuding warmth and confidence. "We've experienced extraordinary events over past months, and many of you are concerned. We understand that. I now have answers to some of your questions."

Susanne pasted a smile on her face as the camera turned back to her. "The opposition leader, Charles Strathfield, is demanding your resignation. What's your response?"

He licked his lips. "I presented the government—the opposition cabinet included—with the material I'm about to share with you. They refused to examine the facts further, so I've decided to bring them directly to the people. That way, they can form their own opinions."

Frank coughed into his hand as he fought for breath. He hoped he wouldn't have a full-blown asthma attack. "All I ask is for the country to keep an open mind until the program ends," he said, "and view the facts as presented. I'm sure your audience will find the evidence conclusive, and will support my proposal."

The camera flashed back to Susanne, and she stared directly into it. "My cameraman and I personally filmed the events you are about to witness," she said. "The footage is genuine and unaltered. You may have already seen the first video, but please listen carefully. Here it is."

On the monitor, the crazy nurse lunged at Imogene as a man pushed her away. The child rose high in the air above Avebury Circle and delivered her speech. The studio camera now panned to Hugh.

"This is the man who saved the girl's life," she said, smiling. "Our own cameraman, Hugh Grantham."

Imogene's voice, strangely low-pitched, filled the studio.

"You'll notice the voice is not a young child's, she said, over it. "Experts agree it's that of a mature woman."

Frank puffed his inhaler off camera, then leaned forward. "This message asks the world to extend love to the disenfranchised, and calls for disarmament. The Council claims mankind's past behavior has led to an unprecedented increase in psychopathic acts of violence, wars, and corruption. Could anyone dispute such a rise? The recent Stonehenge terrorist atrocity is proof enough, I think."

Susanne frowned. "This Council of Elders. Does it exist?"

The Prime Minister's eyes narrowed. "I'll take questions at the program's end." He tugged his tie. "Many believe in God, and naturally question other supernatural events. Others believe only the physical world is real. The next two segments may change all their minds."

The next video started. In it, Dark and Light Beings fought among people in an underground catacomb. A man hit another with a brass candlestick, and he fell. The camera switched to an aged woman lying prone on the stone floor, her throat cut. Several people disappeared down a dark tunnel with the otherworldly beings following.

Frank faced the camera. "Media experts say this video is untouched. The scene you just witnessed really happened."

"My cameraman and I can testify to that," Susanne said, her voice now more intense. "The video, filmed by Hugh, clearly shows I was there. We took this footage as Imogene's father and brother searched for her after the Stonehenge terrorists abducted her. It proves paranormal or other dimensional creatures do exist."

She took a deep breath. Well, she'd said it. Now she had to back it up.

"A group called the Avebury Guardians cares for The Avebury Circle, which is thousands of years old. Imogene's mother is one of the eight guardians, who use the ancient Circle's power to heal locals. This next footage shows such a healing."

Again, the studio monitor became alive. It showed the detective laying his sick wife gently on the altar stone. Guardians chanted and played small drums and tambourines as they encircled her. Light Beings entered from the left, streamed through her body, then moved off-screen.

Susanne waved a sheaf of papers. "These certified papers confirm this woman was close to death, yet today she's perfectly well. The creatures you've just seen are identical to some of the entities depicted in St Michael's church catacombs in the village of Monkton St Michael,

Wiltshire. Others have recently seen these paranormal beings, on the Isle of Angels near the village. That's where Phineas Priesthood members—the people who terrorized Stonehenge—tried to burn Imogene Pembroke's mother Xantara as a witch. The Light Beings appeared to several people."

The cameras cut to break, and Frank turned to Susanne. "How do you think the presentation is going?"

She twisted her necklace and sighed. "I'm not sure. The videos are authentic, but viewers these days believe little of what the media tells them. We'll have to bring in experts on another program as soon as possible."

Within seconds, the cameras came back live. Frank straightened his tie. "This next part plays in audio only," he said. "You'll hear Doctor Ernst Schneider, a world renowned psychiatrist, lead Imogene into her past lives by hypnosis. He specializes in children's disorders, and has conducted many past life regressions. Please reserve judgment until you have heard the audio."

The studio fell silent, and the doctor's interview with Imogene started. Frank's face hardened as the audio recounted her three past lives. Susanne sighed as the final audio faded.

"The Prime Minister will explain how these past lives correspond with the latest disasters," she said. "Prime Minister…"

He nodded. "You heard that with each account, the young girl interacted with an entity called 'Osahar.' We're convinced they worked together to create events in real time. Imogene's first recollection is as a First World War soldier, which matches the latest flu outbreak in which many fine young men perished. The nineteen-year-old men shared the identical birthdate, the birthdate of the soldier in her past life. These deaths occurred worldwide. The odds that the deaths could be coincidental are beyond astronomical."

Susanne mopped away a tear. "And the next, Prime Minister…"

"The great fire of Chicago is well known to our American friends. We can explain the recent, similar fire as an unfortunate chain of events, but

I believe Imogene and Osahar worked on the Council of Elders' orders to set it. When you consider this triple sequence of disasters, you have to give credence to weight of evidence."

Susanne's voice cracked. "And the third?"

"Never has the world experienced such an enormous loss of life. The figure is close to eight million, more than the Holocaust and deaths of our World War Two soldiers combined.

"But how does Imogene's past-life experience as a death camp child relate to the lethal gas cloud?"

"Quite simply, the Gestapo used gas chambers. I guess the Council used the comet's trajectory to deliver the toxic gas cloud which centered directly over the Auschwitz Death Camp. Perhaps they chose this method to illustrate the evil committed against millions of Jews and other so-called 'inferior' people, to show how low mankind has fallen, but the odds of the gas cloud occurring and exactly in this location cannot be calculated."

Blinking rapidly, Susanne adjusted her microphone. "Prime Minster, we'll now play the final audio, your contact with the Council of Elders. Listeners, please stay tuned. This is blow-your-mind scary, but it must be heard."

She prayed people would listen, understand, and accept. The future of her family and theirs depended on this last piece of evidence.

As the final audio came to an end, Frank said "All the people of this country, and indeed the world, must consider this Council of Elders message. We have four months left to meet their terms, which are to disarm and redistribute food and supplies to all. I'll deliver this message to the United Nations and beg—yes, beg—them to authorize action. I ask for your support, to prevent the end of life as we know it."

The cameras stopped rolling, and Frank slumped in his chair. Susanne reached for his arm. "You did well, sir. We'll schedule another broadcast in a week. By then we'll know the nation's mood, and call on experts in view of that. We will succeed. We have to."

CHAPTER TWENTY-FIVE

Jeremiah crept across the unlit yard next to the low lime-washed farmhouse and peered through the window.

Malachi's wife Molly looked as if she were alone. She sat in a rocking chair, a tissue box in her lap. Scattered around her lay white scrunched-up papers, and he could hear her weeping. He checked the other windows, then called softly to his cousin Ezekiel.

He opened the unlocked back door and stood back. Ezekiel pushed past him, carrying the sleeping baby and a large bag. He placed the child on the sitting-room sofa and covered him with a multi-colored crocheted blanket. Jeremiah entered the dining room and moved to behind Molly. His hand clamped over her mouth, and she struggled.

"It's me, Jeremiah. Not a sound!"

Molly nodded, and he let go. She shuffled to her feet as Ezekiel walked in. "What are you two doing here?"

Ezekiel sat heavily on a dining chair. "Be a dear, and put the kettle on."

The kettle whistled and rocked atop the old blackened cook stove, and Molly set out a tea service. She paused, then added fruitcake. "The Guardia have searched both the farmhouse and stables from top to bottom," she said. "They may come back."

Jeremiah nodded. "We're not staying. I'm sorry about Riordan and Sean, both fine young men. The Lord will have his revenge."

She joined them at the table and cut them each a slice of cake. "And now I've lost Malachi as well. He'll never see the green Irish fields again, or his beloved horses. They'll lock him up for life."

Ezekiel stopped chewing. "What do you mean? Malachi and Obadiah were holed up at my Bodmin Moor property, only a few days ago."

"Haven't you seen the news? They've been captured. Inspector 'somebody' crowed about how they'd caught the Stonehenge terrorists, and showed your photos. The whole country's looking for you."

The sound of a crying newborn floated through the doorway. Molly jumped up and rushed into the other room. She gasped and returned, cradling the child.

"Whose baby is this? And why have you brought it here?" As she stroked the child's cheek he caught her index finger and sucked. "The poor thing's hungry. Do you have any formula?"

Jeremiah fetched the heavy bag. "Everything's here. Milk, diapers, you name it. He's my son, and I've named him Gideon. I want you to look after him until I find a permanent home."

Molly's eyes widened as she prepared the baby a bottle. "Your son? I don't understand."

"It's a long story. A young Scottish woman gave birth to him, part of our strategy to expand our Priesthood numbers. We left Scotland in a hurry."

"How did you cross the Irish sea with the police checking the ports?"

Ezekiel downed his tea in one gulp. "Fishing trawler. Money will buy you anything."

Gideon sucked the bottle noisily. "Well, you can't stay here. And what about him?"

Jeremiah smiled at his son. "We'll go up to Uncle's old hunting lodge in County Cork, and lay low for a while. You look after the baby. Pass him off as your niece's child. You'll come up with a story, I'm sure. If the Guardia do return, do your best to keep him hidden."

Molly beamed. "Such a sweet little man. Don't you worry, I'll take good care of him. He'll take my mind off the others."

Jeremiah touched the baby's ginger hair. "I'll be back, son. I promise."

Frank Carrington watched Imogene's eyes roll, then looked across the now-familiar white office to Doctor Schneider. "Is she all right?"

The psychiatrist replaced the syringe and picked up the crystal. "I hope so. She's built up resistance, and I've had to use a stronger formula. Do you want me to stop?"

Images of Frank's own daughter flashed through his mind, and he lowered his head. His throat thickened as he tried to answer.

"Prime Minister?" Dr. Schneider stared at him.

Frank looked up. "No, I have no choice, we have to do this. Let's get on with it." Had he really fallen this low? To use an eight-year-old child? "Let's make it quick."

The doctor pushed his glasses back on his nose. "Sir, hypnosis is not a quick process. I have to be aware of the patient's mental state and gradually guide them."

Frank nodded and grasped the girl's hand.

At last, Imogene focused on the crystal. She followed it, to and fro, and her eyes flickered and closed. Schneider dropped the pendulum into his coat's top pocket.

"Imogene, find the Elders. What can you see?"

Her eyes darted beneath her lids, apparently watching an invisible presence. "Rahmiel's here. She'll guide me."

Her face paled, and her body stiffened. A deep voice echoed around the room.

"Kabshiel speaks, human. What do you want with me?"

Frank's heart leapt in his chest. "People think this is all a trick, that I have a hidden agenda, or I'm crazy. I'll present your message to the United Nations in New York City next week. Can you help me convince them? Perhaps provide another sign, one they can't ignore?"

"I understand and agree to perform one last…"

Imogene's body convulsed, and her hand went limp in his. "Doctor, she's stopped breathing. Do something!"

Schneider pressed an alarm button and performed CPR. Alex followed Security into the office and immediately phoned for an ambulance.

Frank felt the blood drain from his face. He'd killed her! Alex tapped his arm.

"Sir, are you all right?"

He opened and closed his mouth. "Is…is she alive?"

Paramedics entered, and one placed an oxygen mask on her face. He ripped open her dress. "Paddles!" He positioned them on her chest and activated them, and her tiny body lifted off the couch, time after time. "Come on, come on, respond, little girl!" Then: "We have a heartbeat."

The office cleared within moments. Frank again felt Alex tap his arm and shake his shoulder. "Her heart's beating, she's breathing. They'll take good care of her in the hospital."

Frank stood in a daze. "It's my fault. I'll never forgive myself if anything happens to her."

He clutched his throat. His chest tightened, and he couldn't breathe. Alex held his head, forced the inhaler into his mouth, and he puffed Ventolin. "Schneider, call another ambulance."

Braeden met Xantara in the corridor leading to the intensive care unit. She barely glanced at him as they walked, side by side, toward the double doors. He recognized the duty doctor who motioned them in.

"How is she, doctor?"

"Stable, for now. But we still don't know what the problem is. Has she a history of heart problems?"

Braeden's stomach churned as he looked at her slight body. They'd intubated her, and the heart monitor beeped at the bedside.

"No, she hasn't."

"We'll do every test I can think of. Try not to worry."

Xantara kissed her daughter and stroked her arm. "Will she recover?"

The doctor touched her shoulder. "We'll do all we can. She's young. When we find the cause, we can treat her."

Braeden stood at the foot of the bed watching his wife caress Imogene's arm. If he could trade places with his daughter he would, in an instant. Hadn't Ezekiel said that God only gave a person as much as they could bear? Another lie!

He stepped toward his wife. "Xan, I'm so sorry. Can we bury our differences? For now, at least?"

She stood, threw her arms around him and laid her wet face on his chest and sobbed. He stroked her hair. "We have to hang in there. For Imogene, for Alistair, and for us. She's resilient. Surely, Rahmiel will help her…"

The door opened, and they turned. The pale Prime Minister stepped in, followed by the Home Secretary. Braeden clenched his fists. "You and Schneider are responsible for this. She's not going back there. I won't allow it."

Frank's face reddened. "How is she?"

"Not good, thanks to you separating her from her family and allowing Schneider to drug and misuse her."

Alex held the door open. "Let's step outside."

In the corridor, Xantara held Braeden's arm down. "This isn't helping. Prime Minister, please tell us what happened."

Frank paused. "We went through the same procedure as before. I spoke with the Council of Elders again. The situation is dire, time is running out, and I need their help. Suddenly she went limp and her heart stopped, and Schneider gave her CPR until the ambulance arrived. I'm so sorry. It won't happen again."

Braeden moved closer, their faces now inches apart. "You bet your life it won't. When and if she recovers, we're taking her home."

Frank stumbled back. "Of course. I'd never have subjected her to this if the world's future wasn't at stake. If there's anything I can do, please ask, and I'll put whatever resources you need at your disposal. I'm so sorry, more than you can imagine. We won't use her again."

The nurse fell without a sound.

Pressing the correct pressure point in the neck was Lilya's most accomplished martial arts move, quick and silent. She donned the nurse's uniform and dragged the woman into an empty changing cubicle. The young girl's hospitalization had swamped the news channels for days. One reporter had captured her at a private room's window with a long-range lens.

The elevator bell chimed as the door opened, and Lilya saw a constable sitting outside a door at the corridor's end. She strode toward him.

"Hi, I've come to take the girl for another MRI."

The young man looked at his book. "The test's not logged in."

"No? Well, the doctor ordered it. You'll escort us, won't you?"

"Yes, I suppose if he ordered it, it'll be okay."

She smiled brightly and brushed past him into the room. Imogene sat in bed reading a book, her twin dolls lying on each side.

"Good morning, how are you today?" Lilya clicked off the bed's brakes. "Well, off for another test. Just a picture." She took the book from Imogene and closed it. "Lie down, please."

She effortlessly pushed the bed along the corridor and into the elevator. The police officer followed and smiled. "Worked here long, nurse?"

"Ages. Isn't it boring, guarding the door all day?"

The elevator stopped at the next floor, and two interns entered. Lilya's heart raced, but she breathed deeply and calmed herself. They exited at the next floor.

The bell chimed, and she pushed the bed out. The constable frowned. "Isn't this the laundry?"

She smiled. "It's a short cut I always use. Can you help push her through?"

He maneuvered the bed through piles of dirty sheets. When they turned into a hallway, she jumped on his back and pulled a wire garrote around his neck. Imogene screamed as he crumpled against the wall. Lilya clamped her hand over the child's mouth and pushed a syringe into her arm.

She picked her up and pushed through the swing doors into the hospital's rear parking lot. Moments later she swung her SUV's rear door shut and scrambled into the driver's seat.

She grinned, as she thought about the money she would earn from this job and headed for the small private airport just five miles away.

Chapter Twenty-Six

F rank Carrington paced on the sidelines as anchor Susanne Prentice introduced the program. If it didn't convince the people, they were all doomed.

She turned to the experts. "This is Doctor Ernst Schneider," she said, "the well-respected psychiatrist who examined Imogene Pembroke and recorded her messages. Doctor Schneider, could you talk us through the hypnotic sessions you conducted with the child?"

Schneider adjusted his spectacles and squinted. "I can assure the public I carried out all past life regressions meticulously. I've studied the phenomenon for many years, and learned that ninety percent of subject's memories are true. The evidence is overwhelming."

"What about the child's mental state?"

Schneider spread his hands. "Perfect. She's a strong character, mature for her age, well-balanced, and well-behaved. I found her to be a sensible individual."

Susanne learned forward. "How did the places, dates and times she told you about stack up with the actual three past lives?"

The doctor edged forward on his seat. "They tallied with historical reports. For example, there's no denying the flu victims shared the exact date, age, and sex with the World War One soldier. The twin boys tortured at Auschwitz? We found their names in records, and survivors confirmed her version of Mengele's operations. There are few records of Chicago's Great Fire, for obvious reasons. The fire would have destroyed them."

Susanne faced the camera. "Thank you, Doctor Schneider. We'll now hear from Paul Jamieson, a leading forensics expert. Mr. Jamieson?"

The stooped man with dark rimmed glasses glanced at his notes. "After careful analysis, I can guarantee the film and digital recordings were not altered. I've checked every detail, including compression, waveform display, and magnetic signature. Channel five had edited the film to fit its time slot, but they provided me with the raw film, and I can confirm it flows flawlessly. The audios recorded on Doctor Schneider's computer are complete and untouched."

The producer signaled the cameraman to cut to commercials, and Susanne joined the Prime Minister off-set. "Sir, it's going well, don't you think?"

Frank grimaced. "I hope so. Those specialists sounded convincing, but what about the others?"

She nodded. "We're using the same space-cloud expert as before. He'll testify to the event's extreme rarity, but we can't dismiss the possibility of it being a natural act. The Chicago Fire Chief is similar, unfortunately. The unprecedented chain of events that led to the destruction of downtown Chicago can only be linked to her past life account by hearsay. We're saving the best till last. The pandemic expert will confirm the flu couldn't have naturally infected such a narrow group. All in all, I think the testimonies will help your case."

Frank touched her arm. "I can't thank you enough, Susanne. If we survive the four-month deadline, I'll see to it that you get the recognition you deserve."

As the final guest expert finished speaking, Susanne stepped forward. "I thank all our experts and specialists for their time and research. The Prime Minister will now address the nation."

Frank cleared his throat. He hoped to God he could convince them, and that the stress wouldn't bring on an asthma attack partway through.

"This is a time of immense sorrow for our country," he said. "Many of you have lost friends or family members, or know of others who have. Thousands of young men succumbed to the flu pandemic here and around the world. British citizens living or holidaying in Europe and Chicago lost their lives by fire or poisonous gas. Can we afford to ignore the Council of Elders and risk further loss of life?"

He paused. "The documented evidence shows the facts are undeniable. I address the United Nations General Assembly next week in the hope of brokering a deal for disarmament and relief for the poor. The truth is, we should be working harder on these worthwhile aims without the threat from outside agencies. This broadcast will be aired worldwide, and I ask citizens around the globe to support this endeavor and lobby their governments. Thank you, and good night."

Detective McCullage watched Inspector Grant from the back of the incident room. The tall, thin man looked gaunt as he waved his cane at the screen.

"This is Lilya Kaminski," he said, "a freelancer and former Bulgarian State Security agent. She's skilled in martial arts, and is the ultimate killing machine. We don't know who paid her to abduct Imogene Pembroke, or why, but we have to find them. Any questions?"

Jim McCullage tapped his pencil against his notebook. "Any leads on the plane?"

The inspector's face darkened under his bushy brows. "It was a Cessna Citation X, a private jet with a top speed of seven hundred miles an hour. It carries seven passengers, and could have crossed the Channel long ago. By now they could be anywhere in Europe."

Jim's cell phone vibrated in his pocket. He held it under the table and checked the text, then felt the blood drain from his face. "Sir, there's other news. The young woman I rescued from the Priesthood in Scotland? They found her and her mother dead."

Inspector Grant's lip curled. "What happened?"

"The murderer stabbed the mother, and the girl died by apparent childbirth hemorrhage. The baby's missing. The homicide has all the hallmarks of Jeremiah's work." He frowned. "So now we have two missing children."

The Inspector straightened. "You and Sam follow up that case. We'll ask Interpol to help track the Pembroke girl."

Jim stood and motioned to Sam, and they joined the coffee machine queue. Jim bit his lip. The whole affair had become painful. They'd failed to protect Sally Lyons, such a bright young woman. He had failed to protect her. He should have known Jeremiah would return to collect his child. The evil bastard.

They went to his office and sipped their coffee. "Imogene's parents are distraught as you'd expect," Jim said, sitting. "But I'm particularly worried about Braeden. He may be on the edge of a nervous breakdown."

"How's Bryony?"

Jim drained his coffee, then crushed the paper cup. "She phoned yesterday and said Jeremiah turned up at her home a week ago. He threatened to return for the twins, but she refuses a police guard. At least she's installed an alarm and security cameras with a direct feed to the police station." He frowned. "Maybe we should move her to a safe house. If I'd alerted the police in Scotland, Sally Lyons could still be alive."

Sam aimed his empty cup at the waste basket. "You can't cover all bases, so don't beat yourself up about it. So what's next? Scotland?"

"I'm not sure. Maybe we should wait for Forensics to match the DNA. It'll be Jeremiah and Ezekiel for sure, but where would they go with a newborn baby?"

The Royal Air Force jet climbed as Frank Carrington gazed down from it at the countryside. He turned to Alex. "Will they believe me? The girl's missing, so I can't produce her. And I don't know if the Council of Elders will help."

The Home Secretary lay back in his seat. "Kabshiel agreed to just before Imogene collapsed, didn't he?"

He tapped the armrest, then gripped it. "Well, I thought so. But will anything happen? And what will the sign be? Do Imogene or I have to do anything to instigate it, or will it happen anyway?"

"We'll have to wait and see. The Secretary-General has organized the emergency General Assembly, and expects all one hundred and ninety-three nations to attend. You'll have to convince a two-thirds majority. My guess is the African nations are more likely to believe. Many still have a superstitious mentality, plus they will benefit from any wealth distribution. The rich nations won't budge on wealth issues, and the superpowers will never agree on disarmament. Sir, we sure need a sign. An irrefutable sign!"

Xantara unpacked her suitcase while Braeden worked in the clinic. She hated their being apart, and with Imogene missing, it was all too much. She slumped against the bedhead and tried to contact Imogene telepathically, but couldn't. Either she was asleep or—no, she wouldn't verbalize that word. Surely the Light Being part of her would keep her alive. She shook her head and walked downstairs. Maybe tea would help.

Braeden entered the kitchen and flopped back in a chair. She waved from the stairwell door. His eyes widened. "You've back. Are you staying?"

She went to him and lightly kissed his forehead. "I've been thinking. With the end of the world a distinct possibility, your indiscretion is minor. I need you. I can't face Imogene's disappearance on my own."

He stood and held out his arms, and she hugged him and cried on his shoulder. "Nothing will ever happen again," he said. "I'm sorry for the pain I caused. I love you, Xan. Always have, always will."

180

She wiped away her tears. "Will we get her back? My baby girl must be terrified. Will they hurt her? Why did they take her? Oh, Braeden! What can we do?"

Frank Carrington loosened his tie, slipped off his shoes, and lay back on the hotel's king-size bed. He found the remote and switched on cable television. Tomorrow would be a crucial, tough day, and he should relax and get a decent night's sleep. He surfed the channels, recognized Susanne Prentice on BBC, and turned up the sound.

"Breaking news," she said. "Fresh crop circles formed overnight in every county in the UK, and have appeared around the world in places which have never before reported them. Icelandic countries have discovered the same symbols etched in snow and frozen lakes. Each character is identical across the world, a form of ancient Egyptian hieroglyphs."

Frank's heart pounded. Could this be the sign?

The anchor introduced a tweed-jacketed, obese man sporting a silver fob chain across a primrose yellow waistcoat. "This is Professor Blythe-Smyth, head of the Egyptian department at the British Museum. Professor, are these symbols Egyptian?"

He nodded. "They are, and from an early dynasty. Roughly translated, the eye, the bird on an open hand say, 'Practice love and acceptance'.

"Do you have any idea why they've appeared?"

The professor lifted a nicotine-stained finger to his lips and paused. "I believe the Prime Minister's interpretation. Osahar is a well-known name in ancient Egypt, and the child's account of the temple seems accurate. At her tender age she couldn't have read such descriptions, let alone remember them. So I can only assume the crop circles' message is from this Council of Elders."

"Any other reasons?" she asked.

"The use of hieroglyphs is logical. As the audios show, the Council used both the girl and the Egyptian priest Osahar to create the events we've witnessed. It's reasonable they would use symbols from that time and location to validate their message and make sure it was understood the same way all over the world."

Susanne's voice deepened. "Can you explain the symbols appearing in snow? In frozen lakes, and even beds of seaweed in shallow waters?"

Professor Blythe-Smyth fiddled with his watch chain. "I think they intended the whole world to read this message. Crop seasons vary, and a few locations don't grow crops—countries near the Arctic Circle, for instance. It makes sense to use other mediums to communicate."

Frank clicked through other channels, and heard similar reports. He finally switched the set off and reached for his inhaler. Could this be the sign they promised?

CHAPTER TWENTY-SEVEN

J acques de Sales grinned as he walked into the Troth Temple and surveyed his magnificent domain. Lilya Kaminski stood before him.

"Hello, Lilya, well done. Where is she?"

She pointed toward the anteroom. "She's still out cold. It might be another hour or two before she wakes."

Jacques entered the anteroom, and saw Lilya had left the young girl spread-eagled on the baronial table. Goose bumps covered her limbs, bare in the thin flowered dress. He touched an arm, then turned.

"She's cold. Carry her into the guest suite, will you? She's a valuable asset."

His heart raced, and he rubbed his hands together. What were her powers? Could she affect the stock market? Pressure a wealthy mine magnet to sell to him at a rock-bottom price? The possibilities were endless. He needed to find the right hypnotist quickly, one experienced in past-life regression, one who could connect with his Egyptian priestess, Sakhment.

Lilya lifted Imogene and turned. "Where's your guest suite?"

Jacques walked to a wall painting and pressed the eye of Horus. A panel slid back, and he motioned her to enter. "Take her through to the bedroom."

He glanced around the plush accommodation. He'd chosen well. The ornate gold and silver accessories, deep blue carpet, and cream walls would please any discerning eye. High-profile guests had graced this suite on private visits. He smiled as he totted up the millions he'd made from deals brokered right here.

Lilya dumped the child on the bed and drew a padded silk coverlet over her, then stepped to him and held out her hand. "Payment?"

Jacques pressed a number into his cell phone and showed her the screen. "Enough? And I'll give you that much more if you bring me a hypnotist. I'll identify a suitable one, then text you the details. Remember, time is of the essence."

Frank stopped at the massive U.N. entrance door, stroked his tie, and inhaled a couple of Ventolin shots. Thank goodness the General Assembly was broadcast live. The whole world would hear his presentation in just minutes, and he must give a convincing performance.

He entered the large semicircular room and glanced up at the interpreters' booths. His speech would be translated into Arabic, Chinese, French, Russian, and Spanish. The United Nations logo dominated the gold-colored podium. His heart missed a beat as he saw the one hundred and ninety-three First Committee members, already in their seats. They must at least pass his proposal to disarm. They discussed issues six times a year, but often any resolution contained numerous conditions demanded by each country. The results were often weak, useless laws.

He nodded to the United States President, who smiled noncommittally, and sat down. The wait was unbearable. At last, the Secretary General introduced him, and he made his way to the lectern. The room buzzed as he cleared his throat.

"We live in unprecedented times," he said. "The enormity of recent tragedies has affected each country represented here today. I would appreciate your attention as I suggest possible explanations for the flu pandemic, the Chicago fire, and the European lethal gas cloud."

He paused, and the assembly murmured. Well, here goes nothing.

"The films and audio sessions I'll present in moments will astound you," he said. "Experts have independently assessed each one, and without exception attest to their validity."

Frank signaled, and the first film rolled. The assembly sat silently, staring ahead, and he studied each state leader's faces. He then glanced at the interpreters' booth. Many wore stunned expressions as they translated, and stumbled over the strange words. He realized they didn't know the English for an entity or Light Being.

As the technicians changed out each film and audio, the buzz from the delegates increased. The semicircular chamber resembled a giant hive, full of angry bees. Frank felt nauseous. They weren't buying it.

He'd included the two latest television programs to save further explanations. Perhaps he should mention yesterday's crop circles, or maybe not. The final audio ended, and he moved onto the podium. The room exploded with a cacophony of angry voices. The assembly argued for a full ten minutes before he could speak.

A wave of dizziness caused him to rock slightly. "Thank you for your kind attention," he said. "We are fighting on many levels for the survival of humanity, and time is short. I ask each of you to search your conscience. I know the evidence is unlike any you've seen before, but I urge you to seriously consider it."

The room again fell silent. He swallowed, trying to clear the large lump in his throat.

"Unfortunately, we humans are combative by instinct. We must protect our sovereignty and food supply against warmongers who launch hostilities to increase their own land mass and wealth. Prejudice by color, race, and religion also causes conflict, as we have witnessed in recent times between Islam and Christianity."

Frank felt as if an intense stream of fiery air had entered the top of his head and blown through his body. What on earth? He breathed deeply and continued. "This assembly has successfully passed resolutions, for example, to restrict the production of chemical weapons…"

He heard banging, and looked up. The interpreters were hitting their booth windows, frantically waving their headphones. What was wrong? He paused, then continued.

"We have a responsibility to…"

My God, they understood what he was saying. It looks as if he was talking in all the different languages of the Assembly! Now his credibility was shot. They'd think he was mad!

The room burst into chaos, and the Secretary General pushed him aside. "Order, order…." The noise died down as the man held his headphone to his ear.

"Ladies and gentlemen, it appears each of us can hear and understand the British Prime Minister in our own language. I ask the interpreters to stand down while he closes his argument for disarmament."

Frank turned his back and used his inhaler. His heart bucked in his chest. The sign, at last. Thank you, Kabshiel. He turned back and eyed the assembly.

"I asked the Council leader, Kabshiel, for a sign to help me convince you of the situation's seriousness. I believe he has now given that sign, because you can all hear and understand me, each in your own language. It proves the truth of supernatural events. This sign adds credence to the Council of Elders' existence. How else could this be possible?"

He swallowed a mouthful of excess salvia. "These points aside, I ask you to vote for total world disarmament, and propose the First Committee convene within the month. Each world leader will need assurances of their countries' security, and guarantees that all weapons will be destroyed, of course. I ask you to consider this recommendation carefully. My hope and passion are for a safer world, where each man, woman, and child lives in peace. This responsibility rests with you."

Frank felt the strange pressure of air exit through the top of his head. Had he done enough? Surely the Council of Elders wouldn't condemn the entire world while a few good men lived.

～ *** ～

Amelia Mason held her phone receiver at arm's length, stared at it, then held it against her ear. "What's your name again?"

"Jacques."

"And...and you're offering me half a million pounds for two month's work?"

"Correct. Plus all expenses. I've prepared a luxurious apartment for you, and you'll have just one patient to work with. Will you do it?"

She pressed her hand to her chest. "What does the work entail? What's the catch?"

Oh, how she loved a man with a French accent. The sexy voice interrupted her daydreams.

"Hypnosis. Nothing else, I can assure you."

Amelia paused. Her therapy business had dropped in recent months. The recession was driving her regulars away, and the bills mounted. This man was a godsend!

Her knees trembled. "Yes, I'll do it. What happens now?"

"I'm sending a woman—Lilya—to escort you to our headquarters on my private jet. Just pack a bag and your passport. Expect her within the hour. Just one more point, your discretion is paramount. Do not tell anyone about this job."

She giggled. "I understand, no problem. Overseas? Where's your headquarters?" He told her, and she let out a whoop. Wow, a free vacation and enough money to wash her troubles away. Thank you, Universe!

Amelia stuffed her carry-on case and found her passport. She brushed her sleek black Cleopatra styled hair and slipped comfortable jeans over her dainty frame. What an adventure!

 ***

Frank sat in the U. S. President's hotel suite, holding a bourbon shot. "Do you think they believed me?"

The President rubbed his finger around the rim of his glass. "When the interpreters kicked up a fuss I couldn't figure it out, since I'm a native English speaker. But I saw the Russian and Chinese leaders leap out of their seats. The whole scene reminded me of the tower of Babel, in reverse."

The British Prime Minister's stomach sank. "So, your guys aren't convinced? It's the disarmament, isn't it? No one wants to be the first."

"True. But for the record, I'm partway on-board. The evidence and today's demonstration were strong."

Frank sipped his drink. "What's your opinion on the crop circles?"

"The crop circles?" The President shrugged. "Well, they've been around for years."

"But the latest ones are different. They all have identical ancient Egyptian symbols. Thousands of them, even etched in ice and snow. Translators say they mean 'Practice love and acceptance.' How's that possible?"

Frank slumped back and downed his drink. "What does the Council have to do to convince people? I can see this all ending badly."

The President picked up the decanter and refilled their glasses. "Well, the First Committee has to decide. My personal beliefs are irrelevant. Congress has to support me, and I'll do my best to persuade them. But don't depend on the United States!"

Frank's mind raced and the blood rushed to his head. The public would rationalize the whole episode. It was much easier to believe in a trick. They weren't used to supernatural events in their neat and tidy world.

No, the press would crucify him, for sure. They were all doomed.

CHAPTER TWENTY-EIGHT

Amelia's stomach fluttered as she tripped down the jet's steps and saw a gentleman with aristocratic features waiting beside a red Ferrari. Perhaps he was a count, or a foreign prince. The female pilot, Lilya, pushed past her and dumped her suitcase beside the car. The woman appeared distant and unpleasant, but the man wore the most gorgeous smile. As Amelia walked closer, she realized he had at least twenty years on her tender twenty-three. Damn, no romance there, then.

He stepped forward and held out his hand. "I'm Jacques, and you must be Amelia. Welcome."

She shook his hand. He helped her into the car's low front seat, then threw her bag over the back onto the jockey seats.

"Exactly where am I, and who's the patient?" she asked.

"Luxembourg. That's all I'm at liberty to say. The rest? Well, all in good time."

He pressed the accelerator, forcing her body back into the contoured seat. What a thrill, her first ride in a Ferrari! She eyed him again. He must be at least in his forties, but he was suave and elegant, and he radiated an animal magnetism.

The car sped along the highway for miles, then turned into a wooded area. A grassed hump sprouting air vents appeared ahead. Jacques held out a remote and pressed a button, and part of the grass bank opened to reveal a dark tunnel. Open Sesame. What would happen next?

The driveway went down into the tunnel, which soon widened into a large, fluorescent-lit car park. Wow, a Porsche Spyder and a McLaren PI, worth more than million! Her car-enthusiast brother made her watch "Top Gear" when he visited, and at last the crazy show came in handy. She never imagined one person could own so many expensive cars.

"Are they all yours?" she asked.

He helped her out and retrieved her carry-on case. "I have three here, and more in each of my homes."

Good Lord, how rich could he be?

He checked his watch. "I'll escort you to your quarters. You'll be sharing them with your patient, a young girl." He led her down a passage which opened into the largest room she'd ever seen.

"Wow, it's like an Egyptian temple, with all those hieroglyphics." She spied a bas-relief carved door before them. "Is that strange figure an ancient god?"

He said nothing, but pressed the eye of Horus. The wall opened to reveal a foyer. "I'll show you around later. First, let's meet your patient."

She stepped through and gasped. "Is this it? Spectacular! I feel like Cleopatra."

He laughed and casually touched her hair. "You look like an Egyptian queen."

They walked through the antiques-filled lounge, decorated in gold, cream, and deep blue, and Jacques opened one of two doors set in the far wall. "Here's your room. Your patient's next door. Meals will be served in the dining room. I've converted the third bedroom into a consultation room, with a comfortable chaise-longue and chair. Please be aware, each room except the bathroom is fitted with security cameras."

Amelia bit her lip. She didn't fancy someone spying on her, but then her unpaid bills floated into her consciousness. Oh, well, the assignment was only for three months.

"Can I meet my patient? What's her name?"

190

She followed him out of her fabulous bedroom and into the lounge. He opened the second bedroom door, turned, and raised a finger to his lips. "Please be quiet, she's sleeping. Her name's Imogene." He stepped aside to reveal a young girl, her long blonde hair spread out over the cream silk pillow.

"Oh, what a sweet child! How old is she?"

He cradled her elbow and guided her back through the door. "She's eight."

She shook her arm free. "Why on earth would you want me to hypnotize an eight-year-old child?"

He ignored her question, and turned toward the dining-room. "I see your evening meal awaits you. Enjoy, and tomorrow we'll talk again."

He glided across the room and stepped out. The panel whispered shut behind him. She gasped. There was no door handle. She couldn't leave!

 ***

Obadiah Yates heard a voice in his head as he sat alone in his solitary cell at the Wakefield prison in West Yorkshire, which was a super-max security unit a few years earlier. A guard told him the prison's nickname was Monster Mansion because of the high percentage of sex offenders housed there. He thanked God they'd put him in a single cell.

He recalled the guard's words when he'd first entered the small prison room, that a Doctor Harold Shipley had committed suicide in this cell. He'd heard about the serial killer who'd killed up to two hundred and fifty patients. "How did he do it?" he asked.

"He hung himself," the man had said. "They say the cell's haunted. Sleep tight, Mr. Yates!"

Perhaps the voice in his head was caused by the twenty-three hours a day confinement. Perhaps he was going crazy. Or could it be Doctor Shipley who whispered in his ear?

Anger churned in his stomach as he used the corner toilet. It was degrading. They'd pay for this. Everyone! The guards, McCullage, and the government. He completed his ablutions and lay on the grubby blanket covering the bunk. "God, where are you? Get me out of here!"

The voice in his head returned. "The Lord has sent me, Azazel, an angel, to help you. Prepare yourself. Next week you'll be in court, and that will be my chance to strike."

He made the sign of the cross. "Praise the Lord. Of course, He wouldn't let me down."

Over the next few hours, he planned for revenge. He juggled various scenarios in his mind, each one more grandiose than the latter. Yes, they would all pay. How sweet!

Amelia tossed and turned, twisting the cream silk sheets into a shroud. The small girl's name sounded familiar, but from where? She stopped, mid-turn. Yes, Imogene. She was the one who gave the message! But it couldn't be her, could it? The government kept her at a high-security facility.

But she sure looked like her.

Hours later she heard a timid knock, and quickly she pulled on her rose housecoat. "Coming."

She opened the door, and Imogene smiled shyly up at her. "I saw your jacket over the chair. The mean man said someone would keep me company. I'm Imogene, what's your name?"

She paused, squinting. "Amelia. You look like Imogene Pembroke. Are you?"

The young girl's blue eyes crinkled at the corners. "Yes. Have you come to take me home? I miss my Mom and Dad."

Amelia stepped aside. "Come and sit here with me and tell me what happened."

Imogene joined her on the bed, sitting against the headboard and hugging her knees as she did. "A nurse wheeled my bed away, then I woke up here. I don't know where I am, or why. But Mommy will find me, won't she?"

Amelia twisted a hair strand around her fingers. What had she gotten herself into? Her dreams of a free holiday and the enormous paycheck melted away. She should have listened to her mother, when she told her there was no such thing as a free lunch!

"I'm here to hypnotize you, but…" The camera set into the ceiling caught her eye. "I have to get showered. The bathroom's massive, so why don't you sit in there with me?"

They went into the bathroom, and Amelia stepped under the rainfall showerhead. The Hollywood style bathroom with cream and gold-tiles delighted her. She eyed Imogene as she lathered her body and washed her hair. How did the girl get here? And what did Jacques want with her?

She stepped out and pulled the soft, fleecy towel around her, watching Imogene pick up and test an eye shadow before the mirror. Her heart ached. Poor kid, she'd become a commodity, but why? Obviously, Jacques had lied to her. She walked over and hugged her. "Try not to worry," she whispered. "I'll find a way we can both go home."

Someone rapped the bathroom door. "Amelia, are you and Imogene in there?"

She sucked in a deep breath. "Jacques, yes, we'll be right out." She bent close to Imogene's ear. "Let's play along, and await our chance."

The innocent child nodded. God, she couldn't let this girl down. She dressed and unlocked the door.

Jacques didn't look so cute today. She glimpsed a scowl on his face before his features transformed into a wide smile. "Time for the hypnosis session. Please follow me, you can breakfast later."

He opened the third bedroom door, and Imogene stopped in her tracks. "It's just like Doctor Schneider's office," she said.

Amelia looked around and blinked. The whole room was white, the leather chaise-longue, even the desk and chair. No distractions here. She held her elbow and formed a fist against her mouth, then forced herself to relax.

"Jacques, how do you want me to hypnotize her? Should I do relaxation suggestions, a past-life regression, or something else?"

Jacques eyes narrowed. "You know who she is, right?"

Amelia moved to in front of Imogene. "Yes. Past-life regression, then?"

His smile slipped. "Not exactly. Did you listen to Channel five's presentation?"

She twisted her watch band. "Of course. The whole world's talking about the Council of Elders."

He motioned toward the couch and chair. "Why don't you both get comfortable, and I'll explain." He waited until they were both seated, then leaned against the white Formica desk. "You've heard the audio of Imogene's encounters with an entity called Osahar. I'm in touch with a similar Egyptian, a priestess called Sakhment. I want you to induce the girl to find her, interact with her, and then follow my instructions exactly. Shall we begin?"

Frank Carrington loved the Prime Minister's country residence, Chequers. The twelfth-century retreat calmed his soul. Its library housed many treasures, and a space in which he could think. Great minds had graced this house over the centuries, and he fancied their knowledge lived in the walls' fabrics. Perhaps he could absorb their wisdom. He laid his head back, closed his eyes and prayed for a miracle.

A while later a cool draft wafted over him. He opened one eye to see the Home Secretary enter.

"Alex, I'm so glad you could come. Sit down, we have to talk."

The ex-navy commander picked a high straight-backed chair. "Strathfield is causing a stink. He's determined to oust you. But a little good news. The ratings Susanne Prentice supplied show most people support your opinion."

Frank uncrossed his legs and sat straight. "Thank God I confided in her. She's done an excellent job. But now, everything rests with the First Committee's decision."

Alex brushed his hand over his snowy crew-cut. "They meet in three days. Believers and non-believers alike have lobbied their governments, and it's hard to tell which way they'll vote. What if we lose? What then?"

Frank flexed his hands, as if to ward off the panic rushing through his body. "Kabshiel stayed true to his word, but I wish the sign could have been clearer. I'm disappointed. Already the experts are debating how the phenomenon could have been staged."

Alex dropped his head and sighed. "No sign of the girl, so we can't consult the Council again. All seems lost."

Frank shook his head. "I can't understand who would abduct her. What could they possibly gain? We have to get her back. Detective McCullage said her mother has communicated with her telepathically before. Get in touch with her. Maybe she can help find her."

CHAPTER TWENTY-NINE

Amelia sat on the bed next to Imogene, waiting for her to settle. "Relax, this won't take long," she said. She glanced back at Jacques' stony face. "Perhaps if I work with her alone until she's under, she'll be more relaxed."

His face darkened into a fearsome scowl. How had she ever found him attractive? She turned back to Imogene, who now lay still, reached into her purse, and pulled out her favorite pendulum. The mirrored, engraved shield on an elegant silver chain had once adorned her grandfather's fob watch.

"Imogene, you'll be okay. I'll guide you. Relax, and follow the shield."

As Amelia moved the pendulum back and forth, she felt Jacques' thunderous look burning into her back. His negative energy wasn't helping. She turned. "Look, I'm sorry, but she's resistant. I need her co-operation to get her under."

The man lunged and formed a head-lock around Amelia's neck, and bent her face close to Imogene's. "Kid, let her hypnotize you or I'll snap her neck, right now."

Imogene's eyes widened and filled with tears. "I'm trying, honestly. Doctor Schneider does it another way."

Jacques released her. "I'll find out what the doctor does, and then we'll try again." He turned and stalked through the door. Amelia let out a long breath as the panel slid back into place. She rubbed her neck, then helped Imogene off the couch.

"Come on, let's eat our breakfast," she said. "Then perhaps you can explain Schneider's methods."

Imogene grasped her hand and they walked toward the dining table. "I'm scared. I don't know what he does. He swings this crystal, I sleep, then I wake up. The dreams come back in bits and pieces. I'm sorry."

Amelia spread a napkin over the girl's lap. "Don't worry. We'll be rescued soon, I'm sure. Meanwhile, let's do what he says. Okay?"

She picked at her food. Just what was she involved in? Something illegal, for sure, and now he'd threatened her life. They had to find a way to escape, and soon.

The British Home Secretary and The First Committee sat around a large oval table with grim faces, regarding one another. The chairman stood.

"We know the agenda," he said. "The vote will be for total world disarmament. Let's go around the table, and each explain our view. We'll begin with the French ambassador."

Alex Brittan noticed that the ambassador, who appeared jammed between the chair and table, still enjoyed his five-course meals. The Frenchman leaned forward and spoke into the microphone.

"We are one people on one planet," he said. "We owe our children the chance to live in a nuclear-free world. This forum offers us the possibility to live in safety and freedom, to live in peace."

The chairman nodded. "Thank you, ambassador. We'll now hear from the Chinese representative."

Alex looked at the man's impassive face. Would he be for, or against? The leader's hooded lids almost covered his eyes.

"The idea won't work. We need nuclear weapons as a deterrent. If we voted for disarmament, a rogue dictator could build a secret arsenal and threaten us all." He looked around the table and jabbed his finger toward

197

several leaders. "Anyone of you could re-build at short notice. We can't risk China's security."

"The United States President."

The US President cleared his throat and paused. "I'd like to remind you of President John F. Kennedy's words. 'The world was not meant to be a prison in which man awaits his execution.' War could mean the extinction of more than four billion people. The survivors would live on an unrecognizable planet, such that even more would die from the after-effects. This madness has to be stopped. I recommend complete disarmament, along with a dedicated team to enforce the ban."

The chairman stood. "I call upon the South African delegate."

The tall, proud black man reminded Alex of a Zulu warrior. The delegate nodded. "Disarmament would free up resources to end global poverty. Terrorists wouldn't be able to steal nuclear weapons. We would ensure peace and stability for our children and grandchildren. Weapons of mass destruction create more problems than they solve. A hundred and thirteen countries are already nuclear free, we should make that unilateral. We have the opportunity to act now, before other countries already developing nuclear capabilities have their own arsenals."

The chairman nodded. "The Russian President. Mr. President..."

The Russian's pale face made his intense blue eyes gleam. "How can we vote for disarmament? If any country destroyed its arsenal and received a major attack, it would cease to exist. The promise of retaliation prevents such attacks."

The Australian Prime Minister raised a hand. "Nuclear weapons aren't a deterrent," he said, "because they can be deployed by sea after an attack. We're in danger of nuclear proliferation. Once one bomb is released, other countries will send theirs. The world would be utterly destroyed."

The chairman turned to Alex. "We'll now hear from the British Home Secretary, Mr. Brittan."

Alex stood. "Those are old arguments," he said. "But today we must consider another. The world faces a new threat, annihilation from an outside force. The Council of Elders."

The room erupted with strident voices and angry gestures, and Alex waited for the hubbub to subside.

"Please, let me finish. This threat is as real as any mankind has faced before. Think about the lives already lost. Those disasters were real. Do you want to be responsible for more?"

He sat, and watched the debate move from pro to con. How would they vote? So many previous debates resulted in a stalemate, would this end differently?

He doubted it.

The panel slid open, and Amelia turned. Her heart racing, she rested a hand on Imogene's arm. Jacques held a white box printed with a green cross.

"I'm told Schneider uses sodium pentothal, the truth drug," he said. "Now we can get to work."

She felt Imogene cringe, then clutch her arm. "The child's terrified. This is monstrous. Let us go."

Jacques, his face inches from hers, glared at her. "Are you fond of your young brother?"

She stiffened. "What do you mean?"

"You will do precisely what I say, or he will never see tomorrow. Understand?"

Amelia nodded and looked at Imogene. "I don't know how to give an injection, and I can't see her co-operating."

Jacques grabbed Imogene's other arm. "Look, kid, play along, or your parents will suffer. Understand?"

Wide-eyed, the young girl nodded.

"Good. Let's get moving." He pushed them toward the makeshift office.

Imogene lay down, her gaze fixed on the syringe Jacques had just filled from a phial. He crossed the room and swabbed her arm and jabbed the needle in.

"Ouch, you hurt me!"

"Suck it up, kid."

Amelia watched her for signs of physical distress. Imogene's eyelids grew heavy, and she fell into a light sleep. Amelia dropped the pendulum into her pocket, then looked at Jacques. "What shall I do?"

"Talk to her. Induce her into a deeper state, as you would do in normal circumstances. When she's deep enough, I want her to meet with Sakhment, the priestess."

She drew in a breath. "Imogene, imagine you're on a beach. You can feel the white sand between your toes. Gentle waves lap beside you, and you can feel a light, warm breeze. You see palm trees on your left, and hear birds singing in the fronds. In the distance, you see a temple. I want you to walk toward the building."

She glanced at Jacques. He nodded. "You're doing well."

"Imogene, please tell me what you see."

The child's eyes darted beneath her lids. Her blonde lashes barely hid the purple smudges she'd developed over the last two days.

"The temple looks like a small pyramid," she said, softly. "There's a large stone figure on each side of a dark opening."

"Good. That's excellent, Imogene. Imagine a white light forming around you, a protective aura, then step forward and enter the opening."

"The painted walls have Egyptian figures, boats, and animals. Oh, there's someone here."

Jacques nudged Amelia. "That's her. Ask Imogene to speak to her."

Amelia leaned closer. "Imogene, please ask the person's name."

200

Imogene's fingers lifted, one at a time, then relaxed against the white leather. "Her name is Sakhment, and she says she's the temple priestess. She has long black hair, and a twisted golden snake around her head. Her gown catches the light from the candles nearby. She's beautiful, but her energy's dark. I don't like her."

Jacques moved closer. "Tell her I want to talk to her."

Imogene coughed, and her mouth twisted. A deep, feminine voice came out.

"Jacques, my dear, at last we meet. My spirit has been guiding you since your childhood, and I have long wished to communicate. My power is at your disposal. What would you have me do?"

Adrenaline rushed through Amelia, her skin tingled. "What's happening? That's not Imogene!"

Jacques grinned. "I have a simple request today. Is it possible to bring about the appointment of several Troth members to The Environmental Protection Agency, to influence business-related decisions?"

The woman's silky voice arose from Imogene's lips. "Consider it done."

He punched the air, and Amelia shook and clutched her chest. "Can…can we finish now?"

He walked to the door and looked back over his shoulder. "Care for her. We'll have another session tomorrow."

The door swung shut behind him, and she turned back to Imogene. "Relax as I count backwards from ten. When I reach the number one, you will awaken. "Ten, nine, eight…"

The young girl moved restlessly, then screamed.

"What's wrong? Speak to me, Imogene."

"The priestess grabbed my hands. The power, the energy—I can't let…"

Her head fell to one side.

CHAPTER THIRTY

Detective McCullage eyed the two prisoners at the Pontefract Magistrates Court in Wakefield. Mock all you like, but you're both going down! He mentally checked off the security arrangements for their return to prison. The bulletproof prisoner transport van with two motorcycle cops riding behind and two in front should be more than enough.

A lone middle-aged woman coughed behind him, and he turned to her. Who was she? The prosecutor had successfully argued for a closed court, except for family, so she must be some relation. Perhaps Malachi's wife, whom he hadn't had the dubious pleasure of meeting. He opened his case file and thumbed through. Yes, that was her. The Guardia had searched her home, and found nothing. She looked harmless enough.

McCullage turned back to Judge Cadden, who allowed no nonsense in his court and showed offenders no mercy. No, he couldn't have drawn a better judge if he'd tried. Yet now the normally sharp-eyed, stocky man looked pale, and his eyes appeared almost black, as if there were bottomless holes behind them. Cadden nodded to the lawyers. He was ready to arraign the Yates brothers.

Judge Cadden glanced down at his papers, then looked around the courtroom. "I've listened carefully to the prosecution and defense. Obadiah and Malachi Yates claim their cousin Ezekiel and brother Jeremiah pressured them into using the Corsham underground facility. They deny having any part in the Stonehenge bombing. And I must say, I find no direct evidence linking either to it."

The detective stiffened. What was this? He stared at the judge, who avoided his gaze. What was Cadden up to?

Judge Cadden mopped his brow. "Security footage clearly shows the other Yates family members committing the crime. These prisoners simply weren't present."

McCullage felt a rush of blood to his head and stood. "Judge, you can't be serious."

The magistrate glared at him and lowered his voice. "Another outburst and I'll hold you in contempt of court."

McCullage sank back onto the bench. The public would be outraged, and all his hard work would be for nothing.

Judge Cadden pursed his lips. "I find the preponderance of evidence of their involvement in the Stonehenge bombings, the Cardiff poisonings, or the Salisbury arson, inconclusive. However, a court date will be set for trial on the lesser charges, and for that reason I set bail of two hundred and fifty thousand pounds each. If bailed they must surrender their passports, and report weekly in person to the Wakefield police station."

The magistrate nodded to the court clerk, stood, and turned toward his chambers. He swayed slightly, then stumbled as he walked away.

McCullage sat until the court emptied, then called Sam. "Unbelievable! The judge set bail. Let's hope no one comes forward to pay. Obadiah Yates has to face lesser charges for the kidnap and torture of his Swindon victims, and Malachi for aiding and abetting a criminal act. They weren't charged for their part in the terrorist attack on Stonehenge, nor the hundreds poisoned in Cardiff and burnt at Salisbury racetrack. We'd better find the other two fast."

Molly Yates entered the court office, accompanied by the defense lawyer. The officer behind the counter looked up. "Can I help you?"

She pulled out her checkbook. "I'm here to pay the bail bond for Malachi and Obadiah Yates. Half a million pounds, I believe."

The officer stepped back, pulled on his grey mustache, and studied her. "You have that much money?"

She tapped the desk. "Of course, or I wouldn't be here. Where's the paperwork?"

He drew a sheaf of papers from under the counter. "I'll have to clear the check, and I need to know where the prisoners will live and your contact details."

Molly scribbled out the check, and replaced her pen and checkbook. "I have a suite at The Queen's Hotel. My husband and brother-in-law will stay there with me."

The lawyer stepped forward. "How long will it take?"

The officer scowled. "It'll take at least five working days to clear the check. I'll let you know if the location is approved."

Molly and her lawyer left the court, and she shook his hand and stepped into the cab. "Queen's Hotel, please." The cab pulled away from the curb as she called her niece. "Bridget. How's wee Gideon?"

She nodded. "Let Ezekiel and Jeremiah know that I've paid the bail. Tell them to make arrangements nine days from today. Give the baby a hug from me. Bye."

Mommy. Mommy, I want to come home.

Xantara heard Imogene cry out to her in her dream, and woke with a start. At last she'd made contact.

Where are you?

Visions filled Xantara's mind. A luxurious apartment, Doctor Schneider's room... how could that be? Had Schneider got her?

She received another vision of a young woman with black hair, styled like Elizabeth Burton in Cleopatra. The woman wore a kind smile. A friend, then. Good, Imogene wasn't alone. But who was the woman, and why was Imogene with her?

She sensed Imogene's intense fear, and saw the image of a man's hand wielding a syringe. Whoever abducted her also drugged her. Why? The connection faded, and her daughter was gone.

Xantara checked the time. Five-thirty. She hesitated, then picked up her cell phone and called McCullage. He answered immediately.

"I've sensed Imogene," she said. "She's alive. She gave me a vision of an expensively decorated apartment. European, I'd say. But strangely, she also showed me Schneider's office. Why? She's with a young woman who looks like Cleopatra, who appears quite pleasant."

She heard McCullage tap his phone. "Sorry, I'm thinking. Schneider hasn't taken her. I'll check out any missing women who fit the description. Ring me if you get more visions, however small."

"Will do. Please, find her soon."

Xantara sank back against her pillow and glanced at Braeden, sleeping beside her. He looked vulnerable, drained. She turned onto her side. She'd tell him later.

The Prime Minister checked his watch, and drummed his fingers on his desk. Alex was late. Which way had the vote gone?

Alex breezed in, still carrying his overnight case. "I've come straight from the airport. Heavy traffic as usual, let me catch my breath."

Frank's stomach churned, and his chest tightened. He pulled out his inhaler and puffed the Ventolin. "Well?"

Alex shook his head. "It was a stalemate, straight down the middle. We needed two thirds to approve the resolution. The next meeting's scheduled in three months."

He gasped for breath and puffed again. "That's too late for the Council of Elders' deadline. The final consequence will happen before then, and that could be the end. What should we do?"

Alex leaned forward. "We can't give up. We'll find the girl, contact Kabshiel, and gain more time. The Council can't write off the entire human race, can it?"

Imogene snuggled into Amelia's back. "Thanks for letting me sleep with you. Oh—I've heard from Mommy."

Amelia sat up. "What do you mean?"

"We talk with each other in our minds. Pictures, mainly. I've sent her pictures of this apartment and you. She'll find us now."

Amelia frowned. "You can do that?"

A loud knock shocked them both.

"Get up girls, time to roll." The door opened, and Jacques' head appeared. "Today's session is crucial. I expect the best from both of you. You have twenty minutes to dress and eat."

Imogene scrambled out of bed. "Don't worry, Amelia, Mom will find us soon. Maybe this will be the last time I'll meet that horrible Sakhment."

"I hope so. I can't see Jacques letting—" Amelia tapped Imogene's shoulder and pointed at the corner camera. Imogene followed her into the bathroom.

Ten minutes later Imogene watched Amelia pick at her scrambled eggs, and smiled. "Mom will come. She'll rescue us, and we'll be safe."

Amelia stood, pushed in her chair, and held out her hand. "I hope you're right. Come, let's get the session over with."

Imogene's stomach churned as they walked into the white room. Jacques held the syringe at the ready. Her mind drifted to her mother. She'd given her hope, told her to be strong. She could do this!

Jacques helped her onto the couch and tapped her arm, then pushed the needle into her vein. "Good girl. I have a special mission for Sakhment today. Sleep well, my golden goose."

Imogene walked through the soft sand toward the temple. Her steps slowed as she neared the pyramid.

Amelia's voice reached her. "Go in, and find the priestess."

She walked between the sphinxes, squinting as she entered the dim interior. Sakhment moved forward and grabbed her hands. Her body swayed as the woman leeched her energy. The priestess broke contact, and Imogene fell back. She sensed someone else, and scanned the chamber. "Osahar! How did you get here?"

The Egyptian priest stood between her and Sakhment. "Leave her alone. The Council will not allow you to use her."

Imogene watched the woman's face darken. "She's mine. Go, I have her under my control." The priestess held out her palms and released a burst of energy. Osahar flew across the chamber and hit the wall.

Imogene's fists covered her mouth, and she rushed over to him. "Osahar, are you hurt?"

Sakhment reached toward her. "Move, leave him alone."

Osahar stumbled to his feet. "Step aside, child."

Power emanated from his entire body. Shards of lightning crackled and filled the room. Spikes of light bounced off the ceiling and walls, striking the woman. The scene faded, and Imogene awoke and looked up at the two faces leaning over her.

Amelia patted her hand. "Are you okay? You're so pale. What happened?"

Jacques pushed the hypnotist aside and glared at Imogene. "Go back there. I haven't spoken with Sakhment. I must give her my orders. Go back, right now."

Imogene blinked, and sat. "I can't. I think Osahar has stopped her, or maybe killed her."

Jacques roared and hit the desk. "Nonsense! She's powerful, no one can stop her. We'll try again this afternoon. Don't try any tricks."

CHAPTER THIRTY-ONE

Jeremiah rested his boots atop the low table and clicked them together. "I'm bored, Ezekiel."

Feathers floated around his cousin as he plucked feathers from a pheasant and threw them over his shoulder. "In a few more days, we can fetch your brothers and Mollie."

Jeremiah looked around the simple hunting lodge. "No television, no Internet, what's to do?" He pulled out his cell phone, played a game of solitaire, and looked up. "I have an idea."

Ezekiel dropped the bird into a black cast-iron pot. "And what would that be?"

"We'll move the family to the States, and raise Gideon there. I can arrange passage across the Irish Sea, and organize a local Phineas Priesthood chapter to hide us."

"A bit risky, isn't it? You're a twice-wanted man, in the UK and America."

Jeremiah went to the window and looked out across the green hills. "Brilliant, isn't it? The last place they would expect us to go."

Ezekiel added chicken stock and poked the embers in the wood stove. "Could work, I've assets all over the US. Maybe we could have plastic surgery, get new identities, the works."

"No way. I want the authorities to know who we are, how powerful the Priesthood can be. I want them to fear us! My dream of Phineas Priesthood chapters across the UK is on hold for now, but maybe I can unite the American chapters and become their leader. Then we'd have strength in numbers to do God's work, and earn more crowns in Heaven."

Imogene awoke and rubbed her eyes. "I needed to sleep. The stuff they inject tires me so much."

Amelia sat up. "Stress tires me. I've dozed for an hour, but still feel blah. Jacques will be here soon. Can you handle another session?"

"I've no choice, and I know Mom will find us. She told me to be brave, and do what I'm told. Like you said, Amelia, we both need to be safe."

Amelia fetched a glass of water from the bathroom and handed it to her. "I hate to see you used like this. Can this Osahar character protect you?"

She sipped and wet her lips. "I don't know. I'm in spirit when I visit the temple, like being in a dream. I don't even know if they're real."

"What if Jacques asks the priestess to do something horrible? Can you stop her?"

Imogene heard the mean man enter the apartment. "I don't know, I'll try. But—"

The bedroom door snapped open, and Jacques beckoned them. "Time, ladies, and no tricks. I will talk to Sakhment."

Imogene walked along the beach, her mind filled with memories of another beach, South-end-on-Sea. She'd enjoyed the holiday so much— the pier, the fairground—her parents had even arranged a horse trek. She sighed. Would she ever see them again?

She slowed as she neared the temple, then crept into the dark entrance, her back flat against the wall. The chamber looked empty, but

210

the light of the candles flickered across a large black statue, a man with a bird head. Creepy! She moved around the outer chamber wall toward the back, to behind the altar. Another entranceway!

Imogene picked up a lit wax candle, held it high, and slowly made her way down the short tunnel. Another room! Filmy curtains hung around a high platform in its center. She pushed the fabric aside, and gasped.

Sakhment lay prone on a marble slab. Osahar must have killed her.

She moved closer and reached out. The priestesses' arm felt cool. Her face was ghostlike, framed against black hair, and her slender figure showed through the thin gown. Was she dead?

Imogene looked at her chest, still and quiet. She breathed in and placed her hand against the woman's heart. No heartbeat. She felt her healing power surge into the body below her hand. She struggled to control it, but too late. She felt the energy transfer from her body to Sakhment.

The priestess opened her eyes and grabbed Imogene's wrist. "Thank you, child. You couldn't resist, could you?"

Imogene gasped and looked around. Where was Osahar? "Osahar, help, I need you," she shouted.

The woman swung her legs around and sat, still gripping her arm. "He's gone. There's no one to help you. But trust me, I won't hurt you. I just want to use your energy." She stood and dragged her into the main chamber. "Come along, girl. We have work!"

Frank Carrington looked down from his window at Ten Downing Street. The placard-waving crowd outside had grown. Some called for his resignation, and others demanded a crisis solution. A man in the crowd spotted him, and he stepped back.

"Alex, I don't know what to do. Is there any news about Imogene Pembroke's whereabouts?"

Alex shook his head. "Detective McCullage has spoken to her mother. She did contact her telepathically, but couldn't tell her where she was. She's alive and in Europe somewhere, though, with a young woman. The kidnapper is holding her in an expensive apartment, according to her mother, but we have no clue as to what town, or even what country."

The Prime Minister's cell phone rang. He answered, and turned back to Alex. "Susanne Prentice is outside, and wants to see me. Arrange safe passage for her, will you?"

Moments later, the disheveled anchorwoman and her cameraman entered. "Wow, what a crowd. They've even turned on one another. Prime Minister, you need to release a statement."

Frank sat down behind his desk. "You're right, but what can I say?"

Susanne dropped into a chair and frowned. "Let's work something out. We have to keep the people satisfied, and on your side."

A roar from outside filled the office, and all four rushed to the window. Frank pointed. "My God, there's a man down, covered in blood. He's not moving."

He watched the crowd implode. Placards bounced off people's heads, and more fell. People screamed as baton-swinging police surged forward. "There's a full-scale war out there," he said. "I'll have to do something."

Frank pushed the window open and leaned out. A couple soon noticed him, and pointed. All eyes turned toward the window.

"Please, please stay calm," he called. "The situation with the Council of Elders is under control, and you're in no immediate danger. Please go home, and I'll give a statement to Channel Five." He glanced at Susanne, then turned back to the crowd. "I'm sure they'll broadcast it later today."

The police gained control, and the crowd drifted away down the street. A few diehards clutched their banners and sat down defiantly, across from Number Ten. Frank turned away from the window. "Well, Susanne, Alex, what statement do you suggest I give?"

Jacques watched Imogene's every movement, every eyelid flicker. "Amelia. Call Sakhment forward."

Amelia glanced back. "I'll try. Imogene, please let Sakhment speak through you."

The girl writhed. Her eyes rolled, then opened, and Amelia shrank back. "Her eyes are black. They should be blue! What's happening?"

Jacques pushed her off the chair and sat. "Sakhment, is that you?"

The black eyes bored into the center of his soul. "Of course, my dear one. Have you a question?"

His stomach turned over. "Yes, I have. There's an Internet company, a search engine, called 'Powersearch.' I want control. The CEO is Paul Mililani. His second in command wants the deal, but Mililani is blocking us. He's aboard his yacht in Monaco this weekend, the 'Steel Oceania.' Can you arrange his removal?"

The black eyes moved toward Amelia, then back. "Of course, consider the deed done. One small concern, Jacques, the girl grows weaker. She'll need to rest for several days after I use her."

"Yes, I understand. Thank you, Sakhment."

Imogene's eyelids closed.

Lilya Kaminski stood against the low terrace above Monaco harbor, her powerful binoculars trained on the "Steel Oceania." Mililani lounged on deck, glass in hand, laughing with two bikini-clad beauties. Lilya scanned the white buildings and yachts pasted against the azure blue sea and sky. Not a bad retirement town. Sea, warmth, and plenty of marks to practice on if boredom set in.

As she turned back, she saw the waiter serve fresh drinks. Mililani the geek didn't deserve so much wealth. How would his life end today? Why didn't Jacques contract her to kill him, instead of giving her this stupid observer role? Didn't he trust her anymore? Wasn't she up for another kill? Her retirement fund needed a few more mil.

She picked up the beer the waiter had left. The long draught of lager felt good, and the beef sauerkraut roll next to it smelled yummy. Hawk-eyed, she checked the yacht again. He was still on deck. A coke snort would keep her alert. After all, her job was only to observe and report. She sniffed the white powder, and it rushed to her head. She laughed out loud. Life was good, bloody marvelous!

As the day wore on, storm clouds gathered along the horizon. A stiff breeze sprang up, and Lilya pushed her arms into her leather bomber jacket and snatched up the binoculars. He was on the move. She watched him retreat into the vessel's warm lounge with the two women.

The sky darkened, and she checked her watch. Four o'clock. She scanned the horizon with frustration. The storm clouds looked angry. The sea rolled, and choppy waves worried the boats. Owners appeared on deck and furled their sails and tied down moveable objects, casting nervous glances out to sea.

She trained the binoculars back on the "Steel Oceania." Uniformed crew busied themselves, but Mililani stayed below. The seas roughened, and the wind blew a gale. A storm must be imminent. How strange. Tropical storms often arose out of nowhere, but not typically in the Mediterranean.

Vessels of all shapes and sizes rocked, and she imagined the crew's and passengers' queasiness. Seasickness was a weakness, her personal Achilles heel, and she hated it. A boat broke free from its mooring and knocked into the yacht alongside. A siren howled through the harbor basin, warning of a squall or hurricane. Well, Mililani wouldn't be going ashore any time soon.

Lilya's focus stayed on the yacht as she retreated into the villa. The sky blackened, and the humidity bathed her in sweat. Then her heart jumped as she saw it. A monstrous, hundred-feet-tall rogue wave reached the harbor entrance. She stepped back, thankful she stood high in the surrounding hills.

214

The wave hit and silence descended, except for the wind's howl. The wind dropped abruptly, and she ran toward the terrace edge. The empty harbor looked bizarre. Boats, large and small, had simply vanished. The buildings on the harbor's lower levels had been stripped bare. Windows were broken and people and furniture swirled about near the foreshore.

The choppy waves lessened, and finally calmed. The glassy water reflected the white villas, a ghost town, its lifeblood drained away. The "Steel Oceania" yacht and the other boats apparently now lay beneath the ocean.

Lilya stared at the endless calm sea, then called Jacques. "Mililani's dead," she said. "Drowned."

CHAPTER THIRTY-TWO

Frank caught a movement in the corner of his eye, but when he looked around, there was no one there. He rested his chin on his hands, his elbows on his knees. The ornate street lamp cast a halo of light over the office carpet, and he heard the clock chime midnight. Time's so short, what can I do? He and Alex had gone through every possible alternative searching for a solution, without success.

Frank sensed movement again, and the light dimmed as if someone walked in front of the window. He peered through his fingers, and his desk lamp flickered as a figure passed through the beam. His skin tingled as he sat back and scanned the room. The elusive shadow hovered in his peripheral vision. He turned quickly, trying to catch a better view. Heart racing, he scanned the room, but the misty form played cat and mouse with him.

This had happened before on stressful occasions, beginning on the day his parents 'abandoned' him at eight years old. The scene filled his mind - his parents driving away from his prep school without a backward glance, leaving him to the mercy of strangers.

Alone in a small dorm, he'd looked out the window into semi-darkness, the front lawn lit by a single light over the school entrance. The matron told him that the other three boys he would share the room with weren't due until tomorrow. "Be a good boy, and get into bed. Lights out at nine," she said.

As the matron left he'd cried, causing his chest to tighten, triggering an asthma attack. A lump formed in his throat as he recalled the horrific wheezing sensation. He'd been convinced he would die as he gasped for breath, but then he felt a comforting presence. A dark shadow sat on the next bed, emitting an aura of calm toward him.

Now, like then, warmth flooded his body as he realized the presence meant no harm. Reassured, he mentally thanked the extraordinary presence for its support. Since he'd become an adult he'd heard about this phenomenon from his mountain climbing friends, who referred to the sensation as 'the third man syndrome'. It seemed the shadow man appeared when they were in danger.

The famous climber Ernest Shackleton reported such an account, when a third man joined him and two others as they battled for many hours crossing glaciers and mountains. The shadow man guided them and provided comfort throughout their traumatic experience.

Climbers expressed their own opinion about the presence, descriptions varied from a brother, old friend or angel, but all agreed the mysterious third man encouraged them, and led them out of danger. The stories weren't confined to climbers but to many others such as divers, Artic researchers, and lone sailors, and they all shared the same need, comfort and support.

The benevolent presence wanted to help. Reassured, he stood and switched off the lamp and made his way to his living-quarters. Did this mean he'd succeed in his mission? He hoped so and determined he would sleep well tonight, now that he wasn't alone.

 ***

The surgeon's words swirled through her mind as he administered the epidural. "The small baby's heartbeat is weak, which means I'll have to deliver the twins today by caesarian section to save her." Bryony's heart thumped in her chest as the theatre team finished prepping her. Would the twins both survive? Even though Imogene had stopped the larger twin taking most of the blood supply, the second twin was still small and vulnerable.

Her sister Brittany squeezed her hand as the surgeon made the first cut. The green fabric square the nurse had erected earlier blocked her view of the procedure, so she stopped trying to see what was happening on the other side, relaxed and smiled at her sister. "Thanks for your support Brit. I can count on you. I know you're always there for me."

Brittany patted her hand and stroked her hair. "That's what sisters are for, silly. Don't worry, the twins will be fine."

Bryony watched the nurses scurry about behind the screen as the surgeon worked. Their masked faces bobbed back and forth for ages, and then at last the doctor peered over the curtain. "Bryony, we have the first twin out, but she's quite tiny and needs urgent attention. The nurse will take her straight to the neonatal ward."

Bryony heard a feeble cry and bit her lip. "She doesn't sound too strong, will she be alright?"

The surgeon didn't answer as she felt him tug away inside her abdomen. "The second twin is here. Nurse, please note the time of birth, 11.11a.m., for baby one and 11.13 a.m. for baby two."

The large baby gave a lusty cry as the nurse brought her around. Tightly wrapped, the baby's red face looked angry as she bawled. "Isn't she bonny? You can cuddle her after she's washed and weighed."

Brittany's grip tightened on her hand as she heard a commotion. "What's wrong?"

Her sister's face whitened. "You're hemorrhaging, there's so much blood"

Bryony breathed out and closed her eyes, "I feel so tired."

McCullage clicked through the missing person reports, and pictures scrolled down the screen. He shook his head. Who would imagine there were so many women and girls missing? He typed in the filter, 'women aged between 18-25 years'. That's better, just two pages for the last three months. Quickly he scanned the photographs, eliminating those with light hair, and then - there she was!

Jim looked at Sam and frowned, and Sam sheepishly removed his feet off the detective's desk. "Any luck?"

"Look at this, Amelia Mason has a Cleopatra hairstyle exactly as Xantara described. She lives in Stratford-on-Avon, and get this - she works as a hypnotist, specializing in past-life regression. She's our woman, for sure."

Sam beamed. "Where's the nearest airport to the woman's home?"

The detective picked up the phone. "Gloucestershire airport and it's just thirty-eight miles from Stratford." He held up a finger, listened then spoke into the phone. "Inspector Grant, we have a lead on the missing woman who fits Mrs. Pembroke's account, and she's a hypnotist to boot. Will do, yes, we're leaving now."

Sam walked around the desk. "Is this her? How long has she been missing?"

Jim clicked on the print icon. "Less than a month, her brother reported her absence, two weeks ago."

"What're we looking for at the airport?"

Jim grabbed his jacket and made for the door. "My guess is a Cessna Citation X with a female pilot, Lilya Kaminski. Let's hope the airport keep CCTV footage for a reasonable time."

Bryony flicked her hair back as she watched Xantara stroke the baby's cheek. "Isn't she beautiful?"

The baby's fingers curled around Xantara's. "She's a little angel, and thank God you're alright. When you hemorrhaged Brittany was sure they'd lost you. Thank goodness you all survived the birth."

Bryony rocked her baby and cooed. "I'm glad the twins have my coloring, it means I can look at them without being reminded of

Jeremiah." Bryony dangled a lock of hair over the baby's face and smiled. "She's a greedy madam, full bottles already, but such a sweetheart. I can't wait to bring the other baby home, but the hospital says she may be kept in neo-natal for several weeks."

Xantara touched her shoulder. "How are you feeling now?"

The baby grabbed her hair, and she gently extricated the lock. "Good thanks, it's funny, but I don't recall the emergency, the loss of blood made me pass out." She laid the baby back down in the pram and covered her over. "I think I'll park her in the back garden, the fresh air will do her good."

Xantara boiled the kettle and dropped teabags in the pot. "Have you named them yet?"

Bryony nodded. "I feel bad as I promised Imogene she could help me find the right names, but I came up with two I'm sure she'd like."

Her friend placed a cup beside her and sat on the sofa. "I'm sure Imogene will understand. I miss her so much, and hope they'll bring her home soon, she must be really frightened. If I hadn't felt her presence, I would be even more upset, but at least I know she's alive, and they want to use her, so won't harm her. So, what names did you decide on?"

Bryony set down her cup. "The little one is Annysia, it means 'little angel', and the larger one is Azura, which means 'sky jewel'. What do you think?"

Xantara sipped her drink and grinned. "I love those names, and Imogene will too. The twins are gorgeous, and the names will suit their individual personalities. Which one will be the Avebury Guardian?"

"Annysia, they lifted her out first because of her fragile state and guess what? Her birth happened at exactly 11.11 a.m."

"Perfect, the spiritual number doubled, it fits her future role as a Guardian. Imogene will be healing with her at Avebury Circle, when they both come of age, and she can teach her the ceremonies."

Bryony noticed Xantara's eyes fill with tears, and she reached across to her friend. "You will get her back soon. She can only die in Avebury circle so that won't happen, and the Light Being part of her will keep her well. I'm sure Rahmiel will watch over her."

Xantara brushed her tears away. "Yes, you're right, but I miss her terribly. So much has happened in such a short time, will our lives ever return to normal?"

Bryony stood. "Nearly time for Azura's feed. I'd better go home. Why don't you come over for coffee tomorrow, and see the twin's room? Imogene would love it, all pink and lavender, a real girlie room."

Her friend walked her outside to collect the baby. She pulled the covers back. "Oh No! She's gone!" Hysterically, Bryony searched the empty pram. "My child's gone. Someone's kidnapped her. It's got to be Jeremiah!"

She and Xantara ran into the deserted street.

Jim and Sam parked opposite the Security sign at Gloucestershire airport, at Stanton near Cheltenham. Jim clicked the car remote and turned toward the office door. "You know Sam, there can't be many Citation X jets, the machine's high-tech and expensive to fly, a toy strictly for the rich."

They entered the office to see a wall of screens, showing images from every inch of the airport. Jim shook the security officer's hand and turned to Sam. "Looks promising."

They produced their IDs and the officer offered them a seat. "What can I do for you gentlemen?"

Jim pointed at the screens. "How long do you keep the CCTV footage?"

The young man straightened and smiled. "We have the latest technology, and we archive the records. What're you after exactly?"

Sam leaned forward. "A Cessna Citation X, with a female pilot."

The security officer grinned. "Too easy, almost three weeks ago a Citation X landed briefly. I'm a recreational flyer myself, and the Citation X is my dream jet, so much so, I tagged the footage as it landed and took-off."

"Brilliant, can you pull the film for us?"

The officer turned to his keyboard. "There's a coffee machine over there, help yourselves."

They watched the eager young man type furiously as they sipped their drinks. "Did you realize The Citation is the second fastest medium-range executive jet around and costs twenty-one million US dollars? Only the Gulfstream G650 is faster. As you can imagine, there's not many in the UK. Ah, here's the jet." He pointed to the wall's middle screen.

Together they watched the jet land. A slight female figure exited with her cap pulled well down. A customs official met the pilot on the tarmac and examined the paperwork. The screen blurred then focused again on the small boned woman, this time accompanied by Amelia Mason carrying a small suitcase. They climbed the aircraft's steps and moments later the plane moved down the runway.

Jim grinned. "It's definitely Lilya Kaminski, and we can be sure without checking, the flight plan will be false, but there are the jet's identification numbers. Can we use them to find the registered owner?"

The security officer typed in the numbers and sighed. "False identification, they belong to a SportJet 11, a single engine lightweight aircraft."

Jim groaned. "Damn."

The officer pushed his chair back. "There's not many Citations in the UK or even in Europe. The manufacturer would keep an owners' list, and of course there're all registered with the aviation authority."

Jim stood and shook the young man's hand. "Thank you, you're been helpful. Please email the footage to me, here's my card."

Jim and Sam crossed to their car. Once inside, Jim opened his Ipad and searched the net. "They make the jets in Wichita, United States." He glanced at his watch. "It's the middle of the night over there, so we have a five-hour wait. Come on. Let's go back to the station. We're getting closer at last - find the owner and we find the child."

CHAPTER THIRTY-THREE

"I don't want to do it." Imogene struggled as Jacques lifted her on to the couch. "I don't like it, I want my Mom."

Amelia tried to pull Jacques away, but he kicked her so hard she flew across the room, and hit the wall. Then he lifted the syringe and plunged the needle into Imogene's arm. "You will do as I say, or your parents will suffer, understand?"

Imogene looked across at Amelia. Her swollen lip dripped blood down her blouse and white faced, she trembled. "Okay, I'll do it, but don't ever hit Amelia again." She felt her head swim and fought the drug's effect, she couldn't lose control. She tried harder and managed to regain her senses, now she could play the part.

Through half-closed lids, she watched Jacques drag Amelia into the chair beside the couch. "Follow my instructions to the letter," he said.

While Amelia induced her as normal, she ignored the suggestions and directed herself. She willed her spirit into the hall of past-lives and chose a door. The priestess could wait.

Imogene stepped into an incredible wonderland. Brightly decorated pillars arose from a checkered marble floor. Azure blue, burnished orange and gold splashed over the tiled walls, the mosaic formed into lions and strange winged creatures. A man wearing a high crowned headdress sat on a gilded throne, a jeweled scepter rested in his hand. Beside him, a woman played a stringed instrument and sang softly.

For a moment, she thought she'd entered another part of the priestess's temple, but then realized this could be Pharaoh's palace, and she stood in his throne room. She looked down, she liked her intricately designed sandals and the golden strands threaded through her gown. Could she be a princess of Pharaoh's court?

Pharaoh talked to two elderly men, one of whom held a staff. A straggly beard partially covered his simple long-sleeved white robe, which he'd tied with a cord. Imogene moved closer and stood behind a pillar to listen. Suddenly, a hand dropped on her shoulder. Startled, she turned. "Osahar!"

The priest squeezed her gently and whispered in her ear. "Sister, why are you here, someone may see you!"

Imogene frowned. 'Sister', did his words mean that Osahar was her brother in this past life? The connection made sense to her - maybe the Council of Elders picked her for that reason. A sound caught her attention. One of the old men threw down his staff in front of Pharaoh. She gasped as the rod turned into a snake, a living snake.

A high turbaned black man pushed the older men aside, and threw down his rod, which also turned into a snake. She heard Pharaoh snigger. "What say you, Moses and Aaron? My magicians can easily create such a simple trick?"

Other court magicians stepped forward and released their staffs. Quickly the floor slithered with snakes, and then Aaron's snake hunted the others, devouring them one by one.

Moses turned to Pharaoh. "You've seen God's power, now will you let my people go, and allow us to leave Egypt in peace?"

"Never, be gone from my presence." Pharaoh motioned his guards, and they dragged the old men outside the palace.

Osahar steered her toward a side room. "Little sister, what're you doing? Pharaoh's court is dangerous, go now, help our mother."

~ *** ~

Frank Carrington sat with his mouth half open at his office desk, across from The Home Secretary. He gulped several times and took a deep breath. "Alex, the connection you suggest is unbelievable - the report can't be true, can it?"

Alex Brittan gave a half-shrug. "Yes, every word, and just think of the implications!"

Frank's pulse quickened, and he leaned forward. "Tell me again, right from the beginning."

The Home Secretary jutted out his chin. "Detective McCullage phoned me earlier today to give me a progress report. He and the CIA guy tracked down the Citation X aircraft's British owners and came up with a name. Only one owner was privy to Imogene Pembroke's case, none other than our very own Opposition Leader, Charles Strathfield."

Frank shook his head. "No, surely he can't be involved with her disappearance? Why would he risk his position, his reputation?"

Alex stood and paced the room. "He must have a valid reason. Perhaps to discredit you as Prime Minister by removing the girl, she's your evidence after all. Without her he can alienate your people and get them to dismiss you."

Frank felt hot and pulled his collar. "What shall we do?"

Alex paused near the window and turned. "We'll have to tread carefully. Perhaps we could arrange a gentle interrogation on the pretext of Citation ownership, such as who else he knows who owns one, something along those lines."

Frank frowned. "I don't know, we'd be walking over unknown territory, due to his position. And if he's innocent we would be handing him ammunition to use against us."

Alex sighed and wet his lips. "But think, if he's guilty, and my gut tells me he could be, we'd have the means to stop his campaign against you, and get the girl returned."

He nodded. "Alright, but tread carefully. Find out what you can and report back as soon as possible."

Alex picked up the file. "As I said, the jet's identification numbers proved false, so I need to connect Strathfield to that particular jet. I'll work on finding the link before I question him, and don't worry I'll be careful."

The US Phineas Priesthood member, the sole occupant of a minibus parked next to a shadowy private wharf, waited and listened. His heart beat faster as he heard the put-put of the ship's tender, in the distance. He climbed out of the van and walked down the length of the jetty, straining to see through the mist that rolled in off the cold ocean.

At last, the boat appeared and docked. He helped out the passengers, four men, a woman, and two babies. Who on earth had he brought with him? "Jeremiah, how are you? Why have you got kids with you?"

Jeremiah clasped the man's hand. "I'm great Simon, long-time no see. Let me introduce you, Ezekiel my cousin, my brothers Obadiah and Malachi, and Molly, Malachi's wife." He pointed to one child and smiled. "Please meet my son, Gideon, and my daughter, unnamed so far."

Simon took two bags off the sailor, who then turned the dinghy around and headed back out to sea. "Better get a move on, I've made a refuge ready up in the mountains, near a small-town called Elkins, in West Virginia." He led the fugitives to the minibus and helped them aboard. "I've been looking forward to this day, Jeremiah. A great time to build up the priesthood, and I've got a few ideas I'd like to run past you."

Simon settled the group in their seats then started the engine. He indicated for Jeremiah to join him in front. As Jeremiah climbed into the van, Simon noticed he clutched a small bottle. "What's that?" He asked.

Jeremiah's teeth gleamed in the darkness. "It's our ticket to freedom brother, our point of power."

～ *** ～

Alex Brittan sat across from Charles Strathfield the opposition leader, and stared. "Look again, Charles," he said as he tapped his foot against the desk leg.

Strathfield mopped his brow as he studied the three photographs set out in front. "I've done nothing wrong, I tell you. Obviously an unknown person stole the jet, used it, then parked the plane back in the hanger." His gaze darted around the office, then he crossed his arms, his eyes focused over Alex's shoulder.

Alex stabbed at the images. "Look at the matched points, the marks around the engine and along the wing, and of course your plane's nose emblem. You covered up the identification numbers and replaced them, but you forgot your monogram, didn't you?"

Charles' face reddened. "How dare you accuse me of involvement with the child's abduction, and where's your proof? You haven't any evidence here, except a pilot used my jet, without permission."

Alex half-turned his laptop and pressed a key. "Look at this video, taken from your own hanger security system." Together they watched Charles greet Lilya Kaminski and pass over a package. She climbed into the jet as Strathfield walked away.

The Opposition Leader stood and shook his fist. "How dare you invade my privacy, you won't get away with this."

Alex smiled and clasped his hands behind his head. "Well we'll see, Charles. The footage will be aired on Channel five tonight, both here and across Europe, along with a call for the public to locate the girl."

The man sank back into the chair and stared into the distance. "What do you want?"

Alex dropped his arms and leaned forward. "Simple, I want two things. Of course, the girl's location and recovery, as well as your support for the Prime Minister. Drop your campaign against him, and publicly support his belief in the Council of Elders' messages."

Strathfield shook his head. "I don't know where she is, but I can find out. I may need some time to retrieve her, will you wait?"

Alex relaxed. "Yes, but I'm going to be with you every step of the way."

The Opposition Leader glanced at his watch. "That's not possible. She's in the hands of powerful people who value their anonymity. If they get wind of our plans, she'll be killed before our feet leave English soil."

Alex rubbed his ear. "How will we know you'll fetch her and return?"

Charles sighed. "Send men to my country estate, my family will stay there and await my return."

Alex prided himself on judging a person's character. Strathfield was proud of his position, his power and his family - he would do as he promised. "You have two days, but first tell me why these friends of yours kidnapped her and the hypnotist?"

Charles stood. "I honestly don't know, I'm a small cog in a large wheel. If you want me to get her back quickly, I need to start now."

CHAPTER THIRTY-FOUR

Frank Carrington glanced at his watch as the Home secretary entered. "Alex, there you are, switch on the television please, it's time for the six o'clock news."

The Prime Minister closed the file he was reading and moved across to the easy chairs he used to entertain guests. The screen filled with St Paul's Cathedral's familiar white dome and ornate spires. In front, Susanne Prentice stood holding a microphone. The camera panned up the entrance steps, to a crowd pressed against the double doors.

The camera panned back to Susanne as several people pushed past her, and she stumbled. "As you can see people are flocking to churches around the country to pray for deliverance from the Council's final consequence." In the background, Frank heard a choir sing as the congregation wailed and shouted. "With only four days before D-Day, August 19th, widespread panic is endemic across the World. Unbelievers stay home and mock, while people of faith fill churches, temples and synagogues. Crimes have increased exponentially as owners abandon their businesses and whole families head for the hills."

Distant sirens masked her words, and a fight broke out at the church entrance. "People are going crazy, trampling one another in their efforts to enter the church," she said.

Frank raked his fingers through his hair. "This state of affairs will get worse, and I can imagine riots increasing. Is Parliament secure, and how's Strathfield getting on? When can we expect Imogene Pembroke back?"

Alex turned the sound low. "Don't worry, he'll come through for us, and then you can reason with the Council of Elders. They can't deny you've done everything in your power to put forward the case for disarmament."

"Four days, Alex. We're too close for comfort." He heard a muffled cry, snatched the control and turned up the sound. A skinhead group encircled Susanne and pushed her from one to another. "Please stop," she shouted. Her usual confidence and poise crumbled, and she looked terrified.

One tattooed, leather clad biker pushed harder, and she fell. "You're the woman who told us this pack of lies. Putting fear into people, how do you like being scared?"

They watched as police ran toward the group with batons drawn and Bikers and skinheads scattered in all directions. They helped the television anchor to her feet, then the screen blanked.

Imogene's heart soared, as she realized she could control her movements during hypnosis. Jacques' livid face loomed over her. "This time you will meet with the priestess, or else. Understand?"

Imogene looked straight at him. "Of course I'll try, but once I'm hypnotized, I go where I'm told. Perhaps she's not there anymore."

Jacques' hand lifted, and she flinched. He lowered it and half-smiled. "Imogene, my dear, work with the priestess and you'll be doing me a great service. Meet with her a few more times, and I promise you can return home."

Imogene nodded and willed her face to remain blank. She looked at Amelia who shuddered every time Jacques brushed against her. "Ready, Imogene." Her new-found friend stroked her forehead. "Relax, and seek out the beach, feel the sand between your toes."

~ *** ~

Imogene blocked out Amelia's voice and willed herself into the past life hallway. A brisk wind blew against her face as she stepped through a random doorway, on to a parapet overlooking a city. Unnoticed, she stood behind Osahar and his mother. What are they looking at?

She stepped close to the wall edge and looked down. People trailed through the city in a straggly line toward the desert. Colorful clothes mingled with white head coverings and all carried a bundle or a baby. Small children skipped alongside their parents, and old men hobbled along helped by their stout walking staffs. Flocks of sheep interspersed with donkeys and other animals added to the melee. Who are they, and why are they walking into the desert? She watched for hours before the long line thinned and the last people left the city.

Osahar and his mother turned. "Serakh, what're you doing here? Come, let's go inside." She followed them into the palace and through to their private quarters. Questions swirled through Imogene's mind. She wanted to know about those people.

Osahar sat at the table and motioned to her. "Come, Serakh, eat." His mother placed a rice dish next to a bowl of nuts and dates.

She sat and picked up a handful of nuts. "Why are people walking into the desert?"

"They are the Israelites, led by Moses and Aaron. The pharaoh finally agreed to let them leave, after the last plague."

"What plague?"

Osahar swallowed and stared at her. "Never mind, you're too young to worry about the plagues."

The girl shook her head. "I'm not, Brother! I'll soon be in my tenth year. Please, tell me the story."

The priest leaned back and smiled. "You are growing faster each year. Very well, I'll tell you about the Israelites. Do you recall the time I found you in Pharaoh's court and a man threw down his staff, which turned into a snake?

Imogene grinned. "I do, the magicians' rods turned into snakes too, then the first snake swallowed the others."

"Well that was the leader of Jews, Moses, with his brother Aaron. The Israelites are Pharaoh's slaves and responsible for building his cities. They wanted to return to their own country, but Pharaoh refused to let them go."

Imogene folded her arms and leaned across the table. "What happened next? Did Pharaoh let them leave?"

"No sister, he didn't, and I'm sure he regrets his decision. Over the next few months, Moses' God brought down ten plagues to punish the Egyptian people, each worse than the last."

"What plagues?"

Osahar went quiet for a moment, then spoke. "First, all the water turned to blood, the Nile, smaller rivers and lakes, even water vessels, but the Pharaoh still refused."

"What did people drink?"

"Of course, they drank wine, and gradually the blood cleared, and the rivers returned to normal. You may recall the second plague, millions of frogs - they hopped everywhere, in the streets, our houses and in our beds, ovens, even amongst our clothes."

Imogene laughed. "Yes, I do recall, they were funny, hopping over my bed."

Osahar frowned. "The next two plagues weren't so funny, lice and flies. We begged Pharaoh to let the Israelites leave, but to no avail, so the fifth plague descended and proved terrible. Our cattle became diseased and died, causing Pharaoh to bring in new stock from the surrounding countries."

"How horrible, what next?"

"Huge boils appeared on everyone. They covered you too, and you cried with the pain. Next we experienced severe thunder and hail, crops and buildings suffered. Pharaoh didn't relent, and Moses released a locust plague, which ate every living plant."

Imogene bit into a pomegranate. "Yes, I was so hungry my stomach rumbled."

Osahar sighed. "Darkness descended over Egypt for three days, it terrified even Pharaoh and his family, but pride overcame his common sense."

"But there're leaving now, what happened to cause Pharaoh to let them go?"

A tear ran down Osahar's cheek. "The final plague is so devastating that Pharaoh told them to go immediately. Moses did warn Pharaoh, but he ignored him. The firstborn in every family died during the night, including the livestock. Our eldest brother lies dead in his room, and Pharaoh's eldest son lies dead in the palace."

Imogene felt her skin crawl. "My brother's dead? Did the Israelites' firstborns die too?

"No, and we don't know why, but the death angel bypassed their homes".

Imogene felt her spirit waver, the connection faded, and she awoke.

Charles Strathfield greeted Lilya Kaminski as she entered the hanger. "Thank you for coming. I have an assignment for you."

Kaminski looked around. "Where's Jacques, I take my orders from him, and him alone."

The Opposition Leader guided her into an office built into the far corner. "Please, sit. I'm sorry to have to tell you this, but Jacques has lost confidence in you. In fact, he's taken out a termination contract on you."

Lilya paused and clenched her fists. "Why am I not surprised? When he sent me to Monaco to observe a nerd's death, I wondered why he didn't ask me to do the job. Just wait until I get my hands on him!"

Strathfield smiled. "You'll have your chance. I want you to work for me now, and after you've disposed of Jacques de Sales, I shall lead the

Troth Society. But I want you to complete another job for me at the same time, kill two birds with one stone. How does five million pounds sound?"

Kaminski relaxed. "I'm in. What do you want me to do?"

"Jacques is still in Luxemburg with the Pembroke girl and the other woman you flew there. I need those two young women. I want you to enter the bunker, kill Jacques and his butler, and fly the girls back here, to me."

The assassin stood. "What's the timeline?"

Strathfield struggled to his feet and reached for his cane. "Time is short, so I've filed a flight plan, you leave in an hour."

Susanne Prentice climbed the steep hill followed by her camera man, Hugh. "Are you sure there're people here?"

"The villagers assured me they've spotted people hiding up here," he said.

She shuddered as the woods either side emitted a strange rustle. Animals, she realized, and stepped closer to Hugh. The mountains rose high around them as they trekked up the remote Welsh foothill.

The trail deteriorated as they climbed higher. She swatted overhanging branches which snagged her dress, and a thorn scratched her face. Without warning a man appeared ahead wearing camouflage gear and carrying a rifle. "Clear off, this is private property." He leveled the gun, aiming at Hugh.

Hugh held up his hands. "We want to talk to you and others with you, about the Council of Elders deadline."

"Who're you?"

Susanne stepped forward. "I'm Susanne Prentice from Channel Five, and Hugh's my cameraman."

The man listened then blew a whistle softly. A small band of 'Doomsday Preppers' crept out from behind the trees. "We'll talk to you on condition you give us an update. You may have information we don't. Follow us."

The group blindfolded Susanne and Hugh, then lead them through the forest trails, climbing higher till eventually the track felt easier.

They removed the blindfolds, and when her eyes adjusted, Susanne saw dark caves ahead, dotting the hillside. Fires glowed in several cave entrances where women with small children tended pots suspended off metal tripods. The man turned and stuck out his hand. "Welcome to our home. My name's Mike and I'm the elected leader of our little band of merry men, a real life Robin Hood."

Susanne squatted around the larger fire pit while Hugh set up his equipment behind. "Will you answer a few questions? Our viewers would like to hear another perspective."

Mike, a rugged, square set man, sat opposite her. "No problem, but please don't disclose our location." He signaled to the others, and they joined the circle. "We've planned this for years, and practiced wilderness survival. I've always known this day would come, so we prepared. We've gathered food, weapons and shelter to protect our families."

Susanne nodded to Hugh, and he panned around the camp site. "Do you believe the world will end in four days?" She asked.

"The camp's pointless if the end means the end of the world. But look at the lives lost this past year through events incited by this Council of Elders. Not everyone died. Whatever the final tragedy may be, we want at least a chance of survival."

The woman next to Mike shifted her position. "Hi, I'm Candice, Mike's wife. We have four children, all less than ten years old, and we want them to have a future. There're seven families here, enough to repopulate this area if the worst happens."

Mike touched his wife's knee and smiled. "That's the crux of it, but what's the latest news? You are the News. If anyone knows what's going on, you should."

Susanne scanned the group. "You've all seen the news reports and understand our Prime Minister's working hard to solve the problem. An unknown party has abducted Imogene Pembroke, and if he can find her before the deadline, he plans to ask her to reason with the Council for more time."

Mike cupped his chin and stroked the stubble. "And if he can't?"

Chapter Thirty-Five

Jacques looked down on the comatose girls and felt warmth spread through his body. Good, the pills worked. Neither stirred as he carried Imogene from the bedroom. Carefully he laid her on the couch and covered her with a thick blanket. He filled the syringe with a double dose of the truth drug, sodium pentothal and dimmed the lights. Maybe the dose would prove too much, maybe not, but the child hadn't contacted his priestess for days. If she died, she deserved to.

Her body jerked as he slid the needle into her arm, and little by little depressed the plunger. He sat beside her and allowed himself to enter a deep meditative state. Sakhment's features appeared in his mind. So, the priestess lived.

Imogene's chest barely moved and her pulse felt slow, time to guide her. He whispered into her ear. "Imogene, walk along the beach toward the temple."

Imogene found herself near the temple. She shook her head, how was she asleep in bed, and now she stood outside the temple? She crept forward, sidled along the wall and entered. The main room appeared empty and softly lit. She trembled and wiped her palms down her skirt, then curled up in a corner and pictured Osahar. Osahar, I need you, please help me, I'm in Sakhment's temple.

Imogene heard a faint rustle of the priestess's clothing and pressed further into the curved wall. Her knees shook as she watched Sakhment light several candles on a stone table in front of the Birdman statue. The priestess lit an incense burner, wafted the smoke around the room, then knelt and murmured strange words. She arose and swayed, dancing to her own beat with eyes closed, then bowed before the statue.

Imogene held her breath as Sakhment straightened and blew out the candles. The priestess slowly turned. With eyebrows raised, her dark eyes drilled into Imogene's and she approached her. "Imogene, how kind, you've come to visit, I've missed you."

Imogene scrambled to her feet and ran toward the rear doorway, straight into the arms of a tall black man wearing nothing but a loin cloth. "Mistress, I have her."

"Bring her here."

The man twisted her arm behind her back and marched her to the center of the room. She struggled, and a pain shot up her arm as he gripped harder. "What do you want with me?"

Sakhment smiled. "Release her, and leave us."

Imogene watched the man go. His black skin shone like boot polish as he passed by an oil lamp. She gasped, she had never seen anyone so black, unlike the Indians and Pakistani immigrants, back home. Her focus returned to the priestess, who held out her hands toward her. "We have work, little one, hold my hands."

Imogene fastened her hands behind her back and stepped away. "No, never!" Her heart raced as the woman's venomous face twisted. The priestess grabbed Imogene's arms and pulled her close. Imogene screamed, then felt Sakhment release her hold. She looked up and saw Osahar force the woman sideways. Imogene slumped and covered her mouth. Thank goodness, he came!

The priest held a golden cord and wrapped it around Sakhment's neck and pulled. The woman's eyes bulged as she tried to free herself. Osahar uttered strange words under his breath. The magical incantation made the priestess struggle further, and then she relaxed and he let her fall. "She's gone, Imogene."

Dark shapes formed around Sakhment, and snatched her soul as it arose from her body. They dragged her downwards. She and the entities disappeared through the floor, and the air cleared. Osahar stepped forward and comforted Imogene until she calmed down. "Don't cry, little one, she's gone forever."

Imogene's sobs lessened, and she let her arms fall to her sides. "Thank you, thank you, she frightened me so much."

The priest knelt before her and looked into her eyes. "Child, the Council of Elders have issued orders, they want us to release another consequence."

She scrubbed her toe against the stone floor. "I don't want to hurt anyone. Do we have to?"

Osahar's face softened. "At times we have to discipline before people will listen. Kabshiel, the Council leader has a long-term plan, and I promise you from the bottom of my heart, releasing the power is the right action to take. You trust me, don't you?"

Imogene searched the priest's face. "I do trust you Osahar, let's do it." She held out her hands and clasped his. Immediately she felt the universal energy build, the power rushed through every cell of her body. An intense light beam formed between them and rose, then spread throughout the temple. They'd done it! Whatever the energy released there's no turning back!

Lilya crept along the grass bank's perimeter, heading for an air vent. Unknown to Jacques she'd modified this particular vent, for emergencies. Yes, the shaft remained clear! She slid inside and dropped the rope-ladder she carried. Within moments she landed in the bunker. She'd memorized the layout on a previous visit. She had decided to deal with the butler first, and crept toward the kitchen area.

The man servant stirred a skillet next to a range. The bacon's sizzle and aroma made her mouth water as she moved like a ghost across the room. The switchblade hit the mark as it slid between the third and fourth ribs, the man dropped without a sound. Kaminski switched off the gas and moved the pan off the hot ring. She felt it safe to leave him sprawled over the floor - Jacques never visited the kitchen area.

Lilya sneaked through the hallway and emerged into the enormous garage. A large black Hummer stood beside the Ferrari, ideal to transport the girl and hypnotist to the airport. She moved on through the Egyptian themed conference room toward the apartment beyond. Lilya pressed the hieroglyphic tile and the panel slid open. She slipped inside and closed the panel.

The quiet apartment appeared empty as she tiptoed across the lounge and opened the bedroom door. Amelia the hypnotist snored softly, but beside her, the bed showed a dip, and the bed linen pulled aside as if a body had lain there recently. Where the devil was the Pembroke girl, had someone moved her?

Back in the lounge she checked the second bedroom then froze. She heard Jacques' voice behind the third room door, now the consultation office. Lilya listened outside – he talked to the girl. She stood behind the door and settled down to wait.

Frank Carrington's official limousine drove into Porton Down and parked. Alex, the Home Secretary, frowned. "Do you want to do this? I don't like it. Hypnosis can be dangerous, whatever gave you the idea?"

The Prime Minister tapped Alex on the arm. "I can't take the chance. Strathfield may not bring Imogene back in time. I've no choice, our families are at risk, even though it's a slim chance, I have to try, surely you understand?

Alex slammed the car door. "I do, but can you trust Ernst Schneider messing with your mind?"

Frank walked toward the secret base double doors, then turned. "He's a fine psychiatrist, and a man who has suffered the loss of his entire family, he wants to play his part."

The doctor held the door open and they walked through. "I've prepared my office as you asked. Have you any allergies?"

Frank removed his jacket and handed it to Alex. "Just the ones related to my asthma. Did you get my medical records?"

"Yes sir, I can't see any reason medically not to go ahead. Do you want to get straight on with the session?"

The Prime Minister stretched out on the white leather couch and rolled up his shirt sleeve. "Doctor, give me the injection, then follow the identical protocol you used with Imogene."

Frank's head swam, he felt himself fall into a vortex, twisting and turning as the force caught his spirit and whisked him away. He slowed and opened his eyes. Below him he saw his own body, Doctor Schneider and Alex leaning against the desk. A movement caught his eye, the shadow man hovered beside him. What did the 'third man' want, why was he here?

His companion moved away, and he felt a strong need to follow him. Together they rose higher and passed through the roof, higher and higher until Frank could see the patchwork countryside as if from an airplane seat. The shadow man slowed and dropped toward a large city.

Frank heard the somber toll of bells from the church spire. He moved closer, and recognized Westminster Abbey. People carrying coffins formed a long line as they trailed toward the familiar church. He counted each coffin as they passed over the pallbearers, twenty-three. A huge crowd of people behind steel barriers lined the path, watching renowned dignitaries from many countries as they followed the procession. What was going on?

Frank felt the pull of shadow man and they moved away, heading north. Frank willed his thoughts toward the Council, and Kabshiel, but he couldn't leave this experience, whatever it was.

They approached another city, with historic buildings. As Frank flew closer, he recognized Oxford, and the familiar streets he'd walked in as an undergraduate. Now his son followed in his footsteps, and attended the same University. Oxford University's creamy stone and ornate carvings lay beneath him. He passed over Julian's dormitory block, then he saw the large grassed quadrangle amid the university's main structures.

His blood ran cold. The entire quadrangle beneath him was covered in coffins, row upon row. Frank went lower and hovered above each coffin and read the nameplates. His heart constricted as he discovered Julian's friends, young men who had stayed at Checkers for long country weekends, a respite from their studies. He saw the names of children of International public figures who sent them to this renowned University.

His experience must be a dream, hallucination, or worse, a glimpse into the future? He searched harder with dread…

CHAPTER THIRTY-SIX

Lilya Kaminski stiffened as she heard Jacques walk toward the door. She stood ready, knife in hand. Without warning, a loud retort knocked her off her feet. Dazed, she realized he'd shot her through the door. Her left arm dangled, and a bright red stain appeared on her sleeve. She slid backwards as the door crashed open, and held the knife behind her back.

Jacques stood over her, a playful grin on his face. "You're slipping Lilya. I've watched you since you entered the apartment." He flashed his cell phone and showed her the feed from the camera above her head. "Why are you trying to kill me? Haven't we an arrangement?"

She spat, her chest heaving. "We did before you double-crossed me."

Her boss raised his brows. "Double-crossed you? I've no idea what you're talking about."

"Strathfield told me everything. Apparently you've lost confidence in me, I've no idea why you should have, but the Monaco incident proves it, and now you have a contract out on me."

Jacques laughed, then narrowed his eyes. "Strathfield is the one who's playing you for a fool." He held out his hand. "Come on, let me help you up. We're been friends for a long time, don't let the cripple's lies come between us."

Lilya slipped the knife into her belt, grasped his hand and stood. As he loosed her, with a burst of energy, she brought the knife around and stabbed him through the heart. She smirked at Jacques' shocked face. "You may be right, but he pays better. Nighty-night."

She stripped off her jacket and inspected the wound, then searched Jacques' pockets. Lilya bound the flesh wound with her handkerchief, then emptied his wallet and threw it down beside him. She pulled his body away from the door and entered the consultation room. Imogene lay on the couch asleep. Lilya pinched her cheek, but the girl didn't react. Drugged, just as well, the journey will be easier. Her frame was featherweight and she carried her to the Hummer with ease, then returned for the hypnotist.

Amelia stirred several times as she half-walked with Lilya's support. As soon as she helped her across the Hummer's backseat, the woman went back to sleep. Within an hour, the Citation X lifted off from Jacques private airstrip.

The House of Commons erupted as Frank stood to give his address. The Speaker banged his gavel and called for calm, but Frank could still hear the cacophony of noise from the street. Outside, a multitude waved banners and shouted, demanding the government give them a guarantee of safety.

Finally, the Prime Minister spoke. "Today is the Council of Elders' deadline. So far we have no disastrous reports, but there's time. I've been in discussion with Charles Strathfield our Opposition Leader and after a careful review of my reports, he agrees we need to contact the Council through the Pembroke girl, before the day's end."

One member stood and waved his fist. "We've heard the Pembroke girl has disappeared, so how will you contact this Council?"

Frank's head ached, and his neck felt stiff. "It's true, a kidnap attempt was made, but I can assure you she's in our care, and fully co-operating with our taskforce team and Doctor Schneider." Frank glanced at his watch. "I have to go, but I promise you will receive a full report on my return."

Alex steered Frank out into the lobby and led him through a doorway. They clattered down stone steps and entered the abandoned World war two underground-bunker. "To avoid the demonstrators we'll have use the emergency tunnels. Your car's ready. Porton Down is a two-hour drive, but Imogene's already there. As soon as we arrive you can try to contact the Council."

"How is the poor girl?"

Alex rubbed the back of his neck. "She's tired of course, but ready to do her part."

Detective McCullage smiled as he watched Imogene squeal and rush into her parents' arms. Xantara and Braeden looked delighted when he'd picked them up at the clinic. They hugged him in their gratitude and relief their daughter was back, safe and secure. Imogene broke free from her parents' embrace, raced across the room and hugged him. "I see you're feeling well after your little adventure," he said.

She beamed and stood on tiptoes and kissed his cheek. "Thank you for looking after my Mom and Dad, and bringing them to see me." Her smile faded. "What will happen now, can I go home?"

Jim laughed, he felt light for the first time in months. "You can, after the final session with the Prime Minister. You know him as Frank."

She bounced on her toes and waved her arms like a butterfly. "I like Frank, he's been kind to me and promised I can play with his daughter, soon, I hope. I don't mind one more session, as long as I can go home with my Mom and Dad straight after."

Jim crouched down and looked straight into her eyes. "You know what hangs on this session with the Council don't you? The result's important, more than you realize."

Imogene crossed her heart. "I do, and I promise I will do my best to contact them, for Frank."

Alex turned the radio on as they drove across the country toward Wiltshire. The announcer's voice sounded subdued. "Sketchy reports have reached us from the South Pacific. New Zealand and Australian politicians have found their eldest children dead in their beds this morning."

Frank's inhaler appeared in his hand, and he sucked the medication hard. "I have a feeling my worst nightmare will come true."

The radio announcer's voice rose. "There's speculation the deaths relate to the Council of Elders' deadline. The timeline of the Southern Hemisphere is a day ahead of the United Kingdom. The Council's deadline has passed in these countries, and we've received identical reports from Fiji, Tonga and other South sea island nations."

Alex clicked off the set. "Your hypnosis experience predicted this, didn't it?"

Frank felt the hairs rise on the back of his neck. "Press the gas, Alex. I have to stop them before their horrible punishment spreads to the entire world."

Franks looked at his watch. It was six o'clock already, but finally Imogene was ready. He smiled and patted her hand. "Thank you Imogene, you're a real trooper."

Schneider gave the injection, then swung his crystal and guided her into a deep hypnotic state. Within minutes her eyes closed, and her chest rose and fell with regularity. Frank's head fell on his chest at the doctor's gentle tone, till he realized and jerked himself awake. "Deeper, walk down the staircase, one step at a time, one, two, three…"

Frank felt the hypnotic effect again and pinched his arm. What's wrong with me? As he waited he pictured his son Julian and the horrific rows of coffins he'd witnessed at his University. It was a nightmare. Simply a dream, they couldn't be so cruel, could they?

His attention drifted as the doctor spoke softly into Imogene's ear. A deep booming voice startled him back to the present. The young girls' body stiffened, and her eyes darted beneath her lids.

Her mouth opened, and Frank heard Kabshiel speak. "Welcome, human, as expected your world leaders have failed again. We extended the time as requested, but the changes didn't happen. No changes whatsoever."

Frank spluttered and saw spittle spray on Imogene's face. "Wait, I've done all in my power to influence the United Nations, but they move slowly. You have to give me more time, please, I'm begging you."

"We have watched your progress with interest. You have done well and worked diligently on our behalf. We thank you, but we have already released the penultimate penalty, and it's unstoppable."

"It's children, isn't it, like I saw in my hypnosis experience?"

Kabshiel's voice deepened. "Over the centuries we've found humanity to be arrogant and stubborn, like Egypt's Pharaoh, three thousand years ago. He made his people suffer through ten plagues before he let the Israelites go. People don't change unless they experience a personal loss. Because of your heroic efforts and pleas we have limited this punishment to World leaders and their governments."

Frank gripped Imogene's hand tighter. "Did you cause the deaths of the politicians' children in the Southern Hemisphere?"

"Yes, our deadline reached those areas first, and will continue westward until the retribution's rollout is complete."

Frank pinched the bridge of his nose and closed his eyes. "Please stop, we've suffered enough! I'm sure those deaths will be sufficient to turn the tide of public opinion."

"I'm sorry. I have a message for the United Nations, and I would ask you to deliver it next week, after this retribution has completed."

Frank let out a deep sigh. "What's the message?"

"The Council of Elders stopped short of destroying the human race, this time. We believe this penultimate consequence will eat at the hearts of the rich and powerful, the ones we have relied on to make the changes, and they will recognize that we are serious. We have granted the World a reprieve for a year. When that time's up, all of humankind will die, and the Earth will be cleansed if our conditions aren't met."

A knot formed in Frank's stomach. "What do you want us to do?"

"Complete disarmament, wealth redistribution to feed, clothe and house the disadvantaged, and one final condition you may find difficult."

Frank's stomach churned, and bile rose into his throat. "What more do you want?"

"If you recall, when Imogene relayed our original communication, we mentioned the increase in sadistic crime and murders. You must identify these psychopaths, born without a soul, and incarcerate them in a secure facility where they will not be a danger to mankind."

Frank held his breath. "And then, if we do what you ask?"

"The Earth and its inhabitants will be safe, until the next great fall."

He gulped. "The next great fall?"

"It will happen, perhaps years from now, or even centuries. Unfortunately, man is fatally flawed, and will regress because of his arrogance, greed and war-like nature. Farewell, my friend, and we the Council thank you for your courage and struggles over these past months. But now is the time for discipline then redemption."

Frank felt a cold wave wash over him. "Wait, my son, will he…"

Imogene opened her eyes and sat. "Did you talk to Kabshiel?"

Frank forced a smile and helped her off the couch. "Yes, thank you, you did a fantastic job. Now, let's find your parents and get you home."

As Frank and Alex drove back to London, new reports came in over the radio. More politicians discovered their eldest son or daughter passed away, in South America, Africa, and now reports flooded in from America and Europe.

Alex gripped the steering wheel. "I have to admit the Council knows people all too well. This action will turn the tide, and we'll survive as the human race. I can't believe Kabshiel will harm Julian, after all you've done. Thank God I never married."

Frank's eyes filled with tears as images of his son raced through his mind. His cell phone rang, and his hand shook, Julian's number. His finger hovered over the accept button. It must be his tutor, calling to break the news. At last he pressed and held the phone to his ear. "Hello, Dad..."

The End

Book Three coming soon....